BLACK DOG

Simon Corbin

This is HIS land.

This is HIS domain.

TABLE OF CONTENTS

There is a finite number of murder victims discovered by people walking their dogs.

Recently, that total increased by one…

1

DCI Frank Homes of the Norfolk Constabulary had only just poured his morning tea when the call arrived. The body of a young girl had been discovered in a field beside the high school in Hunstanton. Some uniforms and a forensic team were at the site awaiting instructions.

Frank sipped his tea, scorched his lips and slammed his Colchester United mug back on the desk. Hurriedly, he grabbed the keys to his police Insignia.

King's Lynn to Hunstanton is a twenty-minute drive; less if you use the siren. DCI Homes tore out of the police station car park and gunned the engine. The school lay on the outskirts of Hunstanton. It would be the first building anyone encountered as they entered the former Victorian spa town via the A149 from King's Lynn.

Stenham High School (or 'Sten High' as it was known to the 'Sunny Hunny' locals) was a secondary school. The 'students' (as they were ludicrously called – what was wrong with 'pupils', thought Frank) were aged 11-18.

Although it was now the middle of the summer holidays and the school was closed, Frank wondered if the dead girl had been a 'student' there.

The box-like brick buildings of the High School loomed into view as Frank crested one of the few hills in North Norfolk. Such depressing architecture, he thought. It looked more like a military compound than a seat of learning. How were you supposed to inspire a new generation by locking them up in a glorified detention centre for hours each day?

An access road ran beside the school buildings. On the far side were some grassy fields. Perfectly tended, the fields sported bright green grass, smooth as a billiard table. White picket fencing completed the toy town appearance.

As he drove past, Frank noticed a sign attached to a section of fencing: 'Coming soon: an attractive development of 3-bedroom houses and luxury designer apartments. Proudly brought to you by Ballion Housing Ltd.'

More buildings encroaching on our ever-diminishing green belt, thought Frank.

The access road extended only as far as the visitors' car park; a sharp right turn after the last of the school buildings. Then it became a rudimentary dirt track stretching as far as the eye could see, straight as a Roman road, across open farmland, to the horizon.

The final building on the access road housed a power generator. It was heavily fenced off, topped with razor sharp barbed wire and covered with garish yellow hazard stickers that proclaimed: 'Warning: High Voltage Electricity. Danger Of Death!'

Just to make the message clear there was also a crude graphic depicting an electrocuted stick man being fatally pierced by a lightning bolt. Someone – a 'student' no doubt – had used a black marker pen to add a speech bubble inside which was inscribed the single word: 'Ouch!'

Beyond the power generator lay another field. This one was bounded by hedgerow and totally neglected. It was overgrown with weeds and all manner of unkempt crops Frank couldn't possibly identify. The hedgerow featured a smallish gap that had been crudely gouged into it. It was through this space that the unfortunate girl's body had been dragged.

DCI Homes swung the Insignia into the only remaining free bay in the visitors' car park that was otherwise swamped by marked police vehicles and a solitary ambulance.

Frank switched off the Insignia's engine, took a deep breath and helped himself to a Polo mint from the glove box. This was his first murder case in five years and, by God, he intended to solve it. There was nothing worse than the murder of a child.

Blue and white police incident tape had been stretched across the road from the power generator to the white picket fence, designating the roadway as impassable to all but the authorities. A uniformed officer was stationed by the tape, tasked with dealing with any passers-by.

Homes recognised him. It was PC John Sexton – a plod from the Sunny Hunny cop shop. PC Sexton lifted the tape as Frank ducked underneath.

"Morning Sir," said Sexton. "Awful business. She was just a young girl. Local lass. We've not had a murder round here in years."

Despite his veneer of professionalism, the man seemed in shock. Frank clapped him on the arm.

"Keep any unauthorised visitors well away from this one, John." he said. "Especially those bastards from the Press. And don't answer any questions – not from anyone."

There had been no visitors at this stage. Clearly, the hacks had not been alerted yet. Well, it was only a matter of time. They'd arrive soon enough and they'd do so in droves. The Press were nothing but vultures. As if by magic they'd scent a breaking story and descend in droves like a parasitic horde.

Frank nodded to the forensic team who were on their hands and knees beyond the tape, spread out across the dirt road. They were dressed from head to toe in white jumpsuits and matching headgear, looking like a bunch of bewildered astronauts who'd misplaced their spacecraft. They were searching for tyre tracks and other forensic clues.

The assumption was the girl's body had been brought to the site late at night in a vehicle before being dragged through the hedgerow and dumped.

Frank was careful where he walked, keeping as far as possible to the small amount of grass verge. One of the forensic team signalled to him with a wave and a 'thumbs up' that it was okay to proceed normally – they'd finished with the section of road Frank needed to cross. The gravel crunched beneath the soles of Frank's brogues as he approached the gap in the hedge.

At first, nothing unusual could be seen as Frank squeezed through the gap – just waist-high weeds. As he glanced to his left, however, Frank's eye was drawn to two men standing about forty feet away with their backs to him. They were mostly blocking his view but Frank could still see a pale white leg contorted on the ground.

The men turned as Frank approached. One was the imposing figure of his deputy, DI Clive Dempsey. Despite it being a bright summer morning, Clive was wearing a heavy raincoat. Until Frank's arrival, DI Dempsey had been the most senior officer on the scene. The other man was an ambulance driver. As Frank approached, the ambulance driver left. Frank stood next to DI Dempsey and sighed.

"What have we got then, Clive?" Frank asked.

Dempsey said nothing. He merely gestured, palm open, at the ground. Frank stepped forward. There, naked but for a pair of pale blue knickers, and twisted unnaturally, lay the body of a young girl. The white alabaster of her skin seemed completely drained of blood. Instinctively, Frank turned away. Then he forced himself to look again – this time using his professional eye. He crouched by the corpse for a closer inspection. He had to do this. It was his job. It was the only way he was going to catch the killer.

A girl. Fifteen or sixteen years of age at the most, Frank guessed. Long blonde hair tied back in a ponytail. Blue eyes. Painted fingernails. Each nail a different colour. Nails like a rainbow. Rainbow coloured nails, clawing at the earth.

2

"Her name is Sally Hawkins," said DI Dempsey as DCI Homes crouched by the body. "She was a student at the school."

Frank bristled at the word 'student'. You were a student at a university, not in a school, for God's sake.

"Who found her?" Frank asked, standing up.

"Local fellow. Name of Donald Buckingham," Clive said. "An old boy out walking his pet dachshund. He lives in one of the bungalows across the road. Says he brings his dog here every morning, come rain or shine. He knew the girl too. Apparently he's a friend of the family. He was the one who ID'd her."

"And where is Mr Buckingham now? Has he given a

statement?"

"He's with WPC Silver. She's taken him home. What with him living just over the road and being quite an old fellow and somewhat shaken up, I figured it'd be okay to let him give a statement in his own home rather than at the station. WPC Silver is taking his statement as we speak."

"Okay, fine," Frank grunted.

WPC Abbie Silver: the siren of the Norfolk Force. Dark brown hair cut in a neat Cleopatra bob. Chocolate drops for eyes. Every man in the Norfolk Constabulary – married or not – was under the spell of WPC Abbie Silver.

She had a fiancé though. Some halfwit who travelled the length and breadth of the county mending windmills.

"Have all the crime scene pics been taken yet?" Frank asked.

Dempsey nodded.

"Right then," Frank continued. "I'm heading back to HQ to get the Incident Room set up. Who've you sent to speak to the girl's parents?"

"Sergeant Mearns and PC Boyle," Dempsey replied.

"Good," said Frank, nodding.

Sergeant Tommy Mearns already had some experience in delivering the worst news. When there'd been a fatal RTA a few months earlier, it was Mearns who'd had to inform the relatives.

Tommy Mearns combined a certain gravitas with a genuine sensitivity. He was a natural 'people person' – a skill Frank himself often lacked. Not everyone could strike the balance needed for such a delicate task. WPC Silver could have handled it but she was otherwise occupied with the dog-walker, Donald Buckingham.

"You mop up here then, Clive," Frank ordered. "Once Forensics pack up and the body's been moved, you can re-open the access road."

DCI Homes turned and walked away. Suddenly, he stopped, spun on his heel and marched back to DI Dempsey.

"Have we been in contact with anyone from the school yet?"

"PC Sexton checked the place out when he first arrived. It's the holidays, Sir. Everything was in lockdown. The entire area was deserted. However, the school caretaker, a Mr…er…" Clive fished in his pocket for his notebook, hurriedly extracted it and rifled through the pages. "…the school caretaker, er, a Mr Paul Hodson, arrived shortly after I did. He said he checks the school buildings daily – even during the holidays."

"Did the caretaker know the girl?" Frank asked.

"Well, we didn't show him the body, Sir. And I didn't tell him Buckingham had already ID'd her either. I just told him a body had been discovered in the field by the school and that we were closing the road off."

"Good. And where is Hodson now?"

"I sent him home. There was nothing more he could do for us."

"And where is his home?"

"Heacham. He lives in one of the old fishermen's cottages on the sea front. I've made a note of the address…" He began leafing through his notebook once more.

"Good work, Clive. Put it in your report. Have you spoken to the Headmaster yet?"

"Not yet. But I did get his phone number from Hodson." Dempsey waved the notebook as though it were a trophy. "I'll call him from the station, Sir."

"Have you lost your mobile, Clive?" Frank asked.

"No, Sir," said DI Dempsey, looking puzzled.

"Well, call him *now* will you? Ask him to visit me at the station immediately or I can go to his home. I want to get his take on his dead pupil." Frank placed extra emphasis on the word 'pupil'.

"Right away," said Dempsey, pulling out his mobile.

"See you at HQ," said Frank, backing away.

DCI Homes strode rapidly out of the field and back onto the dirt track. There was no sign of the forensics team. Things were winding down.

As Frank approached the police tape he could see a small crowd had gathered: the Press had arrived. Their abandoned cars littered the access road. Frank felt a surge of anger. The instant he ducked below the incident tape, one of the jackals shoved a dictaphone under his nose.

"Norwich Argus," said the oaf. "What can you tell us, DCI Homes?"

Frank brushed the dictaphone aside and kept walking. The mob of Press jackals followed; DCI Pied Piper with his very own trail of rats. Suddenly, Frank stopped. The rats stopped too. Several sets of eyes blinked expectantly at the DCI.

"What I *can* tell you all is this," Frank growled. "If you lot don't move those damned cars of yours off that access road within the next thirty seconds then I will personally arrest every single one of you for obstruction. There's going to be an ambulance coming through here any minute now and you bastards are blocking it. Now, *move!*"

The journalists ran for their vehicles as though it were the start of Le Mans. Frank watched them with a small sense of satisfaction.

However, as he reached the Insignia any lingering pleasure evaporated. The sun was ripe in the sky. It was a bright and beautiful cloud-free morning. And yet, just a short distance away, a child lay dead, dumped in a field like so much fly-tipped garbage.

And somewhere out there, a killer walked free.

There could never be any justice in a case like this. There could never be any closure. Some wrongs could never be put right. But, Frank promised himself as he started the Insignia's engine, I *will* catch this child-murdering scum. I *will* get him off our streets and I *will* throw away the key.

3

The A149 – the main road from Hunstanton to King's Lynn – was largely deserted that morning. Without the usual school run traffic there was barely another vehicle.

A long, flat straight was bordered, for the most part, by fields – principally a mix of lavender and pick-your-own strawberries. With the window down, you could smell the pleasing aroma of both.

The road from the school eventually led to a mini roundabout. Turning right would take you past Sandringham, the Queen's country estate. Frank had seen Prince Philip out driving his carriage on more than one occasion. Beyond Sandringham, another right turn would take you directly to King's Lynn and on towards the police station.

Frank breezed past a petrol station. His window was down. A lazy elbow rested in the open space of the door frame as he steered casually with his fingertips. He reached into to the glove box for another Polo mint and scrabbled for his sunglasses.

He swore as he dropped the sunglasses case in the footwell directly after putting the shades on. Then, for reasons he could not fully explain, Frank happened to glance in the rear-view mirror. And then he saw it.

That is impossible, thought Frank. As clear as day Frank saw, moving from left to right in his rear-view mirror, a gigantic black dog. It emerged from the side of the road and ran – unnaturally fast – across both lanes only to disappear on the far side.

What Frank had seen took only a second but there was no denying he had glimpsed some sort of creature. Immediately, Frank applied his policeman's logic to the vision, seeking only the facts.

The 'facts' appeared thus: this road is straight. It is a perfectly clear summer's day. I can see everything before me all the way to the horizon. I have perfect vision. If a giant black dog – or any other animal for that matter – had been lying in wait before attempting to cross the carriageway, I would have seen it long before I'd driven past it. And there had been nothing there as I'd approached. *Nothing*.

Alarmingly, Frank's logical analysis only *confirmed* rather than denied that he had indeed just seen a gigantic black dog. Yet that conclusion remained impossible to accept. For one thing, no dog is that big. For another, no dog is that fast.

You must have been imagining things, Frank told himself. And yet, instinctively, he knew precisely what he'd seen. He was a policeman after all. He was used to observing and recording every last detail. For years it had been his second nature. And he was not given to imagining things. Cold, hard facts were Frank's daily currency. Still, if it was that difficult for *him* to accept he'd seen a ghostly black dog that vanished into thin air then who else would ever believe him?

Frank pulled the Insignia into the nearest lay-by, slotted the gearstick into neutral and applied the handbrake. He took his sunglasses off and rubbed his eyes.

Maybe he should get an eye test? Maybe his eyes were playing tricks on him? Maybe he had a shadow on his retina? Maybe there was a smear on one of the lenses of his sunglasses?

Frank checked. The lenses on his shades were perfectly clean. Still, there had to be a logical, rational, scientific explanation. He just hadn't thought of it yet. There was no such thing as a giant black ghost dog – let alone a giant black ghost dog that appears out of nowhere, runs across two carriageways and disappears into the ether.

Get a grip, Frank, he told himself.

It was just a symptom of stress. It had to be.

It was the pressure of the case – a dead girl; a child, murdered and dumped. The vision of the ghost dog – or whatever else it might have been – was simply the result of his pressing desire to solve the case. It was a manifestation of the responsibility he felt to track down, arrest and incarcerate a real-life monster. There was nothing more to it than that.

Frank slotted the Insignia's gear lever into first, released the handbrake and chuckled gently at himself. He checked the rear-view mirror carefully before pulling away. No other vehicles and certainly no black dogs.

4

King's Lynn Police Station has two interview rooms. Frank chose Interview Room 2, the smaller option, for the visit of Terence Asquith, the Headmaster of Stenham High.

Room 2 was little more than a glorified broom cupboard – two plain wooden chairs either side of a bare hardwood table, no windows and a grubby skylight.

Frank found the proximity of the room's occupants, the unavoidable intimacy and claustrophobic atmosphere, worked well to loosen tongues. Friend or foe, people tended to speak up in Interview Room 2.

"Tell me about the girl," said Frank.

Terence Asquith fidgeted nervously, clutching his cup of vending machine coffee like a talisman. Frank held a notepad and pen. Asquith coughed and cleared his throat. He'd been shocked when DI Dempsey had phoned to tell him about Sally Hawkins' murder. And to think she was dumped near the school!

Asquith had been gardening when DI Dempsey had phoned. He'd had nothing else planned that day so it was no hardship for him to drive into King's Lynn from his home in Wells-next-the-Sea. He'd driven past the school on his journey and wondered what on earth he could say to the students when the new term began. That first assembly would need careful planning.

"Mr Asquith," Frank prompted. "What can you tell me about Sally Hawkins?"

Asquith took a sip of coffee. His hand shook as he raised the cup. "Sally was a quiet student. One of our better ones. She had seven GCSEs and five of them were A-grade. We were delighted when she told us she'd chosen to stay at the school to complete her A-levels. We've only recently opened a Sixth Form and, to be honest, not that many students have elected to stay with us. Sally would have been due to start her A-level studies next term."

"What subjects had she chosen?"

"English, Drama and Media Studies. She wanted to go to university. I think she had ambitions to become an actress or a TV presenter. She wanted to be in the media and she certainly wanted to leave Hunstanton to see the wider world. Unlike some, she understood how study and qualifications could be a passport to a better life. This is such a tragic waste."

"She wanted to get out of Hunstanton? That's an opinion she expressed directly to you? Any particular reason why Sally wanted to leave her home town with such urgency?"

"Well, no, not exactly. I may have misled you there slightly."

"Misled me?"

"Well, not misled." Asquith took a gulp of coffee. "I mean, it's just a figure of speech. Most people with ambition who hail from a small town want to get out and see the world, don't they? Sally was one of those. Ambitious, I mean. I don't know of any reason why she wanted to get out of Hunstanton as such – nor did I detect any sign of any particular desperation on her part to do so."

Frank wrote a few cursory notes.

"Were there any disciplinary problems with Sally?" Frank continued.

"None whatsoever."

Asquith snorted at the apparent absurdity of such a notion.

"Was she a popular girl?"

"Almost universally, yes."

"Almost?"

"Well, those who are talented and popular will always arouse the envy of those who have neither quality. Some people can always find a reason to dislike others, Inspector…Inspector?…"

"DCI Homes."

"Ah yes, Homes. Homes as in Sherlock Holmes, I presume? The great detective!"

Asquith laughed weakly. The Sherlock Holmes comment – and its attendant whiny laugh – was no doubt a clunky attempt at an icebreaker.

"Sherlock was my nickname at school," Frank replied. "With a name like mine, what else could I become?"

"Indeed. There's no 'L' though, is there?"

"No, there's no 'L'. So, who had it in for Sally Hawkins then? Staff or students?"

"Certainly not staff." Asquith grunted. Again he laughed; this time with a note of hysteria. Frank had seen this inappropriate skittishness in witnesses before. Usually, it was shock. "No, no, no, certainly not the staff." Asquith continued. "I can assure you, DCI Homes, if they were *all* like Sally Hawkins my job would be much easier."

Asquith drained his coffee.

"To my knowledge, Sally Hawkins was only disliked by Mary Harris."

"Mary Harris?"

"A tearaway. Mary Harris had her own gang. Mary and a couple of the other girls used to give Sally a hard time on occasion."

"So, this Mary and her gang were bullying Sally?"

"I don't think it amounted to bullying as such. The school has a strict and effective anti-bullying policy. There was a bit of name-calling at one point. I nipped it in the bud. I suspended Mary and her sidekicks for a couple of weeks."

"And where is Mary Harris now?"

Asquith laughed again, this time with a hint of malice.

"I believe she's working part-time at the local docks, gutting fish. Personally, I wouldn't let that girl anywhere near a job that allowed her to wield a knife."

"You think she might be violent?"

"That was a joke, Inspector. I apologise for my levity. It wasn't appropriate in the circumstances."

"The point, Mr Asquith, is that even the smallest detail may be pertinent. This is, after all, a murder enquiry. So, what about Sally Hawkins' home life? Can you tell me anything about that?"

"Well, I…as you will know…indeed, must surely know… anything that's said between a school and the parents of a student is confidential and…"

"I repeat: this is a murder enquiry, Mr Asquith."

"Have you spoken to Sally's parents yet, Inspector?"

"I'm asking *you* Mr Asquith."

"Oh God…"

"What is it, Mr Asquith?"

Terence Asquith put his head in hands.

"I just realised…" Asquith began, raising his head at last.

"Yes, please continue…"

"Those poor parents. It's only just hit me – Sally Hawkins was an only child. The extent of their loss is unimaginable."

"I was asking you about Sally's home life, Mr Asquith. Anything untoward? Anything unusual? Anything that either Sally or her parents had confided in you that might now seem relevant?"

"No, there's nothing. I'm sorry, Inspector. I really don't think I can be of further help in this matter."

"Well, thank you, Headmaster. I appreciate you coming to see me. However, I still need to speak to other members of your staff."

"Of course. A couple are out of the country on holiday but I have their contact details – mobile numbers, emails and so forth."

"Are you also going away in the next few weeks, Mr Asquith?"

"Sadly not. Contrary to popular belief, most teachers, including Headmasters, work through the so-called holidays. There are lessons to plan, meetings to be held, preparations to be made for the coming term. For the few days I have to spare, I shall simply potter round my garden."

"Thank you, Mr Asquith. We'll be in touch." Frank stood up and offered his hand.

The Headmaster had barely crossed the threshold when WPC Silver barged into the room. *Well now*, thought Frank, *there's a fine sight for an old copper's eyes!*

5

Frank stared across his desk at WPC Silver.

"Good afternoon Abbie," said Frank. "What can I do for you?"

Frank smiled indulgently. Abbie smiled weakly. She pushed a few sheets of A4 paper across the desk towards her DCI. Frank used his index finger to slide them back in her direction.

"Tell me, don't show me," Frank barked.

"It's Mr Buckingham's statement, Sir," said Abbie. "You said you wanted to see it the moment I'd typed it up."

Frank leaned back and stretched, locking his hands behind his head.

"Why don't you give me the gist."

Abbie picked up the papers, smoothed them out and prepared to read.

"Witness statement of Mr. Donald Buckingham of 14 Hillcrest Drive, Hunstanton…"

"Yes, yes," Frank interrupted. "Just the gist, Abbie, thank you."

There was a pause while WPC Silver scanned the document, searching for an appropriate opening.

"…I take my dog, Alfie, across the main road from my bungalow every morning at 7am sharp. It is a routine I have followed for years. I walk my dog beyond the visitors' car park at Stenham High School where I know there is open ground free of traffic. I usually let my dog off his leash for a run as soon as the road becomes a dirt track. I used to let Alfie run free in the fields now owned by property developers but, since they were fenced off, we need to walk further."

Frank circled his finger in the air, gesturing for Abbie to fast-forward her report.

"What about the discovery of the body?" Frank asked.

"I'm getting to that, Sir," Abbie replied, a tad tetchily.

"Facts, WPC Silver," Frank cautioned. "This statement may be used in a court of law. We need to stick to the facts about what happened. We are not writing a treatise on dog-walking or town planning."

"Shall I continue, Sir?"

"Be my guest," Frank replied.

"As soon as I let the dog off the leash he disappeared through a gap in the hedgerow and vanished into an overgrown field. The field was located immediately beyond Stenham High School. The gap had been created in the hedge approximately fifteen feet beyond the electricity generator that lay beyond the last of the school buildings. The gap was barely large enough for an average-sized adult man to squeeze through. Although I walk my dog along this lane every day, I had never seen this gap prior to that morning."

"Interesting," said Frank. "Now move on to the discovery of the body."

Abbie shuffled through more paperwork. "...when Alfie did not return immediately I called to him again. When he did not respond after calling his name several times, I began to feel concerned. It is very unusual for my dog to ignore my commands and I began to fear for his well-being. I decided to enter the field to look for him. I squeezed through the gap in the hedge and..."

Frank circled his finger. He sensed Abbie's irritation but this lesson in brevity was for her own good. It was a maxim that held true in both written statements and the witness box. Focus on relevant facts *only* – any gaps could be filled by anyone with half an IQ. Nothing extraneous must be allowed to obscure the facts. Then, from the facts, you extrapolate. That is how cases get solved and, thereafter, are successfully prosecuted.

"…I saw Alfie sitting beside the body of a young girl. She was obviously dead. Her corpse was naked save for a pair of light blue panties. The body was on the ground approximately forty feet from the gap in the hedgerow, immediately to the left as you entered the field. As I approached I had a terrible shock when I saw the dead girl was someone I recognised. It was Sally Hawkins. Her parents own a newsagent's shop in Hunstanton. The newsagent also contains a sub-Post Office. I would sometimes see Sally when I collected my pension. She was fond of dogs and made a tremendous fuss of Alfie. After I had got to know her and her family, she would sometimes walk Alfie for me when I was ill or the weather was inclement. I believe this is why my dog rushed straight to her body and waited there once he was allowed off the leash…"

Frank circled his finger.

"…as I do not possess a mobile telephone, it was necessary for me to return home in order to contact the police. As I left the field I looked at my watch. It was 7.20 a.m. I decided to phone the local

Hunstanton Police rather than dial 999 as I knew the number and realised that a local officer would, in any case, probably be first on the scene. As instructed by the police, I left Alfie at home and returned to the scene to await the arrival of a police officer. I arrived at 7.45am and was met in the access road by PC Sexton, who I already knew, who had been checking the school buildings. I showed PC Sexton the gap in the hedgerow but I did not wish to re-enter the field. At approximately 7.55am DI Dempsey and other police officers from King's Lynn Police Station arrived. At 8.15am WPC Silver accompanied me to my home to take my statement."

Abbie dropped the papers back onto the desk. Frank sat up, straight-backed and attentive.

"Good work, Silver. Now, shorten it. Concentrate only on the facts. When will we get the forensics and pathology reports?"

"They're doing them now, Sir."

"See if you can jolly them along, will you?"

"Yes, Sir," Abbie replied, gathering up Donald Buckingham's statement. She paused at the door and smiled briefly at Frank.

Ordinarily the gesture would have filled Frank with joy. However, on this occasion, the DCI did not notice. He was leaning back in his chair, staring at the skylight, lost in troubled reflection. His mind was awash with unanswered questions concerning a murdered girl and his own sighting of a mysterious black dog.

6

It always seemed absurd to Frank that he could walk home in twenty minutes yet still had to drive. However, he needed access to a car at all times – never knowing where the job may take him at any moment. But, with lodgings so close to King's Lynn Police Station, it seemed an indulgence to get behind the wheel.

It was different when was married. In those days he lived in a large detached house in 'Constable Country' on the Essex-Suffolk border. Timber beams, gravel driveway, all mod cons. Driving made sense as he lived in the countryside but worked in the town centre.

However, everything had been different then. Life itself had made sense.

Then came the upheaval and Frank had to pack his bags. Sue still lived in the big house, along with his shop mannequin replacement and their bonny, bouncing baby. Winner takes all. Loser moves to a new county and rents a grotty bedsit in a grimy maisonette by the railway line.

A divorced DCI renting a tiny flat in one of the less salubrious parts of a small town is not a status Frank readily advertised. Still, Norfolk was the only unit with a vacancy when he applied for a transfer.

Frank drove past the football stadium and over the level crossing. Almost immediately the search for a parking spot began. He'd never fully appreciated having a driveway when he'd lived with Sue. Now it had become one of his most desired luxuries.

A parking space was never easy to find in a street in which most of the houses had been converted into flats and there were often two, if not three, cars per household. Frank would often have to park at least two streets away and tonight was no exception. He cruised past his front door. No chance.

He hung a right. Nothing. Another right. Aha! Frank jumped on the brakes. It was a tight squeeze but Frank felt he'd become so adept at parallel parking he could probably reverse a juggernaut into a matchbox.

With the car parked, Frank began his walk home.

The route took him past Mr. Singh's convenience store. Frank went inside. He emerged with a loaf of bread, a shrink-wrapped sachet of streaky bacon, a chilled can of lager and a Mars bar. Dinner!

Frank rented the upstairs apartment in a two-flat house conversion. It was the last house by the railway line from King's Lynn to London King's Cross. The rattling of trains was something you got used to. However, late at night, the line was also used for goods trains making deliveries and shunting spare carriages into a yard. It was the goods trains that would stop Frank sleeping or, worse still, wake him up moments after drifting off.

The downstairs flat was occupied by an old lady named Mrs. Gostage. Having bought the upstairs flat from its previous owners, Mrs. G (as Frank called her) was also his landlady.

I've not had a landlady since my student days, he'd told her when he'd first moved in. Mrs. G was overjoyed when she'd heard Frank was a policeman. She'd immediately offered to reduce his rent.

The added security of a policeman on the premises would more than compensate, she'd said. Frank wouldn't hear of it. The rent was peppercorn already.

Mrs. G and her late husband, George, had been dog breeders. It was just a hobby, she'd said. However, her front room was full of trophies, photographs from dog shows, breed certificates, even a couple of Crufts rosettes. Unable to have children, she and George admitted the dogs were initially child surrogates. But the breeding bug had bitten and they'd subsequently travelled the length and breadth of the land to advance their breed.

When George died, it was his life insurance that had enabled Mrs. Gostage to buy the upstairs flat. But the dog breeding had to stop. She didn't have the heart, she said. And she was getting old herself, she added. Mr. and Mrs. G had bred Affenpinschers. Mrs. G explained to Frank that this was an ancient 'toy' breed that originated in Germany and played a direct role in the creation of the Griffon Bruxelloises. '

Affen' is German for 'monkey' and the Affenpinscher is known as a 'monkey dog' not just for its appearance but also for its cheeky, spirited character. Affenpinschers – about the size of Yorkshire Terriers – are small, shaggy, coal black bundles of mischief and energy. Mrs. G now had only the one dog: Spider. Her loyal companion, Spider had taken an instant shine to Frank and vice versa.

Frank had always been a 'dog man' and would happily have had a dog at home with Sue but the fact they both worked full-time had always prevented this. He'd never considered owning a small dog, though. An Alsatian, a Rottweiler, or perhaps a Staffordshire Bull Terrier – those were *proper* dogs, he'd thought. But Spider had changed his mind. On occasion, Frank would walk Spider for Mrs. G – much as poor Sally Hawkins had done for that old fellow, Buckingham, and his dachshund.

The door to Mrs. G's flat opened as Frank stood in the corridor fumbling for his keys.

"Hello, Frank love," Mrs. G said.

Spider shot past her and launched himself at Frank, tail wagging furiously. Frank crouched and the dog jumped up at him, licking his hands, nose and chin.

"Spider, behave yourself!" Mrs. G cautioned jovially.

"Would Spider perhaps like a W.A.L.K. later?" Frank asked, spelling the word letter-by-letter, knowing the little dog would otherwise become even more berserk the instant he heard the first syllable.

"That would be very nice of Mr. Homes, wouldn't it, Spider?" said Mrs. G, continuing to speak to the dog as if it were human. Frank stood up. Spider continued to leap at his leg. Frank and Mrs. G laughed.

"I'll fix myself some tea first," said Frank, holding up his bag of groceries.

"I'll have him ready for you in an hour," said Mrs. G.

Frank smiled and turned to walk up the steps to his flat. He'd barely reached the stairs when Mrs G. called to him.

"Oh, Frank, isn't it awful about that poor girl up at the school in Hunstanton? It's been on the news this evening. Is that your case?"

"I can't speak about police business, Emily," Frank said gravely. "And not a word shall pass my lips on the matter, I'm afraid. But as to the question of whether it is my case or not…" He nodded emphatically.

"Terrible business," said Mrs. G, shaking her head. "She was just a poor wee mite. Whatever is the world coming to?"

"I think it was ever thus, Mrs. G," said Frank. "But the killer *will* be caught. I can promise you that."

Frank hurried to his flat, shoved the bacon under the grill, buttered two slices of bread and went to change out of his work clothes. He washed his face with a hot flannel, used a roll-on deodorant and added a good splash of aftershave.

After selecting some neatly pressed chinos and a fresh shirt, he returned to the kitchen, opened his can of lager and took a long swig. Then he began laughing loudly at himself. He shook his head and slugged more lager.

Of course, *that* was it.

How could he have been so stupid?

Now it all made sense. The 'gigantic' dog in the rear-view mirror earlier was just an overgrown mind's eye vision of *Spider*! God alone knows why it had happened but it now seemed totally obvious.

Well then, I'd better take the little fella for a nice long walk, thought Frank. After all, I wouldn't want to upset his alter ego!

7

The little dog trotted enthusiastically beside Frank, dashing to keep up with the man's strides.

There was a pub – The Railway Arms – at the top of Frank's road, but that was not their destination.

"Come along Spider," Frank coaxed. "Speed it up."

Frank broke into a jog and the little Affenpinscher began a spirited run, his tongue lolling from side to side as he frolicked at his companion's side. The pair ran past the supermarket then pelted flat out as far as the War Memorial, where Frank paused to draw breath. Spider, unconcerned by his exertions, leapt happily around Frank's legs.

Frank hoisted Spider into his arms and crossed the road, setting him down with a playful ruffle of his head. They were now on the road heading directly out of town. To continue on the main road would have taken them in the direction of Hunstanton and the Sally Hawkins case. Frank sighed. For just a few hours he hoped to put that slaughter out of his mind. He wanted one evening's relaxation before devoting every waking moment to catching the girl's killer.

"Come on Spider," Frank said. "Not far now."

Frank and Spider strolled past a row of large detached houses. Sweeping driveways led up a steep slope towards the dwellings, giving you the impression you were walking along the bottom of a valley.

Some of the houses had whitewashed pillars and elaborate arches. Apart from a row of old Edwardian terraces in the centre of King's Lynn, these houses were among the most desirable residences in town.

After another ten minutes' walk, man and dog arrived at Frank's destination – a proper, old-fashioned, country boozer: A large wooden sign stated: "Linnet Tavern. Free House. Food Served. Children and dogs welcome." The building stood at the top of a small hillock, even further from the pavement than the expensive houses had been.

The pub was entirely surrounded by carefully manicured grass. Several wooden benches and tables topped by parasols created a spacious beer garden. A few happy families occupied the tables, their children rolling on the grass while the parents sipped cold beer. However, the pub was less crowded inside than Frank had expected.

A few heads turned as Frank strode to the bar with Spider. Frank recognised some of the elderly regulars, their weather-beaten faces looking forlorn as they nursed a solitary pint for hours, remembering the days when you could smoke in pubs, when lager was considered exotic and when you received a fair day's pay for a fair day's toil. Frank nodded to them.

It's a changing world boys, he thought.

A small group of college students crowded round the pool table, whooping it up. A barmaid emerged from out back, carrying a box of crisps. As soon as she saw Spider she put the box down, gave a shriek of joy and held out her arms.

Frank passed the little dog over the bar and watched approvingly as the barmaid hugged Spider as though he were a soft toy. Frank knew the girl – Monika; a Polish lass.

There were hundreds of Poles in nearby Peterborough but Monika and her partner, Lech, had chosen to escape 'the ghetto' and move up the road to King's Lynn.

Lech was a skilled electrician, in great demand among the locals. Frank watched as Monika filled a small bowl with pork scratchings and a large bowl with water and set them on the floor in front of Spider.

Once the dog was happily wolfing down his treat, Monika turned to Frank. "And what I can get for you?" she asked pleasantly.

"Pint of Guinness, please, Monika," said Frank.

"Normal or extra-cold?" She pronounced it 'extra-colt.'

"Oh, on an evening like this, I'll take an 'extra-colt', please," Frank chuckled. Once the pint had settled, Frank took an appreciative swig. "I'll go through then, shall I?" he said.

"Yes, you go." Monika replied, lifting the serving hatch so Frank had access behind the bar.

Frank walked past Monika and entered the private house section at the back of the pub.

"I'm upstairs Frank," a woman's voice called. "If that *is* Frank down there?"

"It sure is," Frank called back, a chuckle catching in his voice.

Frank finished his Guinness. He placed the empty glass on a side table and dashed up the staircase.

"I'm in here," a female voice called from behind a half-open door.

Frank opened the door to reveal a feminine boudoir – white bedding, flowers on the wallpaper. Jo was waiting for him in little more than a grin, a negligee and a cloud of perfume. Her blonde hair had been sculpted into a towering beehive. In many ways she was his ideal woman.

Jo was a divorcee – no kids, no ties *and* she owned a pub. She had no desire to make the same mistake twice so she wouldn't be nagging him to put a ring on her finger.

Thank the Lord he'd let her to carry on with that lock-in when he'd been drinking late that night in the Tavern. And thank the Lord again that she'd taken a shine to him as they'd chatted into the small hours. Now he had a sex life again for the first time since his divorce.

Frank pulled Jo close to him, tipping her head back and kissing her neck. They fell onto the bed. Afterwards, they lay side by side, each staring at the ceiling.

Jo reached across Frank for a pack of cigarettes. Frank tickled her roughly. Jo squealed and rolled away. Presently, she tried to grab her cigarettes again. Frank tickled her even harder.

"Cut it out, you bastard!" Jo complained, half seeming to enjoy the torment.

Frank relented and let her reach her cigarettes. "That's a dying habit," said Frank.

Jo held out the pack and offered him one.

"You know, if I can quit the cancer sticks, you can too," Frank replied. "I can help you."

Jo blew a thin trail of smoke at the ceiling. "Maybe one day," she said wistfully.

Frank kissed her on the shoulder, gathered his clothes from the floor and began to get dressed.

"I...er...I'm probably going to have to stay away for a while," Frank muttered.

"Oh, I see. It's wham, bam, thank you Ma'am?" Jo teased.

"It's a big case, Jo. A child killer. It's going to take every waking moment. I'm sorry. Listen, I'll take a few days off when the case is over. We'll take a trip. Somewhere nice. How'd you fancy Paris?"

"Relax," Jo cautioned. "I knew the score when I got involved with a cop. Paris would be nice though."

"Paris is a deal." Frank said firmly. "Meanwhile, text me, phone me. Don't be a stranger."

The pub was a far busier when Frank returned to collect Spider.

"How's he been?" Frank asked Monika. "Any bother?"

"No, he never bother," said Monika. "I wish much to keep him!"

"Sorry, no can do," Frank smiled.

Frank took Spider outside. It was quiet and peaceful. Frank felt happy. The families had abandoned the outside tables and Frank and Spider stood alone.

"Come on Spider," Frank said, slapping his thigh in encouragement. "Home time."

As they strolled down the slope away from the pub, Frank glanced into the distance. Then he stopped in his tracks, pulling on Spider's lead in his shock.

There in the distance, on top of a hill on the far horizon, was a gigantic black dog. Even at that distance, its silhouette was unmistakable – serving only to reinforce its outlandish size.

"Surely not. It *can't* be!"

Frank said the words aloud even though Spider was his sole audience. Frank looked at his small companion. Spider was straining at his leash, growling and shaking as he stared in the direction of the huge black dog.

That could mean only one thing: if Spider could see it too, it had to be *real*. Frank considered he'd only had one pint of Guinness – he could hardly be drunk.

There was, then, no other explanation. The thing on the hill was real. And if the thing on the hill was real, then the thing he'd seen in his car's rear-view mirror had been real too.

Frank crouched, gathered Spider into his arms and began to soothe the frightened animal.

When Frank looked up, the huge black dog had vanished into the ether from whence it had derived.

8

Frank did not sleep well that night. His dreams were overrun by huge black dogs with luminous red eyes, dead schoolgirls and Sally Hawkins with her arms outstretched receding from him screaming, screaming, *screaming*. Three times Frank awoke to the clatter of goods trains outside his window, their dull, monotonous clanking adding insult and injury to his futile attempts to achieve some rest. After his third nightmare, Frank awoke sweating profusely. Moonlight was seeping through the curtains. Frank felt tempted to get up, draw back the curtains and peer outside. However, he didn't dare. He feared he might see 'it'.

The hulking black dog might be there, staring at him with its red eyes; snarling, prowling, *waiting*. The thought was ridiculous, he told himself. He was behaving as though he were six years old, not a grown man.

Frank kicked out, sending the duvet flying. He pulled his alarm clock into view: 3:37 a.m. There was still a chance of a few hours of rest. However, the frustrated policeman experienced only three solid hours of further tortured thoughts.

Somewhere out there, Frank reflected, a killer was on the loose; a man who was no doubt enjoying a better night's sleep than Frank himself.

At 7.05 a.m precisely, DCI Homes sprang from his bed a little more energetically than he'd intended. A wave of sleep-deprived nausea washed over him. It would have been so easy to slip back under the duvet.

However, there was no such thing as 'throwing a sickie' in the Force. Frank walked to the window and pulled back the curtains. There was no lurking devil dog – just sunlight and a pile of police work awaiting him. Frank had to tough it out. He'd worked on zero sleep before. True, it was harder as you got older but the trick was not to think about it. Just fix yourself a hearty breakfast with plenty of strong black coffee. When all this was over there'd be that trip to Paris with Jo.

Maybe they should get married after all? Pool their resources. Then again, maybe a lack of sleep really was affecting his judgment.

Breakfast was an egg and bacon sandwich and three cups of strong black coffee. The coffee convinced him he was okay to drive. Out in the Insignia, Frank switched the radio on to help him stay focused. Some third rate crooner was singing 'Fly Me To The Moon.' Frank punched a button. A classical music station sprang into life playing 'Ride Of The Valkyries.' Frank hit the button again. This time a local news station came on. It was his case! He'd caught the announcer mid-story. He turned the volume up.

"...the girl's body was found in open land beside Stenham High School by a man walking his dog. It is believed the victim had been strangled. Police are appealing for anyone with information to contact them at King's Lynn Police Station..."

Frank jabbed another button. Silence reigned. There would be quite enough of that once he arrived at work.

One by one they assembled; solemn, resigned faces, each clutching a cup of coffee, notebook and pen. Dempsey, Silver, Mearns and Boyle arranged their chairs in a semi-circle around the whiteboard Frank had positioned at the front of the Incident Room.

Crime scene photographs were taped to the board. Next to the images was a tangled web of spider diagrams in red marker pen.

Frank felt the adrenaline surging through him. It was time for action. Frank stood in front of his colleagues and waited for silence. Once the murmuring subsided, Frank spoke.

"Sally Elizabeth Hawkins was sixteen years old, two weeks from her seventeenth birthday. She was a student at Stenham High, the school beside which her body was found. Sally was looking forward to progressing to the Sixth Form and A-levels. She was highly praised by her Headmaster and was, by all accounts, a model student. Sally had her whole life in front of her – a life that was callously snuffed out. This much we know. Tommy, what can pathology add?"

DS Mearns shifted in his chair. He flipped some pages in his notebook, ran a hand through his dark curly hair, rubbed his nose and began to speak.

"The victim was asphyxiated; strangled. Contusions on the neck confirm strangulation as the method of execution. Ligature marks indicate the victim was strangled using a fabric such as a scarf or a towel."

"Cut to the chase, Tommo," Frank snapped. "Time of death? Anything to help identify the killer?"

DS Mearns flipped to a new page in his notebook. His fingers were long and slender, echoing his tall, ungainly frame. If you'd seen him on the street you'd never have thought he was a copper.

However, appearances can be deceptive – DS Tommy Mearns possessed a wiry strength that had been the undoing of many a sneering heavyweight brawler.

"The body had been washed in what appears to be commercial bleach," said Mearns. "We appear to have a killer with some knowledge, or at least a basic awareness, of forensic procedures. The bleach was likely an attempt to disguise any traces of DNA or other forensic material. There were some metal frag marks in open wounds on the back of the deceased where she'd been dragged across concrete of some sort – possibly a pavement or patio. This occurred post mortem. Further tests are being conducted to determine the precise identity of the metal compounds. As yet, no hair or DNA traces have been found. Not even under the fingernails."

"Time of death?" Frank asked.

"Er…" Tommo flipped backwards through his notebook. "About eighteen hours before the body was discovered. So, it seems she was killed around lunchtime the day before. There were no signs of sexual assault. A non-sexual motive indicates a close family member or…"

"*Facts*," Frank yelled. "Facts first, then extrapolate. Don't rule anything out at this stage. Consider every possibility but allow the facts to lead you to the truth."

Tommo coughed uneasily and flipped to a new page in his notepad.

"Given the time of death, it's fair to assume, Sir, that the victim was killed elsewhere, her body soaked in bleach, then transported in a vehicle of some sort before being dumped in the field."

Frank nodded.

"Scene of crime report. Anything to add?"

PC Jack Boyle sat forward in his seat as DS Mearns sat down. Now it was Boyle's turn to start flipping hurriedly through his notebook. The dome of his bald head shone brightly under the harsh electric light of the Incident Room. Boyle's narrow blue eyes scanned his notebook rapidly.

"Most of the approach road to the dump site is loose gravel, Sir. There was not much in the way of useful tyre tracks or footprints on the gravel section. However, heading away from the school, about fifty yards beyond the field in which the body was found, is the gated entrance to a fallow field. We found some tyre tracks in front of this gate – evidence of a vehicle, with smaller tyres than a tractor but larger than a passenger car. It's possible the killer drove to the dump site in a van of some sort, dumped the body and drove further up the track to perform a U-turn before heading back to the main road. We're checking the tyre treads against the database. We also completed a thorough line search of both fields and tagged and bagged every fag end, sweet wrapper and used rubber Johnny we could find. Results are pending, Sir."

"Thanks Jack." Frank nodded.

"What about CCTV?" Frank continued. "Anything useful along the A149 that could show a lone vehicle in the vicinity in the small hours?"

"There's a petrol station with 24-hour CCTV," PC Boyle replied. "I'm on it, Sir."

"Excellent. Okay, listen up folks," Frank barked. "I'll speak to the girl's parents this afternoon. Abbie, you pay a visit to that Headmaster….what's his name again?"

"Asquith." Abbie replied.

"Yes, that's the fellow. Abs, you go and see Asquith. Get that list of Sally's teachers and their contact details he promised us. Jack, check the CCTV. Tommo, you come with me to the parents. Clive, jump on Forensics again. I can't believe they've not yet found a single hair or the merest trace of the killer. He's not a bloody ghost, is he? Okay, let's catch this murdering scum, and let's do it pronto."

9

Barbara Hawkins sat on the edge of the sofa clutching a tissue so tightly her knuckles were white. Her husband, Derek, paced by the window, too agitated to sit still. Frank and Tommy occupied an armchair each, directly opposite Mrs. Hawkins. Tommy balanced a notebook on his knee while Frank sat forward and asked questions. They'd both declined the cup of tea Mrs. Hawkins had offered.

The poor woman was in no state to be making tea for anyone. She could barely choke out answers to Frank's questions.

She was, however, utterly determined to provide the police with any information that might help them apprehend the killer of her only child.

"Mrs. Hawkins…" Frank began.

"Please, call me Barbara."

"Barbara, did you notice anything strange about your daughter's behaviour in the days or weeks leading up to her disappearance?"

"No, nothing." Mrs. Hawkins shook her head and dabbed her eyes.

"There was nothing out of the ordinary at all, Inspector. We had absolutely no clue what was coming." Mr. Hawkins added suddenly. "If only there *had* been some sort of sign or if Sally had confided in us about anything that might have been troubling her then maybe we could have saved her. It's…it's…" His voice trailed off.

"Did Sally have a boyfriend?" Frank asked.

Mr. Hawkins rounded angrily on Frank. "They don't all start at sixteen you know!" Mrs. Hawkins grabbed her husband's hand and pulled him to the sofa. He sat meekly beside his wife.

"Derek, the Inspector has to ask these questions. It's the only way he's going to stand any chance of catching the person who… who…"

Barbara Hawkins burst into tears. Her husband held her tightly as her thin body convulsed with sobs. Frank waited awkwardly for an opportunity to resume his enquiries.

"Did Sally have any friends in particular?" Frank asked, rephrasing the question as best he could. The ensuing silence was unusually long.

"Antonia Hollins – otherwise known as 'Toni,'" said Derek. "She was Sally's best friend. The girls were inseparable. They belonged to the Drama Club the school ran after hours on Thursdays. Toni was often round here at our house for meals and Sally was just as often round at the Hollins' place."

Tommy wrote the name 'Toni Hollins' in his notebook, added an asterisk and the letters 'BFF' in capitals.

"If you speak to Toni, I'm sure she can tell you more about what they got up to in their free time." Derek continued. "I'm sure it was all perfectly innocent. They really weren't those sort of girls, Inspector." He looked pointedly at Frank.

"Sally didn't have many friends." Barbara said suddenly, recovering her composure. "Certainly not boys. She found them difficult and some of the ones at school sometimes teased her. Toni was definitely her best friend. Poor Toni, she's almost as devastated as we are."

"Could we see Sally's room, please?" Frank asked.

Barbara Hawkins stood up and straightened her skirt. It was a knee-length brown skirt with a plaid design. She'd paired it with a pale green cardigan that she hugged to herself despite the summer warmth. Derek wore navy blue chinos and a pair of High Street brogues – the same sort of shoes Frank himself often wore.

These were solid lower middle-class people, thought Frank. They ran the local post office and dressed in an off-the-peg approximation of the land-owning class but couldn't afford to send their daughter for private education. They must have instilled a great many of their own hopes and aspirations in young Sally. Her 'dream' of going to university was also their dream. Now it had been snatched away by an act of evil.

For an extended moment the four people remained rooted to the spot, seemingly standing to attention as though a royal dignitary had entered the room. Eventually, Derek Hawkins gestured with an open palm and his wife led the way out of the front room and up a narrow staircase. "Did Sally walk to school every morning?" Frank asked as they climbed the stairs.

Mrs. Hawkins stopped and turned. "Yes, most mornings she did, yes. After all, it's so close. Just fifteen minutes up the road. Ten if you really hurry. On the few occasions Sally was running late, she'd take her bicycle but she didn't really like leaving her bike in the school sheds. Things got stolen or broken and all the rough sorts would hang out in there, smoking and so on. If the weather was very bad, Derek would give Sally a lift in the car, wouldn't you Derek?"

Mr. Hawkins grunted his assent.

At the far end of the landing, Mrs. Hawkins gestured to a closed door bearing a small decorative china plaque that read "Sally's Room." Frank pushed the door open. It revealed a compact space that, due to a sizeable single bed, was too small for the four of them to enter together. Sally's parents waited outside and allowed the two policemen to look around for themselves. It was a typical teenage girl's bedroom – soft toys on the bed, posters of pop stars (bland-looking fresh-faced boy band members Frank could never hope to recognise) on the walls. A 'Cute Puppies' calendar was proudly displayed on the back of the door.

"Sally was fond of dogs wasn't she?" Frank asked, directing his question to the waiting parents huddled together on the landing. Barbara Hawkins smiled wistfully.

"She was forever pestering us for one. I wish to God we'd said 'yes' now. She seemed to find solace in walking Mr. Buckingham's dog, Alfie, for him sometimes. My God, Mr. Buckingham was the one who...who..."

"...found your daughter, yes." Frank finished the sentence for her. "We've spoken to Mr. Buckingham. He's been very helpful."

"He's a nice man," said Barbara sadly.

As the conversation continued, Tommy opened and closed drawers. Frank stared momentarily at the bookshelves. Acting and the theatre dominated. 'The Complete Works Of Shakespeare' sat next to a range of drama textbooks including 'Method Acting Made Simple', 'The Art Of Stagecraft' and 'A Concise History Of The Theatre Of The Absurd'.

"Acting really brought Sally out of herself," said Derek, craning over his wife's shoulder to make eye contact with Frank. "She was a shy girl, really, but she seemed to come alive by pretending to be someone else. Give her some lines and she somehow became that person. It was a rare talent. Her drama teacher often said as much. Her mother and I could only stand in awe sometimes."

Frank nodded before quickly snatching up the item the two policemen were really after – Sally's laptop. Frank held the computer in the air.

"Do you mind if we take this to the station?" Frank asked. "We'll issue a receipt, of course."

Barbara Hawkins waved a hand in assent. Derek Hawkins nodded solemnly. Back in the car, Frank handed the laptop to Tommy.

"It's an evil thing, the internet," Frank said grimly. "And they're all at it these days, the kids. Facebook. Twitter. Social networking. Who knows who they're contacting or what they're up to when they're on it. Paedos, perverts, weirdos, stalkers – you name it, they're all on the internet; grooming young girls like Sally Hawkins. Younger even."

DS Mearns nodded sadly.

"Tell me about it, Chief. My two are always on it. I've warned them endlessly. But this is the tech generation. They can program a computer before they can walk. I had to use a logarithm book in my school Maths class. The internet hadn't even been heard of when I was a kid. In those days, a computer was something that occupied an entire room and spat out a strip of binary code on ticker tape once in a blue moon."

"Logarithm book?" Frank laughed. "You were lucky. I had to make do with an abacus. But look, if young Sally Hawkins – shy, introverted, boyfriend-less young girl that she apparently was – was sitting up in that bedroom making contact with someone on the internet who she then arranged to meet…well, we need to know exactly who that person was…"

"I'll give this to Harry, pronto," Tommy said, placing the laptop across his knees. "He'll have its secrets laid bare in no time."

"Pure evil, the internet." Frank repeated, sparking the Insignia into life. "If you're a young kid messing about on the world wide web then, sure as eggs is eggs, all roads will lead to Rome."

10

A quick drink after work was in order. Abbie and Tommo had agreed to accompany Frank although the others had cried off. The three colleagues walked out of the police station and turned right.

Abbie had changed out of her uniform and was now wearing a brown leather jacket, blue jeans and ankle boots that made a clicking sound on the pavement. Her bobbed hair bounced as if in a shampoo commercial.

"Why do you womenfolk always wear such impractical shoes?" Frank teased.

"It's called 'fashion', Sir," Abbie replied, with a grin. "Something you menfolk don't seem to bother with much."

"Oh, I don't know," said Tommy, adjusting his orange tie. "I've still got it!"

Abbie laughed.

"Yes, Tommy, you've still got it if it's 1975. Then again, this is King's Lynn. You're probably about five years ahead of things in these parts!"

"She's not wrong there," Frank laughed. "I thought I'd stepped from the Tardis when I moved here."

"Hang on a minute, Boss," Tommy protested. "You only came from Essex – that's hardly a million miles away."

"No, but I'd say it's about ten million light years," Frank laughed.

The banter continued as they crossed the Tuesday Marketplace. Full of bustle, commerce and parked cars by day, Frank always felt the Marketplace evoked a deeply eerie quality by night. It was the scene of the town's public executions from medieval times.

In 1590 an infamous execution had taken place in the Tuesday Marketplace during East Anglia's notorious witch trials. Margaret Read, a local 'witch', was burned at the stake there. Legend had it that, during her execution, her heart had burst from her body, ricocheted into the wall of a nearby house and, still beating, bounced out of town and directly into the river.

As it sank, it caused the water to boil, bubble and turn red, while giant clouds of noxious fumes rose up. House No. 15 in the Marketplace still had a crudely cut diamond shape etched into its red brickwork, said to be the exact spot that Margaret Read's still-beating heart had struck.

It was superstitious nonsense, of course, thought Frank, but tourists still liked to take photographs of the 'witch's heart' to this day.

The pub Frank frequented after work was called The Ship. It was located in a narrow cul-de-sac off the Marketplace, right by the Old Docks.

The Ship was an old-fashioned 'spit and sawdust' pub. It was the sort of pub that still had free roast potatoes on the bar on Sunday afternoons and served beer that was pulled slowly, allowed to settle and inspected for clarity before being handed over.

Appropriately, The Ship was decorated with all manner of seafaring paraphernalia: flags, buoys, capstans, ropes, compasses, maps, galley pans. There were also large, full-length reproduction portraits of Norfolk's two most famous maritime sons – Admiral Lord Nelson and King's Lynn's own George Vancouver.

However, in Frank's view, the main attraction of The Ship was its three locally brewed real ales – Gaoler's Curse, Linnet Best and Sandringham Mild.

"Pint of Gaoler's please, Jeff." Frank said to the barman. "His shout," he added jovially, clapping Tommy on the back.

"Right you are, Frank," Jeff replied. "Fresh on, this barrel. Not seen you here for a while, my friend."

"Been busy." Frank growled. "You know how it is. No peace for the wicked – even less for those trying to catch the buggers."

Frank steered Abbie to a quiet table by the fireplace. Presently, Tommy arrived with two pints of beer and a glass of white wine. A pack of crisps dangled from his teeth.

"Ugh!" Abbie groaned. "Salt and Vinegar."

Frank stood up and shouted across to the bar. "Jeff, chuck us some Ready Salted will you? Add it to Tommo's tab!"

A fresh pack of crisps flew towards the table. Frank made a perfect catch.

"On second thoughts, make it two packs will you? This is supper, after all."

Tommy caught the second packet equally deftly. Once the crisps had been opened and the drinks had been sipped, it was Tommy who spoke first.

"So, what do we think? Did Sally Hawkins know her killer or are we looking for a total stranger?"

"Are we talking facts or hunches?" Frank asked, through a mouthful of Salt and Vinegar crisps.

"Let's try a hunch." Abbie interjected. "What does your intuition tell you, Sir?"

Frank stared into the distance. There was a long pause as he continued to munch his crisps. Eventually Frank spoke, as much to himself as his companions.

"My feeling is Sally knew her killer. They arranged to meet. She went to his place. He wasn't what she thought he was. Somehow she wound up dead; strangled. What I can't figure is whether he was an older man or a boy roughly her age. My hunch says he's an older man. The facts tell me this is someone who knows about using chemicals for a clean-up and someone who can drive the vehicle used to dump the body. The motive, given there was apparently no sexual assault, is unclear at this time. So, Abs, what does *your* intuition tell you?"

"I agree entirely, Sir," said Abbie, excitedly. "And, unless it was a straightforward abduction by a stranger – and the injuries, or lack of them, are not consistent with such a scenario – I'd say Sally went willingly to her doom, which means she knew and trusted her attacker."

"Is the father a suspect?" Tommy asked.

"*Everyone* is a suspect," said Frank, sipping his beer. "Unless there's a cast iron alibi and, even then, I don't completely cross them off my suspect list; false alibis are ten-a-penny. Keep an open mind. Follow your hunches but don't try to make the facts fit a theory, Grow the theory from the facts."

And so it continued until closing time. Fact: the girl was found beside the school she attended. Possible implications: the school was somehow connected; the killer had local knowledge.

Fact: the girl was a model student – a paragon who caused neither her parents nor teachers any grief.

Possible implications: she was targeted because she was seen as easy pickings or she led a double life neither the school nor her parents knew anything about.

Fact: much more would become clear when the girl's laptop was examined by Harry and statements had been taken from the school's staff.

Eventually, Tommy stood up and announced he needed to head home. He offered to let Abbie and Frank share his minicab. Abbie accepted, Frank declined.

"You two lovebirds run along," Frank said. "I'll have one for the road with Jeff then I'll walk. It's only a short stroll through the park to my gaff."

"If you're sure, Guv?" Tommy asked.

Frank nodded and watched with a beery smile as his colleagues left the pub. Frank sauntered to the bar. He hoped a drop of the hard stuff might help him get some decent sleep.

Anything to shut out those damned goods trains.

"Neat Jameson, please Jeff."

"On the house, Frank." Jeff replied, tipping a measure of brown liquor into a small tumbler.

"You don't have to, Jeff. Just 'cos I'm Old Bill…"

Jeff laughed.

"You're alright, Frank. It's not free because you're a copper. It's free because it's your last drink for tonight. After all, we don't want our Chief Inspector arrested for being 'drunk and disorderly', do we? The local rag would love that one."

Frank knocked his drink back and slammed the glass on the bar, Wild West style.

"Cheeky beggar," Frank laughed. "I'm sober as a Judge."

"That's precisely what I'm worried about." Jeff replied with a wink.

Frank smiled and stepped out into the night.

11

Although it was summer, the air felt bracing. For a moment Frank thought about picking up the Insignia from the police station car park. However, drink-driving as a copper would be even worse than being found on the street drunk and disorderly. No, it was Shanks's Pony for him.

Frank checked his watch: 11.05 p.m. If he was walking to work in the morning, it would mean an even earlier start than usual. Perhaps that after-work drink hadn't been such a great idea.

Frank swayed as he entered the Tuesday Marketplace. Maybe Jeff had been right and he'd had one too many. He'd only had four pints, though, or was it five? Still, age was catching up on him.

He was past fifty now. You can't pack it away like you did in your twenties, he reminded himself. And crisps for dinner hadn't helped.

Something – some instinctive urge – made Frank look up as he crossed the Marketplace. He had no idea why – his gaze simply felt drawn upwards and to his left.

Frank stood aghast. There, on the wall of No. 15, the witch's heart was glowing. It was palpitating obscenely, as if beating. Frank turned away and blinked.

He looked back. The heart was still pulsing. Suddenly blood began pouring from the heart – rich, coagulated blood cascading down the wall like a crimson river. What trickery was this?

Frank hurried away, half-running, not daring to look back. Presently, he reached The Walks. Frank hesitated at the entrance to the park to collect his thoughts.

Focus on the facts, he told himself. There was no such thing as a witch. There was no such thing as a gigantic black ghost dog. This was all insanity. He had a real-life murder to solve. *That* was reality. That was all he needed to be thinking about.

Frank strode purposefully into the park. There was no lighting in the park. He'd mentioned it to the council before. It was a hazard to lone women to have an unlit path through empty parkland. Yes, the moonlight provided a little illumination but it wasn't enough. Funding, they'd said. Their answer to everything they didn't want to do was 'funding.'

What were they waiting for? Someone to get murdered?

They always found the money for their bonuses and pension pots, Frank thought angrily.

The DCI was now deep in the park, the distant street lights could no longer be seen. It was pretty damn dark, thought Frank, as he reached the bowling club. He could just about make out the silhouette of the clubhouse on his left and that was only a few yards away.

It was strange how blackness could always become blacker still – no matter how dark the shade, there always seemed to be an even greater depth of oblivion waiting to engulf you.

As Frank hurried past the clubhouse, the building appeared to become a void; a black hole of nothingness. The unnatural cold Frank had felt in the Tuesday Marketplace now returned. Extreme unease threatened to overwhelm the lone policeman.

The silence was eerie.

The blackness was threatening.

A sense of foreboding permeated the atmosphere.

Frank had not felt this way since he was a small boy sent upstairs to bed without being permitted to switch the light on. For a moment Frank thought of turning back. However, he was more than halfway to the exit. Turning back now would mean an even longer journey than simply pressing on.

"Don't be so bloody stupid, Frank," the DCI told himself.

As Frank reached the children's playground, he heard the rusty squeal of the roundabout turning on its axis. He heard the creaking and clanking of the chains on the swings. The hollow sounds were horribly magnified by the silence they penetrated.

Who could be using the playground at this hour and in pitch blackness? Frank did not want to turn and look but the desire to do so was irresistible. Frank walked on a few more steps then spun round. The roundabout and swings were moving by themselves!

The roundabout was spinning at a demonic rate as if, at any second, it might fly from its moorings. The swings were swaying violently back and forth, to the outer limit of their capability.

Then, more outlandish sounds assailed him. Mocking, laughing voices tormented Frank from the ether. These were not the happy, innocent sounds of children at play. These were malevolent, threatening, guttural voices; mischievous and chilling.

A shiver ran the length of Frank's spine. Surely this *had* to be the effects of alcohol? Perhaps Jeff had spiked his beer for a laugh. There was no other explanation. No rational scientific explanation.

Frank turned and ran, little caring who might see a grown man fleeing in terror. He ran pell-mell like a child, stumbling and uncoordinated from dread. As he ran, Frank became aware of another sound – close behind and gaining ground. It was the unmistakable sound of scrabbling paws; large animal paws. Frank could hear the creature's claws scraping at the concrete pathway and a galloping that signified four legs rather than two.

Frank ran faster. He could see the exit – only a few desperate strides remaining. He could see the street lights; a promise of sanctuary. He quickened his pace with an energy he didn't know he possessed.

Right on the verge of safety Frank felt a powerful rush of air, and the heat and stench of animal breath; the beast was upon him! And then, there it was – the *beast*; a gigantic black dog. Its massive head was level with Frank's shoulder. Frank could see its red eyes blazing.

The dog sped past him, so close the pair almost touched. The speed of the creature was beyond imagining; so fast it looked like stop-go animation.

In a mere blink, it was 'there and gone' so suddenly that Frank wondered if he had even seen it at all. The shock and force of the animal as it rushed past him sent Frank tumbling off balance.

Now the policeman found himself falling and knowing, with a sense of helpless dread, there was nothing he could do to prevent himself crashing to the ground.

Frank's skull hit the concrete with sickening force. And then the blackness that had been all around him became blacker still; blacker than black, until the blackness itself became nothing at all.

12

WPC Silver took the limply proffered hand of Terence Asquith before seating herself in an armchair. The Headmaster of Stenham High School sat opposite and crossed his legs. His pale blue eyes watched the policewoman impassively.

Asquith was coldly polite in a way that managed to be courteous yet also distinctly frosty. WPC Silver wondered whether this was simply due to the man's demeanour or whether he had something to hide.

"Are you sure you won't have some tea and cake, Officer?"

Abbie shook her head.

"I'll try not to take up too much of your time, Mr. Asquith. I'm hoping you can provide me with contact details for Sally Hawkins' teachers, especially her Form Tutor."

"Yes, of course. I'll be glad to help."

The Headmaster stood up and walked to an old roll-top desk. He opened a drawer and removed a small leather-bound address book. Once he'd sat down, he began to flip through the book's pages. This continued for some time. Abbie coughed. Asquith looked up and smiled.

"I imagine most people store this type of information on their mobile phones or computers," Asquith chuckled. "I'm terribly old-fashioned, I'm afraid. Last of the Luddites. I still write everything down in longhand; everything important, that is. Old habits die hard. I often tell the students: what if the electricity failed? You'd be glad of your handwritten notes then. I've got all this on the school PC, of course. However, my home PC is kaput. It's all in here somewhere though."

The Headmaster continued to flick the pages back and forth. Abbie smiled in an attempt to demonstrate her apparently never-ending patience – instead it emerged as a rictus grin. "Ah, yes, here we are." Asquith exclaimed at last. "I've found the first name you'll be wanting." He proceeded to read out a series of names, addresses, emails and mobile phone numbers of members of the

School's staff.

WPC Silver's pen skated rapidly across her notepad.

"I fear most of them will still be on holiday," Asquith sighed.

"We'll catch up with them," Abbie replied.

She closed her notebook and stood up. Asquith stood too.

"One last thing," Abbie said.

Asquith drew himself up an inch.

"Would you say, in your opinion, that Sally Hawkins had a particularly good or even a particularly bad relationship with any individual member of your staff?"

The Headmaster placed his hand on his chin and stared briefly skywards in a classic mime of a thinker's pose.

"No, no. All was normal," Asquith said at length. "Quite normal."

"Normal?"

"Yes, normal."

"And how would you define 'normal', Sir?"

"Well, *normal*! As in, nothing out of the ordinary."

"Sally used to attend an after-school Drama class, didn't she?"

"Yes, with Mr. Powell. She was very fond of Drama. But you'll have to ask Mr. Powell about their relationship, as it were. As I've said, everything was quite normal, Miss Silver."

"*WPC* Silver."

"Indeed." Asquith grunted.

Abbie was relieved when the front door closed behind her and she'd returned to her car pool Astra. She felt as if she needed a shower just from talking to the man. If her own Headmaster had been even half as creepy, she'd have bunked off school every day.

Back at HQ, Harry Wilkins was waiting in the Incident Room with a report on the contents of Sally Hawkins' laptop. Harry's nickname among his colleagues was 'The Mad Professor.' His bald head, thick specs and flyaway tufts of white hair was primarily responsible for the unflattering title. The fact he also habitually wore a white lab coat while dissecting and reassembling various gadgets had further cemented the tag. Everyone had gathered to hear Harry's findings.

Only Frank was conspicuous by his absence as he now resided in hospital following his unfortunate fall in the park. Tommy glanced at Abbie as she dashed in.

"Afternoon Abs, you're just in time for the Mad Professor. D'you want to tell us what Asquith had to say or shall we hear Harry's laptop gen first?" Tommy asked. He had no qualms about addressing Harry as the Mad Professor directly to his face.

"Asquith only gave me a list of names to chase and a bad case of the creeps," Abbie replied. "I'm sure the laptop stuff is far more interesting."

"Over to you then, Professor." Tommy said.

Harry Wilkins rubbed his hands in excitement.

"Righto," Harry began. "Gather round, gather round. It appears that young Sally Hawkins had bit of a social life going on the internet. Social networking sites and the like."

"You mean the type of sites where kids talk to total strangers?" Tommy asked.

"And then agree to meet up," Clive continued.

"And then are never seen again." Tommy added.

"Facebook. Twitter. And so on," said Abbie.

"Yes," said Harry. "That's precisely what I mean. Sally Hawkins was indeed present on both the sites you mention – Twitter and Facebook – and I have transcripts of her tweets and her Facebook posts. However, what might be far more interesting to our enquiry is the third social networking site she used. It's little known…"

"Come on, then," said Clive, growing irritated at the teasing drip-feed of information. "Spit it out, Professor!"

"Anyone here ever heard of smellofgreasepaint.com?"

"I beg your pardon," Tommy said. "Smelly what?"

"smell…of…greasepaint…dot…com" Harry said slowly.

Blank faces stared back at Harry Wilkins.

"Call yourselves cops?" Harry teased. "Come on, what was

Sally Hawkins' only known out-of-school interest?"

"Walking dogs." Clive exclaimed.

"The other one." Harry snapped.

"Acting." Abbie squealed. "Greasepaint! Of course, the smell of greasepaint. It's a social networking site for actors."

"Hurrah. Give the girl a prize!" Harry chuckled. "Yes. Young Sally Hawkins was active on a social networking site for actors, producers, directors, scriptwriters – all manner of thespian types. I've got print-outs of transcripts waiting to be read from all three social networking sites. I'll drop them on your desk pronto, DI Dempsey."

"Fine," said Clive. "But what did you find on Facebook and Twitter? Or on the laptop itself? Can you give us a summary?"

"There wasn't much of value on either of those sites, I'm afraid." Harry continued. "Sally only had a couple of friends on Facebook. One was an Australian girl I don't think she'd ever met and the other was that best friend of hers, Terri or…"

"Toni," said Abbie.

"Glad someone's paying attention," Harry smiled. "No, trust me, this smellofgreasepaint site is way more promising as a lead than anything else. In fact, Sally gave away her mobile phone number to at least three other users of this particular site. And she'd posted an email address on the site too. She used a Gmail one privately and an AOL one on the greasepaint site. Luckily for us, she'd also saved some of the email correspondence with the greasepaint users on her laptop's hard drive including – and, you'll like this, folks – a record of her plans to meet up in person with one of these actor types."

"Good work, Prof. Have you got a name for the greasepaint bloke Sally was planning to meet?" Clive asked.

Harry shook his head.

"Not as such. But I've got some of my team talking to the site's administrators. Most users on the site post fake names alongside an equally fake picture – avatars they're called. They then hide behind these fake identities to post all sorts of messages on the site's forum. However, we're hoping to soon have IDs – real names and real addresses – of all those Sally corresponded with."

"And did Sally use a fake name and an avatar?" Tommy asked.

Harry nodded.

"She called herself 'Tomorrows Girl' and her avatar was a picture of a dachshund."

"Mr Buckingham's dog, I presume?" Abbie asked.

"Sally's mobile phone has never been found," Clive interrupted. "Anything back from the phone company yet?"

"It's in the file, Clive."

Harry gestured to the pile of paperwork on the desk.

"Every number called and every call received for the past six months – all itemised and cross-referenced. Knock yourselves out, my friends."

"So, you reckon this greasepaint thing is a promising line of enquiry?" Tommy asked.

"Not just promising, Very bloody promising indeed, I'd say." Harry stated.

"Can I feed this to the Press, Boss?" Tommy asked, turning to Clive. "I've had the local rags sniffing."

"No way," Clive snapped. "If the killer is still lurking on that greasepaint site we sure as shite don't want to scare him off. Just give the hacks the usual 'pursuing all lines of enquiry' bollocks and tell 'em to jog on. Meantime, Harry here will keep the greasepaint website's activity monitored, won't you Harry?"

Harry saluted in answer before leaving the room. Everyone stared at the pile of papers he'd left behind. Clive sat down and sighed. Hours of eyestrain awaited.

"Right then," said Clive. "We'd better make a start on this lot. But first, who wants to buy some grapes and visit Frank in Norfolk General? Someone needs to bring The Boss up to speed."

Tommy stared at his feet. Abbie glanced at her watch.

"Bloody Hell! Don't all rush at once!" Clive barked. "Right

then, I'm nominating you, Abs. The Chief will no doubt appreciate a dose of the 'gentle touch' while he's stuck in traction."

Abbie shot Clive a 'screw you' grin. Tommy breathed a sigh of relief.

"Before you go, Abs, leave me the details of those teachers Asquith mentioned. I'll sort out the interview itinerary. And send a couple of uniforms in to help me sift through all this cak."

Clive gestured unhappily at Harry's print-outs. Abbie spun on her heels. As she reached the door, Tommy called out.

"Oh, Abs."

WPC Silver stared back at Tommy expectantly.

"Make sure Frank's grapes are seedless. Don't want him spitting the pips at you!"

13

Frank's head hurt. The pain was worse than any hangover. It felt as if his cranium was on fire. A cracked skull with bleeding on the brain, the quacks had said. Concussion too. Rest needed. Further tests pending. Take it easy for a while, Mr Homes.

Well, bugger that, thought Frank. This was *his* investigation and yet here he lay, hospitalised and useless. If he stayed here too long, the Chief herself would come down from Norwich to take charge.

How had this happened? Was he drunk?

He couldn't remember. He'd left the pub – he recalled that much – and then he woke up in a hospital bed.

The whole thing was a nightmare. He hadn't had that much booze, surely. Just a quick drink after work. The last thing he needed was senior brass investigating him for a drink problem, putting two and two together, making five and taking him off the Sally Hawkins case. The prospect was an even bigger headache than the one he'd inherited from the concrete.

Frank tried to sit up. His skull felt as though it was gripped in a vice. Admitting defeat, he sank back into his pillows. He looked down at himself. He was dressed in a long white nightshirt – the sort of thing Scrooge wore. The hospital bed had sheets and blankets rather than a duvet. The blankets had seen better days.

Pity the poor NHS, thought Frank.

He'd been tucked in tightly, like a baby in swaddling.

He cast his eyes sideways. His left thumb was shoved into some sort of plastic cylinder. A wire led from the cylinder to a heart monitor. Oh, for God's sake, thought Frank. He used his right hand to feel his forehead. He was bandaged like a mummy. Some type of space helmet-cum-turban gripped his head. He must have looked like a Mekon. If he was trussed up like this, they clearly weren't planning on discharging him anytime soon.

Had anyone let Jo know he was here? How long had he been here anyway? *Jo*! Part of him didn't want her to see him like this but another part of him wanted her by his side.

And then – so suddenly it was shocking – Frank remembered *exactly* how the 'accident' had happened. Every awful event from the moment he left the pub came rushing back.

The glowing witch's heart in The Marketplace. The possessed children's swings and roundabout. The huge black devil dog hunting him down. The horror and the insanity of it all swamped his consciousness and Frank barely stifled a scream.

How could he possibly tell *anyone* any of that?

Swings with no-one on them thrashing about wildly? The witch's heart glowing neon and spilling blood? A gigantic phantom hound? Get real, Frank, you really are thinking like you've had a bump on the head!

No, he couldn't say a word about any of this. They'd take him off the case in a nanosecond. They might even get him sectioned. There was no choice. He had to stay silent.

He'd tripped. That's all. Nothing more to it. Silly old me. It was dark, it was late, I was in a hurry. I'd not had much sleep the night before. I should have paid more attention. No, I wasn't drunk. Just clumsy. I should sue the council. I've been saying for years they should install proper lighting in that park. It wasn't safe for lone women walkers. It wasn't safe for anyone.

By God, his head hurt. It felt as though his head was ripping itself apart from the inside. Frank closed his eyes.

The agony was almost unbearable but the darkness provided a momentary respite. Frank hadn't closed his eyes for long when he gradually became aware of a face taking shape within the darkness.

Thin, wispy mists of smoke swirled around him until a solid shape formed. It was a face. A young girl's face. God, no! It can't be! Sally Hawkins! It was Sally Hawkins, as solid as if she'd still been alive. Her face was a perfect death mask; porcelain white, inert and fragile. Her eyes were closed. Then, all of a sudden, her eyes sprang open! They were blood red and incandescent – just as the witch's heart had been, just as the ghost dog's eyes had been.

Sally opened her mouth to speak. However, instead of speaking, all she did was bark! She was barking at him like a wild dog. Over and over she barked; vicious, feral, uncontrolled. She was frothing at the mouth, white spittle emerging from between razor sharp teeth. In spite of himself, Frank began to scream.

"Frank! *Frank!*"

It was a woman's voice but not one he recognised. He dared not open his eyes.

"Frank! Come on now, Frank!"

Frank took a deep breath. Gripping the sheets in fear, he forced himself to open his eyes. A woman with long red hair and a blue uniform was leaning over him – a nurse. She was holding his wrist. She had a firm but motherly touch.

Frank looked to his side. His heart monitor was spiralling through the roof, the numerals on the screen spinning so wildly Frank thought the device might explode.

"That was some nightmare you were just having, Inspector," said the nurse. "Here, take these," she continued, handing Frank some pills and fetching a tumbler of water from a side table.

Frank did as he was told and handed the empty glass back to his red-haired Florence Nightingale.

"Those should give you a peaceful sleep...and far nicer dreams." The nurse smiled before leaving.

However, Frank had no wish to return to sleep. Not while it carried a risk of repeating of the horrifying visions he'd just escaped. He fought the urge to close his eyes.

Eventually, though, he succumbed. This time, however, Frank's dream was not horrific. This time it was erotic. Jo was in the hospital. She was astride him, naked, riding him with wild abandon. He could smell her perfume. He could feel her breath on his neck. She was here!

Oh Jo, *honey*, oh yes!

Was this really just another dream? It seemed so real.

Frank sensed a woman standing beside him and this time it definitely wasn't the nurse. "Jo, honey," Frank said, reaching out a hand. "Come here, you sexy..."

"I've…er…I've brought you some grapes, Sir," said Abbie awkwardly. "They're seedless, just the way you like them."

Frank laughed heartily as his consciousness took hold once more. He laughed so hard the bed shook. What a sight: WPC Abbie Silver, in full uniform, dangling a bunch of grapes above his bandaged head, a panicked expression on her face.

"Bit of a cliché bringing grapes, isn't it, Silver?"

"It's the healthy option, Sir,"

"Is it now? Well, you eat 'em then," Frank growled. "Now, pull up that chair. I want to know everything that's been going on with this investigation…and I mean *everything*."

14

DI Clive Dempsey sat behind Frank's desk and replaced his boss's Colchester United mug with his own Norwich City mug, shutting the Essex club's china into a drawer. Part of him wished he could close Frank in the same drawer.

Clive leaned back in the chair and placed his feet on Frank's desk. I could get used to this, he thought. It's a DCI's life for me! He pulled his mobile phone from his pocket and began scrolling through his messages.

Just then WPC Silver walked in.

"Making yourself at home, Clive?" she asked.

"Christ Almighty, Abs. You shouldn't creep up on people like that. It's enough to give a guy a heart attack."

Abbie sat down opposite Clive, who begrudgingly removed his feet from Frank's desk.

"How's the patient?" Clive asked. "Did you feed him his grapes one by one?" He chuckled lustily.

Abbie was about to tell Clive about all the ill effects a bump on the head can cause – how Frank had mistaken her for Jo and whispered a plethora of embarrassing small nothings at her in his semi-conscious state.

Then she'd thought better of it and decided she'd save her boss any embarrassment. Clive wouldn't understand. He'd simply have concluded Frank was losing his marbles and, close colleague or not, the episode would later resurface in their endless banter or, worse still, be reported further up the chain of command to bolster Clive's promotion ambitions at Frank's expense. Abbie crossed her legs and sighed deeply.

"He's like a bear with a sore head," she replied.

"No change there then," Clive laughed. "So when are they setting him free?"

Abbie shrugged.

"He seems to think he'll be back behind that desk in a day or two but I think that's pretty optimistic. He's bandaged up like a mummy from a tomb. He's also concerned The Chief will send someone down from Norwich to take over the case. Or, worse still, that she'll take over herself."

"What? He thinks I can't handle it?"

Abbie shook her head. "No, it's not that. Quite the opposite, in fact. Frank has every faith in you. He just thinks Norwich will jump on any excuse to take the case away from us. It's going to be a high profile collar. You know how competitive they can be."

Clive grunted and placed one foot back on the desk. "So what's the plan then, Abs? What did The Mummy From The Tomb tell you?"

"He says we need to complete all the interviews within the next couple of days and send the full transcripts to him at the hospital. I'll take them over when they're ready. He also wants copies of those website transcripts Harry gave us. He's got plenty of reading time on his hands. Can you get a few more copies made?"

"Bloody Hell," Clive groaned. "As if we don't have enough on our plate. It's like having your manager sent to the stands."

"I'm sorry?" Abbie said, puzzled.

"Nothing," Clive replied, with a dismissive wave of the hand. "A football metaphor, that's all."

Abbie ignored the comment. She uncrossed her legs and sat forward. "So, who's interviewing who then, Clive? And when can I get a few transcripts to take to Frank? It does appear he's chosen me to be his personal 'runner' for all of this."

"I bet he has," Clive grinned.

Abbie scowled.

"I didn't go looking for this, you know." Abbie snapped. "You're the one who nominated me to visit the hospital. You could just as easily have chosen Tommy."

Clive laughed.

"Tommy?" Clive sneered. "You think Frank wants *Tommo* feeding him grapes when he could have a nice WPC..."

"What about those transcripts, Clive?"

"No worries. I'll ask Julia to print off a few more copies of Harry's bumph..."

"And the interview schedule?"

"I'll take the English teacher, Collins. Tommo can chase up the Drama teacher, Powell. What else was Sally studying for GCSE?"

"History and French. Asquith taught her Maths and I've already spoken to him."

"Right. You take the History man. What's his name?"

"Clarke...with an 'e'."

"That's the chap. He's yours. We'll draw lots for the French bird."

Abbie glowered.

"The 'French bird' as you so charmingly put it is actually a woman called Claudette Palmer."

"Palmer doesn't sound very French to me."

"That's because she married an Englishman, Carl Palmer. He's the school's PE teacher."

Clive nodded.

"Okay, we'll need to speak to both of the Palmers then. Get them together if you can. We can kill two birds with one stone, so to speak."

Clive placed a deliberate emphasis on the word 'birds' and grinned provocatively at Abbie. Abbie ignored Clive's goading and stood up, ready to carry on with her duties.

"Hang on," Clive said.

Abbie sat down again.

"I also want you to speak to that best friend of Sally's, Toni Hollins. See if she'll open up to you – girl to girl and all that. Get her going on that greasy paint website stuff. See if she'll tell you about any secret boyfriends we haven't heard about."

"What's all this about girl-on-girl action?" a voice called from the doorway.

Clive looked up and Abbie swivelled in her seat. Tommy was in the doorframe, grinning broadly.

"Is your mind permanently in the gutter, DS Mearns?" Abbie asked Tommy angrily.

"Children, please," Clive interjected. "We've got work to do if we're going to keep Norwich off our backs. Come on. Chop, chop!"

Clive clapped his hands.

"How's Frank?" Tommy asked.

"Oh, he'll be back behind his desk soon enough," Abbie replied, staring pointedly at Clive.

"And he'll be back to teach *you* some manners too," she said to Tommy as she stalked smartly past him.

Tommy grinned at Clive and shrugged his shoulders.

"Women, eh?" he said with a chuckle.

"Agreed," said Clive. "But *what* a woman!"

15

Tim Powell was short, fat and effeminate. 'Camp' or 'theatrical' was probably the right word, thought Tommy.

Powell had dark, greasy hair cut in a bizarre hybrid of a Beatles mop and a short back and sides. When you added the fact it was plastered to the man's head, DS Mearns wondered if it might be a wig. It was hard not to find yourself staring at it to try to establish whether it really was a 'syrup'. However, staring at the 'wig' was preferable to looking at the man's bloated, acne-scarred face. Poor sod, thought Tommy. He really didn't have a lot going for him. Not much chance him playing any romantic leads. More likely Quasimodo.

Two small wide-set blue eyes blinked expectantly at DS Mearns above a somewhat porcine nose. From graffiti on a wall, Tommy knew the kids' nickname for the man was 'Porky Powell' and it was hard not to think of this while he was interviewing the Drama teacher.

DS Mearns had arranged to meet Mr. Powell at the school in Hunstanton as he felt it may help to focus the teacher's mind more readily if they spoke in proximity of the body dump site. Powell had met Tommy at reception and led him to the Drama Studios – a converted gym space behind the main school buildings. With the summer holidays at their height, the deserted school evoked an eerie sense of abandonment.

Tommy looked around the drama studio. Chairs were stacked high against three walls, creating a large expanse of open floor space. A makeshift dais functioned as a stage.

A half-open door led to a small ante-room in the far corner – Powell's office. Curtains hung loosely on a rail above the stage. Behind them, all manner of stage lighting clung to rigging, like giant spiders waiting to descend.

Light from a skylight ran the length of the roof, a legacy of the building's former life as the school gym. Finally, towards the back of the stage, a whiteboard on which a student had written (in indelible green ink) the following sentence: "Porky Powell shags sheep." Powell noticed Tommy raise an eyebrow at the graffiti.

"Year 10. A difficult age." Powell shrugged, leaping onto the stage and attempting to wipe away the offending words. Unfortunately for him, the marker ink was the wrong type for the surface and the stain seemed ingrained. Powell licked the palm of his hand and began rubbing furiously at the whiteboard. He smeared the words somewhat, transferring plenty of green ink to his hand but Tommy could still read "shags sheep."

"Little scallywags, eh?" Tommy said, trying to disguise his amusement.

While Tim Powell continued to rub frantically at the whiteboard, Tommy pulled two chairs from a nearby stack and set them opposite each other. Eventually, having smeared most of the offending script, Powell rubbed his green-inked palms on his trousers and sat down opposite the policeman. Tommy held his notepad at the ready.

"So, young Sally Hawkins," said Tommy. "Tell me about her."

Tim Powell shook his head sadly.

"Such a tragedy." Powell wailed.

Tommy nodded and waited for the man to elaborate.

"She lived for Drama," Powell continued. "The stage was her world. She came alive in the spotlight. You'd never have guessed it. Offstage she was such a timid, mousey little thing. On stage, well, a talent like that only emerges once in a generation."

Tommy chewed the end of his biro. As yet he hadn't written a single word in his notebook. Tommy nodded, encouraging Powell to speak further.

"You could give her any part," Powell continued. "She'd immediately embody it. Comedy. Tragedy. Shakespeare. Kitchen Sink. Any genre you'd care to mention, she was fantastic. She inspired the others to raise their own game. In the twenty years I've been teaching Drama, I've never seen a talent quite like Sally Hawkins."

"Twenty years here?" Tommy asked.

"No. Ten years here. Nine years previously in Cambridge and a year's teacher training before that in West Sussex."

"And Sally was the best you've ever seen?"

"Without a doubt. I was hoping she would go to RADA after A-Levels. I know she was considering it. But now..."

Tommy asked, "Have you ever heard of a website called smellofgreasepaint.com?"

Tim Powell blanched and swallowed. He began to speak, hesitated and tried to disguise his false start as a cough. "N-no. Sorry. Can't say that I have. Should I have?"

"Well, apparently it's the leading social networking site for actors," Tommy replied. "Naturally, I thought with you teaching Drama..."

"Ah, well, now," Powell continued, regaining his composure. "You're talking about the internet. I'm not a fan of the internet. It's a necessary evil, I grant you, but one I prefer to keep at arm's length. Give me some props, some actors, a script and a stage and I've got everything I need. I tend to leave the internet and all that social networking malarkey to the kids. I show them clips on YouTube, of course – great actors in memorable scenes. But social networking? No, no, no. That's not my scene at all."

"I see," said Tommy, scribbling a few notes.

"Yes, I leave all that to the youngsters," Powell rambled on. "On it for hours, some of them. Can't be healthy, can it?"

"Did Sally ever discuss her own internet use with you, Mr. Powell?"

"No, she didn't. Not at all." Powell said, shaking his head. "I've absolutely no knowledge whatsoever concerning whatever Sally Hawkins got up to in her free time, Sergeant. We worked on her acting together and that's all. Let me be quite clear about that."

"Well, thank you for your help," said Tommy, standing up. He handed the teacher his card. "This is my direct line, Mr. Powell. Give me a call if anything else occurs to you. Anything at all – no matter how trivial it might seem."

Nodding earnestly, the drama teacher folded the card and shoved it in his back pocket. Tommy started to walk away but then stopped and turned to face Tim Powell once more.

The drama teacher trembled with anticipation at whatever else the policeman might be about to ask. DS Mearns jerked a thumb in the direction of the smeared graffiti on the whiteboard.

"Try Turpentine," Tommy said with a grin. "That ought to shift it."

16

Jasper Collins was tall, thin and wiry with a nervous manner that reminded Clive of a meerkat. Although he was in his thirties, Collins had an eternally youthful face, requiring him to grow a wispy beard and thin moustache in order to be taken seriously as an adult by his students. Clive sipped a mug of milky tea as he sat watching Collins in the cramped kitchen of the small bungalow the English teacher rented near the cliffs of Old Hunstanton.

"Very scenic right by the cliffs," said Clive, as an opening gambit.

"That's why I chose it," Collins replied, pleasantly. "No good for anyone with vertigo, though."

"Indeed." Clive muttered. "So, you taught English to Sally Hawkins?"

Collins nodded before sipping his own milky tea and throwing the teaspoon in the sink.

"And you helped Tim Powell with the after-school Drama group Sally attended on Thursday afternoons?" Clive added.

Collins murmured his assent, seemingly preoccupied with his tea.

"So you must have known Sally Hawkins very well?" Clive smiled.

Collins raised an eyebrow as he joined DI Dempsey at the kitchen table.

"Reasonably well. I knew her reasonably well, poor lass."

"So, how often do you help Mr. Powell with his after-school Drama classes?"

"Oh, at least once a month, sometimes twice," said Collins, dropping a cube of sugar into his tea before getting up to retrieve his discarded teaspoon from the sink.

"More frequently when we're rehearsing for the school play."

Collins stirred his drink, threw the teaspoon back in the sink and took a large gulp of the sugary liquid.

"And on those rare occasions when Tim's ill or absent, I run the after-school drama class by myself."

Clive scribbled in his notebook as Jasper Collins returned to his seat. "And you recall Sally Hawkins attending the after-school Drama Club on many occasions?"

"Absolutely. Sally was our star performer."

Collins looked glassy eyed. He stood up and walked to the kitchen cupboard. After rummaging for a while, he sat down again with a pack of digestive biscuits and offered one to Clive. DI Dempsey held up his hands in the universal sign language for 'no thanks.' The man cannot sit still for five seconds, thought Clive.

"What was Sally like in your English classes? How did she behave?" Clive probed.

Collins dunked a digestive in his tea. Only half the biscuit emerged, the remainder sinking without trace.

"Oh bother!' the teacher exclaimed, staring sorrowfully into his mug. "Sorry, what were you saying?"

"What was Sally Hawkins like in your English classes, Mr. Collins?"

"Very quiet – in stark contrast to the Sally you'd see at drama club. It's not as if I didn't try to include her. I did try, I can assure you. The school has clear policies regarding inclusion and…"

"Did Sally display any behavioural traits that stood out to you or did she have any particular friendships or any clear enmity with anyone in the class?"

"As I said, Sally was quiet. Like a church mouse. She kept such a low profile in class that one could easily forget she was there. She'd never volunteer to answer a question and only spoke when directly questioned. That's just how she was. But her written English was excellent. Most students copy and paste stuff from the internet these days but Sally's thoughts were all her own. Brilliant, original insights into whatever we were studying."

"Didn't it strike you as odd that she had so little to say in her English class and yet she was an amazing actress in the drama workshops?"

"Not at all. As I've been telling you, there were basically two versions of Sally Hawkins. One in the classroom and one on the stage. It was only when she was acting that Sally came to life. Many actors are like that, you know. Acting can be a kind of therapy. It takes you out of yourself, gives you permission to be someone else. It frees you up to live and breathe in an alternate universe. That appeals, especially if you're not happy in everyday life."

"So you think Sally Hawkins was in need of therapy?"

"No, that's not what I was saying."

"Or that she was desperate to escape from something?"

"No, that's not what I meant either."

"So, what exactly *are* you saying Mr. Collins? I'm sorry, I'm not an art critic, I'm a police officer investigating a murder. If you can speak plainly, please."

Clive was annoyed at himself for losing patience with Jasper Collins. It was just the constant fidgeting, the distracted manner, the grandiose pronouncements. Were all English teachers like this? Probably, he concluded, as he thought back to his own schooldays.

"Apologies." Collins said glibly. "Sally had no issues. There was nothing that we – the school's staff – should have noticed or investigated and nothing we could have done differently. To be plain, there was nothing that could have given any of us any clue that Sally Hawkins would end up being murdered. If only there *was* something I could have seen or done…"

"So you didn't find it in any way strange that Sally appeared to have a deep-seated need to hide her light under a bushel; that she somehow needed to play acting roles to…to perhaps escape her situation, as it were?"

"No. No, Detective. I just saw this as a facet of her character. It's a very interesting question but it's not something I can help you with. I suspect Sally's parents are best placed to speak about that."

Clive was regretting alienating Jasper Collins – the man's manner was now decidedly frosty. Clive would get no more help from him unless he changed tack. "Did you do much creative writing in your classes?" Clive asked. "Do you perhaps have some examples of Sally's work you could share with me?"

Jasper Collins shook his head and placed his empty mug on the kitchen table.

"Sorry, no. We don't have room on the curriculum for creative writing these days. You'll find it still happens in the Primary schools but no longer at Secondary level. It's all technical and analytical writing now."

"I see. Do you know who Miss Hawkins might have confided in on a personal level? Did she ever speak to you in confidence about anything – anything at all, Mr. Collins? Please think carefully. You were her Form Tutor as well as her English teacher?"

"I was Sally's Form Tutor, yes, but she didn't confide in me about anything, Inspector. As I said, it was hard enough getting her to answer a question in class, let alone confide in me outside of it. She knew she could turn to me if she needed help, though. All my students know that. It's constantly reinforced in tutorials. I believe Sally's best friend was Toni Hollins – Antonia Hollins, that is. By all accounts the girls were inseparable. So, if Sally spoke to anyone in confidence, it would be Toni Hollins."

Clive opened his mouth to ask another question but Collins, seemingly anticipating Clive's line of questioning, kept talking.

"Miss Hollins did not study English with me, though, so I didn't encounter her very often. She and Sally were in the same History class so I suggest you speak to Jim Clarke, the History teacher, about Toni and Sally. Have you spoken to Jim yet?'

Clive shook his head.

"Not yet. However, Mr. Clarke is next on the interview list following your good self."

Clive stood up and Jasper Collins took that as his cue to also rise. The two men shook hands.

"One last thing, Mr. Collins." Clive added, still shaking the English teacher's hand.

"Yes?" Collins asked furtively, suddenly releasing his grip.

Clive asked, "Have you ever heard of a website called smellofgreasepaint.com?"

Jasper Collins looked relieved. His good humour seemed to have returned now the interview was at an end.

"Yes, I have, actually. It's a social networking site for actors. Can't say I've ever used it myself but Tim Powell, the drama teacher, well, he's on it all the time. Your best bet is to have a chat with Tim about that. I'm sure he can tell you everything you need to know."

17

Jim Clarke was a small, dapper man in his late fifties with bouffant grey hair. He seemed very pleased to have WPC Silver calling on him at his ivy-clad cottage by Old Hunstanton's bay. He puffed himself up like a rooster when he opened his door and found her standing there, notebook in hand.

"Do come in WPC?..."

"Silver."

"Silver. Splendid, splendid. Please come in, WPC Silver." Clarke purred.

The pair entered a small sitting room with chintz curtains and a matching three-piece-suite. Jim Clarke sat on the sofa nursing a glass of sweet sherry while Abbie sat opposite on a wing-backed chair. A fluttering canary in a cage maintained an incessant chirruping from the far corner of the room.

"Oh, a canary," Abbie remarked, feeling somewhat stupid for blurting out the obvious.

"Yes," Clarke grinned, twisting his head to look at the bird as if seeing it for the first time.

"That's Jim Junior, as we call him, or 'JJ' for short. Not many people keep canaries any more. They used to be widely kept in these parts. They're the emblem of Norfolk, you know. Then again, you're a Norfolk girl aren't you? You probably knew that."

Abbie smiled politely and nodded.

"JJ's my wife's bird," Clarke continued. "I can throw a cover over his cage if he gets too noisy."

JJ squawked loudly.

"Where is your wife, Mr. Clarke?"

"In King's Lynn, doing the weekly shopping. She'll be back soon if you need to speak to her."

"No, that's okay, Mr. Clarke. It's you I came to see."

Clarke drained his sherry and placed the glass on a side table.

"Well, I'm all ears and I'm at your disposal, my dear. How can I help?"

"You taught History to both Sally Hawkins and Toni Hollins

didn't you? How would you describe the relationship between the two girls?"

Jim Clarke settled back on the sofa and looked pensive. The silence was unusually long, punctuated only by more fluttering and chirruping from JJ. Eventually the teacher spoke.

"Those girls were undoubtedly very close. More like sisters than friends. It was as if they shared a secret somehow."

"A secret?"

"Well, I don't mean that literally, of course. It's just a figure of speech. Let me put it another way. What would you call the female equivalent of blood brothers? I'd say they were something like that. Soul sisters I guess." He smiled weakly.

"Would you say Sally was especially dependent on Toni or was it more that Toni depended on Sally?"

Clarke shook his head and looked puzzled.

"It wasn't like that. To be honest, I didn't pay all that much attention to the state of the girls' relationship. They were just two students in a class of twenty others I happened to be teaching. But, I suppose, if I was pushed, I'd characterise it as a true friendship – very balanced and very equal. However, it's fair to say their friendship did exclude the other students in the class to some extent. I think that made a few of the others jealous. Resentful even. Especially the boys."

Abbie stopped writing in her notebook and looked up.

"Which boys? In what way resentful?"

Jim Clarke shifted uncomfortably.

"Well, you know, it was just boys being boys. Nothing serious."

"You can let the police be the judge of that, Mr. Clarke. Now, which boys in your class took exception to Sally and how did that manifest?"

JJ suddenly began flinging himself madly around his cage, pinging off the bars in a burst of excitement. Jim Clarke stood up, walked to the cage, picked up a grey plastic cover and draped it over the agitated bird. JJ's noisy commotions ceased immediately. Clarke returned to the sofa and ran a hand through his hair.

"I'm sorry, where was I?"

"You were about to tell me about the boys who resented Sally."

"Ah yes, well. Really, it was nothing important. You know how boys are – well, some boys anyway. They'd call the girls lesbos, lessies, lezzers – that sort of thing. It was just immaturity..."

"Which boys in particular did this, Mr. Clarke? Can I have their names, please."

"Well, quite a few of them joined in with the general teasing but, if you want the ringleaders, it would be Danny Booker and Gavin Hurlock. They were the main culprits. They kept on doing it even though I'd told them in no uncertain terms to stop."

Abbie wrote the names in her notebook.

"To your knowledge, did either of the girls have a boyfriend?"

Jim Clarke shook his head.

"Well, if they did, it certainly wasn't any of the boys in my class – unless they hid their relationship extremely well. As I've said, Sally and Toni kept themselves isolated from the other students – especially the boys. And I simply didn't see these girls outside class. You're better off asking their Form Tutor, Mr. Collins. I must say, though, I can't imagine Sally Hawkins ever having a boyfriend, even though she was a very pleasant-looking young lady. She was simply too insular. Boys tend to find girls like that off-putting; more unapproachable than usual, you see. Of course, either girl might have had a boyfriend *outside* school. But you'll have to ask Toni or the parents."

"Are you aware of either of the two boys you mentioned – Danny Booker or Gavin Hurlock – ever making a pass at Sally Hawkins; perhaps getting a knock back?"

Jim Clarke laughed dismissively.

"WPC Silver, really. I teach in a History class not a dance hall! No, to my knowledge, nothing like that occurred. I really don't think those particular boys would have been interested in either of those particular girls. As far as I'm aware, nothing untoward happened between them beyond a few choice comments on a few rare occasions. There was simply too much mutual dislike."

"So the level of dislike was noticeable and significant then?"

"Noticeable, yes. Significant – I'm not so sure. As I've told you, the students were all far too busy learning about the Norman Conquest for there to be any other type of conquest on their minds."

Abbie folded her notebook, put her pen away and stood up.

"Thank you Mr. Clarke, you've been most helpful. One final thought – how do you get to school each morning?"

"I cycle. It keeps me fit and it's the only real exercise I get."

"And what route do you take? Along the main road?"

"Oh no, definitely not. It's far too dangerous for a cyclist given the reckless way most drivers charge along the A149. No, instead I follow the coastal path that runs behind the cottage. It starts off in the wrong direction but soon sweeps back on itself. It's very quiet and mostly cross-country. Shortly after passing the last of the fields it widens into a dirt track that leads directly to the school gates. You never meet any traffic along there besides the occasional tractor."

"Would that be the same dirt track that approaches the school from the rear and goes right past the…"

"…electrical generator and the fields where they're building those new houses, yes."

"And past the same field where Sally Hawkins' body was found?"

Jim Clarke looked ashen.

"Well…er…yes, exactly," he stammered. "That's the route I take, WPC Silver, almost every day."

18

Frank was seated in an armchair by his hospital bed when WPC Abbie Silver entered the room. The huge turban-style bandage he'd been wearing when she'd last seen him had been replaced by a more modest version.

"No grapes this time, Silver?"

"No, Sir. I've learned not to bring you any healthy stuff. I've brought you a King Size Mars bar instead."

"Excellent," Frank chuckled. "Now, sit yourself down."

As Frank was occupying the room's only chair, Abbie perched on the bed. She rummaged in her bag and pulled out a stack of print-outs. "Here are the transcripts you wanted," Abbie said, handing Frank the paperwork.

"Thanks," said Frank. "I've must've read the sodding newspaper fifteen times. This'll be a welcome change."

"When are they letting you out, Sir?" Abbie asked.

"I believe the term is 'discharging', Silver. I'm not an inmate in an asylum. I'll be *discharged* over the weekend, which means I'll be back at my desk first thing Monday morning."

"Very glad to hear it, Sir."

"Right, well, let me say from the get-go that I fully appreciate you coming here to see me on your day off. But, as you know, Abs, this is not a social call. I asked specifically for you to be the one to visit me to provide a full update on the investigation. So, fire away, I'm all ears."

"I'll do my best, Sir," Abbie replied.

"Consider this as overtime," Frank continued. "Put it on the books."

"Thank you, Sir. Yes, Sir."

"But before you begin," Frank said, clapping his hands. "Where's this Mars bar?"

Abbie laughed, rummaged once again in her bag and handed over the chocolate bar.

"You talk, I'll eat," said Frank, tearing at the wrapper. "The food in here's a disgrace. This'll keep me going."

There was a pause while WPC Silver collected her thoughts. Frank unwrapped the Mars bar and took a bite.

"Since you were admitted to hospital, we've spoken to three of Sally's teachers; the Drama teacher, Tim Powell, the English teacher, Jasper Collins, and the History teacher, Jim Clarke. We've still got to interview the married couple – the Palmers – who are the school's French and PE teachers respectively. We've also got a few students we need to see – Sally's best friend, Toni Hollins, and a couple of boys who teased Sally. There's also a girl with a grudge against Sally."

"A grudge?"

"Well, not a grudge exactly. I'm talking about Mary Harris – you might recall her being mentioned before your accident? She led a girl gang that allegedly gave Sally a hard time."

"Yes, I remember. The Headmaster, Asquith, mentioned Mary Harris when I interviewed him. Okay, these all sound like promising leads. Don't let the grass grow – get all of the interviews wrapped up ASAP. Any clear suspects emerging among the teaching staff?"

"Well, not as such but…well, there are some anomalies."

"How so?"

"Well, for one, the Drama teacher, Tim Powell, told us he'd never heard of the social networking site for actors that Sally had joined and yet the English teacher, Jasper Collins, told us that Powell was on it…and I quote: 'All the time.'"

"Which website?"

"smellofgreasepaint.com."

"Okay, that's definitely interesting. Have we got Harry onto this?"

"Yes, he's tracing all the users Sally was in contact with on the website. We've also got stacks of correspondence from Sally's internet and email activities. Clive and the others are going through it now."

"Sounds like we're on top of things. So, what else is new?"

"Jim Clarke, the History teacher, is a strange fish. I interviewed him myself. He lives in a cottage by the cliffs and cycles to work each day…right past the body dump site."

"Okay. Powell sounds especially promising, though. Where does he live?"

"Tim Powell rents a cottage in Heacham, on the beach front."

"Right. Well, we won't haul him in for further questioning just yet. Monitor his movements, though. See if he trips up in some way. Anything more from Forensics?"

"Most of it's in the paperwork. However, we're still awaiting a couple of updates. We're chasing the CCTV along the A149 to see if we can spot the vehicle used to transport the body. We're also still checking tyre tracks against the database to see if the vehicle that performed a U-turn near the dump site is the one we're after."

"Okay, things are taking shape nicely. Any theories of your own yet, Abs?'

Abbie shook her head before sliding off the bed and preparing to leave. Frank threw the empty Mars bar wrapper onto the bedside table. It landed on Clive's print-outs.

"It's too early to speculate, Sir." Abbie said.

"You taught me that. There aren't enough facts on the table yet. I do think Tim Powell's denial of any involvement with the smellofgreasepaint website is significant, though. There's a reason he's trying to cover that up.'

"Yes, there is." Frank agreed. "I'll give it some thought. God knows, there's little else to do in here."

"I'll update you again soon, Sir," Abbie said, opening the door and taking half a step outside. "That's if you're not back with us on Monday."

"Oh, I'll be back by then, Abs." Frank grunted. "You can bet your house on it."

"I'm not sure I'd want to wager my house, Sir, but it will be good to see you."

Abbie had barely left the room when Frank called out.

"Hey, Abs!"

WPC Silver popped her head back around the door.

"Yes, Sir?"

"Be sure you tell Clive to get his bloody size nines off my desk!"

19

Clive's feet remained firmly planted on Frank's desk – at least until lead pathologist, Kate Ross, burst in. Clive sat up straight immediately. He coughed nervously and tried to look busy. Kate's eyebrows, raised on seeing Clive's feet on the desk, remained raised.

"Frank's still in hospital then?" Kate said archly.

Clive smiled weakly.

Besides Abbie, chief pathologist Kate Ross was another of the Norfolk Constabulary's unofficial pin-ups. Whereas WPC Silver had a dark bob and was petite, Kate was a tall, willowy blonde of almost six feet tall with a decidedly Amazonian profile. Clive had been for a couple of drinks with Kate a few weeks back. It hadn't gone as he'd hoped but he felt the door wasn't completely closed. Frank had been pursuing Kate Ross before Jo had appeared on the scene and Kate's notoriously hard-to-get affections were another area in which Frank and Clive had clashed. Now, however, Frank was out of the running – in more ways than one. Clive's feeble smile soon became a cheesy grin.

"Kate. How're you doing?" Clive boomed. "Please, have a seat."

"Not a social call, I'm afraid, Clive." Kate replied, sitting down and throwing a sheaf of papers onto the desk where Clive's feet had so recently been.

"The Sally Hawkins case," Kate continued, gesturing at the pile of papers. "I've got some more info."

Clive stared at the paperwork and sighed. Kate leaned back in her chair.

"I don't suppose you could precis that lot, could you?" Clive asked, a puppy dog expression replacing the chancer's grin.

"You coppers don't change do you?" Kate chuckled. "That's what Frank always wants from me too."

I bet he does, thought Clive.

"Okay," Clive said. "I'm all ears."

Clive sat back in his chair, mirroring Kate's posture. A

psychological profiler had told him to do that in suspect interviews. Mirror postures build empathy, said the shrink. It was probably bollocks but it was worth a punt, Clive figured. Perhaps at the end of the conversation he could test the waters by asking Kate out again. However, for now, it was strictly business. Clive flipped his notepad open and searched the desk drawer for a pen.

"Okay. I've collated the forensics from all the various sources into the documents I've just given you. However, having spoken to both Harry and Vijay, I can summarise across all areas. I'll give you my own stuff first. As per my previous report, I can confirm Sally Hawkins was strangled using an item of clothing, perhaps a scarf, as a makeshift ligature. There was no sexual assault and the killer had attempted to remove all forensic traces by immersing the body in water and applying a bleach wash."

"You're sure it was bleach?" Clive asked, looking up from his notes.

"Yes, a strong industrial bleach – the sort used by office cleaners, schools, public loos, institutions, commercial premises, factories…"

"Schools?"

"Yes," Kate could see Clive's line of reasoning. "We've identified it as a type of bleach sold in large quantities to institutional customers. Not weak supermarket stuff."

"I'll get Abbie to contact the school and find out where they get their bleach, who has access etcetera. If I get a sample from the school, can you match it?"

"Ruth Marie can, yes. She's the chemicals expert in our department."

"Great. So, did the bleach cover all the forensic traces or can we nail this bastard?"

Kate was silent for longer than Clive expected.

"Well, ordinarily, a bleach wash wouldn't be enough to hide everything of forensic value. I'd still expect to find perhaps a single hair clinging to the body, some skin cells under the fingernails – some tiny but significant clue to identify our perp. However, our killer was either extremely thorough or extremely lucky. It appears the water and bleach rinsed off even that trace evidence. If there'd been a sexual assault there'd have been far more to go on but…"

"So, what *did* you get?" Clive asked, trying to keep the irritation out of his voice.

"As I've said before, there were some metal fragments stuck in a series of wounds and grazes on the underside of the body – small particles that had dug in when the body was presumably dragged across some sort of flooring."

"Metal?"

"Yes. It's quite curious. There were tiny splinters of metal, some of which had traces of paint. It suggests Sally was kept – or killed – in a warehouse. Somewhere industrial at any rate. It might also explain the availability of the extra-potent bleach. All speculation at this stage, of course..."

"Thanks, Kate. That's very helpful. Can we get a handle on the type of metal and type of paint?"

"That's Ruth Marie's department again." Kate smiled. "She's on it."

"Excellent. Anything else?"

"Yes, Vijay's been checking the tyre treads of the vehicle that U-turned by the dump site. He's been through the databases and, well, he's found quite an interesting match."

Clive looked up from his notepad.

"Go on."

"Well, we only found treads of the two rear tyres at the site, not all four tyres. However, it seems both tyres we've identified fit a van – a Transit or suchlike. One of the tyres is a Goodyear but the other...well, that's the interesting one."

"Come on, don't *tease* me, Kate." Clive grinned.

He wondered if his careful intonation had allowed her to pick up on the double-meaning in his comment. Kate, however, ignored the provocation.

"The other tyre is a fairly rare beast. It's a cheap as chips model from South Korea, called a Koo-Rog apparently. There aren't too many of them around. We should be able to track where one of those was sold or fitted locally."

"Brilliant. How about CCTV? Did we capture any Transits or similar vans on the A149 in the middle of the night?"

Kate shook her head.

"Sadly not. Vijay asked the petrol station just outside Sunny Hunny for their recordings and, well, it turned out their CCTV wasn't working that night."

"Shit, fuck and bugger."

"My thoughts precisely. However, Vijay also found some other CCTV from Lynn town centre and the Lynn end of the A149."

"And?"

"Tumbleweed, I'm afraid. There was one small car we spotted in the early hours but it turned out to be a bunch of nurses heading for their night shift at the hospital. None of them had seen anything untoward. And that's your lot. It's all in the documents."

Clive frowned. Some of it was good but, in truth, it was much less than he'd been expecting. Frank would not be pleased.

"Okay, thanks Kate. Appreciate you bring me this." Clive said.

Kate stood up.

"Soon as I get anything new, I'll bring it straight down."

She ran a hand through her blonde mane. Clive secretly wished he could do the very same thing. Kate headed for the door. This was it – time to chance his arm. Faint hearts and fair maidens and all that.

"Oh, Kate," Clive said, the inflection rising as he said her name.

Kate turned, the door half open.

"Thanks again. Good work." Clive grunted.

Kate smiled.

"Oh and…" Clive continued.

Kate arched an eyebrow.

"We can release the body back to the family for burial now."

Kate nodded solemnly and left.

Clive could have kicked himself for being such a bottler. Instead, he placed both feet angrily back onto Frank's desk, sending Kate Ross's carefully assembled paperwork flying.

20

It was late on Sunday evening when Frank arrived home. He wasn't going to spend one minute longer in that hospital. The quacks had cautioned against a self-discharge but, Frank reminded them, it was his legal right. He had a murder case to solve and every second counted. The medics acquiesced. After all, it freed up a hospital bed.

"Good to have you back, Frank," said Mrs. Gostage when the DCI stepped into the entrance hall. "Now then, you come along into my front room and tell me all about it. I'll put the kettle on."

"Well, I…" Frank began.

"No buts," said Mrs. G. "In you come."

Reluctantly, but feeling too polite to refuse, Frank stepped into Mrs. G's flat. He caught sight of Spider jumping up and down excitedly behind the frosted glass of the kitchen door. The little dog was overjoyed to hear the voice of his big friend.

The sight of Spider's undulating shape, oddly distorted in the glass, triggered a sudden, unwanted memory of the giant black ghost dog silhouetted on the skyline opposite Jo's pub.

Frank froze. Was that what was wrong with him lately? Was he simply hallucinating with disturbing regularity? Could that be the true explanation for these ghost dog sightings – just a series of bizarre hallucinations?

"Frank. *Frank*!" Mrs. G. was tugging at his sleeve. "Frank, are you sure you're alright? Should I call the hospital?"

Frank laughed loudly and rapidly came to his senses. "No, no, no! Please don't do that, Mrs. G. Don't call the hospital, for goodness' sake. I've only just got out of there! Honestly, I'm fine. I've just got a lot on my mind before I go back to work in the morning."

Mrs. Gostage studied her tenant with benign scepticism. "They don't take care of people in hospital these days like they used to. They let people out far too soon just to free up the beds. You can't take chances with a head injury, Frank."

"There's nothing wrong with me that a good strong cuppa

won't put right." Frank grinned. "Now, did you say you've got some biscuits somewhere too?"

"Shortbread," Mrs. G. replied.

"My favourite," Frank chuckled, rubbing his hands in anticipation.

As soon as Frank had sat down in the front room, Spider was released from the kitchen. The little dog went into a fit of mad celebration; jumping up at Frank, tail wagging, yapping and yelping loudly.

"I think someone is pleased to see me," Frank chortled.

"Spider! Leave the poor man alone!" Mrs. G. laughed.

Frank scooped the dog into his arms and stood him on his chest. Spider began licking Frank's face and wriggling and squirming so crazily that the burly policeman struggled to contain him. Eventually, Frank held the over-excited animal at arms' length and made hushing sounds at it.

"I'll tell you what, Mrs. G." said Frank, juggling an over-excited Spider. "I'll skip the tea and take Spider for a walk right now. I could do with some air and it might help to calm him."

Right on cue, Spider began barking and howling with even greater levels of excitement.

"Well, I suppose, now you've mentioned the 'w' word, you'll have to!" Mrs. G. laughed. "Hang on, I'll fetch his harness."

Frank placed Spider on the floor and the Affenpinscher stood stock still, tail wagging. Mrs. G. returned with a red leather harness and began fixing it to the dog. Suddenly, she stopped and looked up at Frank.

"Are you sure you're up to this, Frank, love?"

"Yes, definitely. It's just what the doctor ordered. Get back in your normal routine as soon as possible, he said. Those were his exact words."

"It's just that...well..."

"What is it Mrs. G.?"

"Well, I...I don't really know how to say it."

"Say what, Mrs. G.? I won't go until you do say it, whatever it may be, so you'd better tell me."

"It's just that, well, you look worried, Frank. You look as though you could do with talking to somebody. I've seen that look before and I know what I'm seeing. Listen, Frank, if you ever feel a need to unburden yourself, to get a worry off your mind...you can always talk to me, you know."

Frank tried not to betray his irritation. His elderly landlady was only trying to be kind and she was genuinely concerned about his well-being. That was all. But now a further doubt assailed him; did he really look *unusually* perturbed? Had she somehow picked up on his unspoken fears about the mysterious ghost hound?

"I've been in hospital, Mrs. G. I've missed some important developments on a major case and I need to get back to work. That's all that's wrong with me, I assure you. But I thank you for your concern and, I promise, you and I will definitely have a cup of tea and a good chin wag very soon. But now, if you'll excuse me, I'd better give this little fellow his walk."

As soon as the word 'walk' was again uttered, Spider once more began yapping and jumping. Distracted, Mrs. G. ushered them to the front door.

"See you later, boys," the old lady said as she closed the door.

"Right then, Spider," Frank said in a conspiratorial tone. "Pub."

Frank really needed to see Jo. The emotion of the past few days had welled up inside him and he hardly knew how to express it – he just knew *who* it was he wanted to express it to.

As man and dog walked towards the Linnet Tavern, Frank reflected on all the things that had been troubling him: the bizarre dreams, the visions and sightings of the gigantic black ghost dog, the incident in the park that left him hospitalised.

And, overshadowing all of this; the senseless murder of a young girl. It all seemed to be crowding in on him. Suddenly, he just needed to be with Jo, telling her how much she meant to him, even if he was no damn good at showing it most of the time.

It was some way past 9 p.m when the pair arrived at the pub. Happily, the pub's kitchen was still open. Frank didn't usually eat at the Tavern unless it was something Jo was cooking for them out the back. However, after all that dreadful hospital food, Frank had an overwhelming urge for a huge plate of honest-to-goodness pub grub – some sausage, chips and beans with plenty of English mustard and perhaps an extra sausage for Spider.

Frank picked the dog up. He could feel the little animal's heart beating happily. Frank could sense a new spirit of resolve flowing through his veins.

Could he really get up next day and devote all his energy to this murder case? Yes, he bloody well could.

Could he really tell Jo about the gigantic black ghost dog that had been haunting him? No, he bloody well *couldn't*!

In fact, there was no way he could ever tell anyone about that. In fact, Frank reflected, the only living soul he *could* share that particular secret with was a small black dog called Spider.

21

Frank was pleased to find Jo working behind the bar that evening. She smiled broadly as he and Spider approached.

"Hello strangers," Jo said. "Nobody told me you were coming out of hospital today, Frank. I'd have collected you."

Frank waved a hand dismissively.

"Self-discharged this morning. Honestly, I didn't want any fuss. In fact, I wasn't even going to come here tonight. I've got to be back on the case first thing in the morning."

"Self-discharged?" Jo shrieked. "Are you sure that was wise?"

"Not you as well," Frank chuckled. "I've just had Mrs. G. going on at me in the same vein."

"Well, you know best," Jo said curtly.

Spider began wriggling in Frank's arms.

"Here…take him, will you…" Frank said, handing the dog across the bar.

Spider yapped with excitement as Frank passed him to Jo. Once the Affenpinscher was happily ensconced in the rear of the pub with a bowl of water, Jo summoned Monika to mind the bar while she joined Frank at one of the pub's corner tables.

Frank was soon presented with a pint of Guinness and a plate of sausage, chips and beans. In spite of his earlier resolve, Frank ended up telling Jo far more than he'd intended.

He told her she meant the world to him and then he told her far more about the Sally Hawkins case than he should have done. However, despite his loosened tongue, he told her nothing whatsoever about his sightings of the ghostly black dog. He wasn't *that* crazy!

Eventually, mindful of Mrs. G. waiting for the return of her beloved pet, Frank glanced at his watch and made his excuses. Monika brought Spider to him and assured Frank the dog had enjoyed not just a bowl of water but also two complimentary sausages. Jo stood outside with them as they left.

"We must talk like this more often," Jo said, leaning in to Frank for a lingering kiss.

"Next time we'll do more than talk." Frank whispered.

"No, next time we'll do *both*," Jo countered.

"Just you find your passport," Frank offered as a parting shot. "Paris *is* going to happen."

Darkness had fallen as Frank and Spider began their walk back to Mrs. G's. It had been a perfect evening and Frank felt ready for the challenges that lay ahead. There was a child killer roaming free and, by God, DCI Frank Homes was going to nick the bastard and bang him up for the rest of his days.

Frank began whistling as Spider trotted by his side. They were setting a decent pace. Everything was fine until they reached the King's Lynn War Memorial. All of a sudden the night sky seemed to darken even further. However, this was not a normal darkness.

This was an all-encompassing claustrophobic blanket of blackness; the blackness of the grave, the oblivion of the void. At the same time the temperature dropped, and Frank and Spider found themselves enveloped by an icy cold. Spider was rooted to the spot, his small body shivering.

Frank picked the dog up and held him close, although the tiny animal continued to shudder, his teeth gritted in an almost comical grimace. Then, an ethereal shape began to emerge from behind the stone façade of the War Memorial. The 'thing' was composed of a grey mist that swirled and coalesced like vapours from a magic lantern. Frank was transfixed as the shape continued to grow. Frank's mind told him it was a physical impossibility that something so large could have been concealed behind a stone the size and shape of the War Memorial yet the clear evidence of his eyes (and the wholly independent reactions of Spider) told Frank this was exactly what had just happened…and was *continuing* to happen.

Time seemed to slow as the thick fog began to take on a solid shape. Then, emerging unmistakeably from the opaque mist was the head of a gigantic black dog. The dog's head featured huge, red glowing eyes and they were both trained on Frank!

"Good God, no! This *cannot* be happening. Not *again*!" Frank was uncertain whether he'd said this aloud or merely thought it.

Gradually, the torso and legs of the huge ghost hound emerged from the swirling smog until Frank was confronted by the entire spectral beast, standing triumphantly on a floating carpet of churning vapour. Then the horrific vision began to glide slowly towards Frank and Spider. Frank felt the air rushing from his body as he struggled for breath.

He tried not to look in the beast's direction but an overwhelming compulsion meant he simply could not avert his gaze. The huge ghostly hound was akin to a shaggy, jet black version of a rabid Great Dane crossed with a Pit Bull and yet it was larger than any earthly dog Frank had ever encountered. The spectre floated closer. Its jaws were roughly the size of a lion's although, Frank sensed, infinitely more powerful. Its teeth were twice as sharp as that of any shark.

It was a truly demonic entity; it was the stuff of nightmares; it was Cerberus with a single head. The ghost dog floated up to Frank until it was almost upon him. It was drooling obscenely. Then it began to growl – a guttural force so strong it almost knocked Frank off his feet. Suddenly, Frank caught the creature's breath – a fetid stench; the smell of decomposition and rotting flesh; the odour of the grave.

Spider twisted in Frank's arms, frantically trying to bury himself in the policeman's chest. Frank feared the little animal might die of fright. The DCI closed his eyes and waited for the fatal attack that must surely follow.

Frank waited. And *waited*. Eventually, when Frank dared to open his eyes, the phantom had vanished. The temperature had reverted to normal. There was no sign of anything untoward having just occurred. The Kings' Lynn War Memorial stood undisturbed. Frank spotted a lone man walking on the other side of the road. In desperation, Frank called out.

"Hey mate."

The man turned and looked at Frank.

"Did you see that?" Frank asked in a panicked tone.

"See what?" the man asked.

See what? For God's sake! Surely he *must* have seen it? The guy was walking towards the monument in the exact direction from which the ghost had manifested. There was no way the man could *not* have seen it!

"Did you *see* it?" Frank asked again, in a tone of increasing desperation.

Unless the man was blind he couldn't possibly have missed seeing the ghost. But how could Frank even begin to describe his bizarre visions to a complete stranger and so soon after his release from hospital?

"Did you *see* it?" Frank yelled again. "Tell me!"

The man tapped the side of his head and hurried away.

Spider was still shivering in Frank's arms. Something had definitely happened. Spider was not suffering this much distress for no reason. Frank carried the little dog through the streets, speaking soothingly, trying to calm it before returning it to Mrs. G.

All the while, Frank was trying to quiet his own nerves and make some sense of what he'd just experienced. Why did he keep seeing this ghost dog? What did it want? What could this *mean*?

Two streets from Mrs. G's house, Frank judged that Spider was sufficiently recovered to be able to walk by himself. He set the dog on the ground and glanced nervously around. Empty streets met his gaze at every turn.

Sensing he was home, Spider puffed himself up and pulled at his lead with all his tiny might, urging Frank onwards. In that resilient way animals have, Spider appeared to have suffered no ill effects from his recent ordeal. If anything, it was Frank who was in need of some consolation. Too shaky to put his key in the front door, Frank rang the bell.

Eventually, Mrs. G. appeared.

"Forgotten your key again Fra…" Mrs G began.

Something in the policeman's expression made it impossible for her to complete her sentence. She looked quizzically at her lodger. "Are you alright, Frank, my dear? You look like you've seen a ghost!"

Frank scooped Spider up and placed him in Mrs. G's arms. Unable to speak, he touched the old lady's face gently before running up the stairs to his own flat.

22

Carl and Claudette Palmer rented a small cottage in Heacham at the edge of the lavender fields. Pretty as a picture, thought Clive, as he parked his car-pool Astra in the driveway. However, that lavender smell would be enough to stop him living there. It was decidedly floral but also somehow sickly and unappealing. Old ladies' bathwater sprang to mind.

The front door opened before Clive had a chance to knock. He was confronted by a small, mousey-looking woman. Her sleek ebony hair was tied in a bun and Clive detected a nervous flicker within her dark eyes. Well, hello there Olive Oyl, thought Clive. Lurking directly behind 'Olive' was a six foot six muscle man in a contour-hugging white T-shirt, dark grey joggers and scruffy trainers. His peroxide blonde hair was carved into a military crew cut. Okay, thought Clive, Dolph Lundgren and Olive Oyl are shacking up. It was hard to guess their ages – late 20s, early 30s perhaps. Either way, they ranked among the younger members of the school's staff.

"Inspector Homes?" Olive Oyl asked. She had a foreign accent of some sort.

"No, I'm afraid the Detective Chief Inspector is on other duties at present." Clive muttered, giving a perfunctory wave of his ID. "I'm DI Dempsey. May I...?"

"Yes, of course," said Olive, stepping back to allow Clive to enter. Olive's hulking partner placed a supportive hand on her shoulder – a meaty fist, Clive noted, much like that of a heavyweight boxer.

As they left the shadow of the entrance hall, Clive could see the woman's hair was brown rather than black and her eyes were hazel. Instantly, her resemblance to Olive Oyl passed.

"Won't you please come through, Inspector?" said Mrs. Palmer, leading the way into the sitting room. The Incredible Hulk followed.

The room was threadbare and dilapidated, far more run down than Clive expected from the cottage's fairytale exterior and storybook location. Clive, however, showed no reaction to the squalor – a degree of self-control gained from years of entering derelict properties to pursue 'lines of enquiry'.

The 'furniture' consisted of a picnic table and three folding garden chairs. The moth-eaten drapes appeared to be about thirty years old and the grimy, unwashed net curtains they partly concealed looked even older. There was no sofa, no armchair and no pictures on the peeling walls.

After a few seconds, Clive realised the 'carpet' was actually composed of squares of carpet store samples that had been stitched together to form an unsightly mosaic.

Bare wooden floorboards poked out from the corners of the room where the 'carpet' fell short. There was no TV but there was a small iPod dock attached to a set of desktop speakers and an old radio plugged into a wall socket.

Mrs. Palmer seated herself on one of the picnic chairs and invited Clive to do the same. The chair creaked ominously when Clive sat down.

"Can I fix you a brew, Inspector?" asked Mr. Palmer, who remained standing in the doorway.

"No, no thank you. Please, come and join us, Mr. Palmer. My questions are for both of you. I'll try not to take up too much of your time."

Clive took out his notebook as Carl Palmer sat on the third creaking garden chair. Those chairs are stronger than they look, thought Clive. "Right then, Mr. and Mrs. Palmer…"

"Please, call us Carl and Claudette," Mrs. Palmer interrupted.

"Thank you, Claudette," Clive smiled. "And Carl."

Claudette smiled, Carl nodded.

"As you know, I'm here investigating the murder of Sally Hawkins – a student from your school."

"Dreadful business," said Carl, wringing his out-sized hands.

"Indeed," said Clive. "This is just a routine enquiry. I'm here in case you may have something – no matter how small or apparently trivial – that might aid the investigation. So, Carl, if I might come to you first. You teach PE at Stenham High?"

Carl Palmer nodded.

"Did you, at any time, teach Sally Hawkins?"

"No. The girls have their own female games teacher. I only teach the boys."

After Carl had spoken, he glanced at his wife and they both struggled to suppress a fit of giggles. Clive raised his eyebrows.

"I'm sorry, did I just say something funny?" Clive asked, puzzled.

"No, not at all. I'm sorry, Inspector." Carl said, still chuckling. "It's just that the girls' games mistress, Beatrice Morgan, well, she's a bit of an old cow, to be honest. A right old battleaxe, if you'll pardon my saying so. My wife and I sometimes joke that Beatrice is even more masculine than I am!"

"I see," said Clive, chewing the end of his biro. "So, you, Sir, had nothing to do with Sally Hawkins on a day-to-day basis at the school?"

"That's right, Inspector. Nothing at all."

"Did you see Sally Hawkins outside of school, Sir?" Clive asked sternly.

"No. No, I most certainly did not. As a matter of fact, Inspector, I didn't even know what the poor lass looked like until I saw her picture in the local paper. I honestly can't help you with this, I'm afraid. Perhaps my wife has something of greater value she can tell you."

Carl Palmer stood up.

"Is it okay if I make that brew now?"

Clive nodded and Mr. Palmer left the room.

"What would you like to ask me, Inspector?" Claudette said.

"What part of France are you from, Claudette?" Clive enquired. Her foreign accent seemed to be growing stronger by the sentence.

"I am Belgian, not French." Claudette snapped moodily.

"Oh, I see, begging your pardon *Madame*," Clive stumbled,

taken aback by the strength of her sudden hostility.

"It's okay," she said, with a wave of her hand. "It's a common mistake a lot of English people make. They always assume…"

"But you do teach French at the school?"

"That's right. Of course, no-one English would detect any difference in the two accents so they always think I am French but…" She attempted a smile.

"Did you know Sally Hawkins?"

"Not very well, *non*. She came to speak to me briefly at the end of last term to discuss the possibility of taking French A-level. She'd been taught GCSE French by the school's other language teacher, Mr. Hughes, and now she was thinking about doing A-level. I only teach A-level French to the Sixth Form. You see, my contract is only 0.5 – half of a full-time timetable."

"When exactly did Sally Hawkins come to see you, Mrs. Palmer?"

"About a week before term ended. She thought it could be useful to have an extra A-level – a fourth one – and she wanted to know how much reading was involved; whether she'd need to read any plays or novels in French. And then – *bof*! – she was dead."

"Did you notice anything out of the ordinary about Sally when she came to speak to you? Did she appear troubled in any way? Was she unduly nervous?"

"Well, she was a quiet girl. Very timid. It seemed in contrast to her love of acting and the stage."

"Yes, we've had a lot of reports saying that," Clive murmured.

"But no, there was nothing I would describe as unusual."

"Did Sally Hawkins ever visit you here at the cottage?"

"No, *non*. No way." Claudette laughed at the apparent absurdity of such a suggestion. She waved a hand at her surroundings.

"You can see for yourself how we live. We don't ask too many people to come and bear witness to our poverty."

"Teaching doesn't pay much, you see," said Carl Palmer in a deep baritone as he reappeared in the room, stirring his tea in a chipped Manchester City mug. He sat on the creaking chair and placed his wet teaspoon on the table.

"Basically, we rent this place because it's cheaper than renting in King's Lynn or even Hunstanton." Carl continued. "It looks pretty nice from the outside but…well, as you can see, it's a bit of a shithole on the inside, if you'll pardon my French."

Clive smiled politely. Claudette grimaced.

"And this is how our landlord furnished it – from a frigging skip!" Carl Palmer laughed loudly at his own joke.

"Well, at least you have a pleasant view," said Clive.

"So long as you like bloody lavender," Carl snorted.

"But it is pretty," Claudette sighed. "Heacham is world famous for lavender, you know, Inspector."

"Not just lavender," Carl continued.

"Oh?" Clive asked.

"Yes, there's more to the place than that. I could tell you plenty. In fact, I suppose you could say, in some ways, I'm Heacham's present-day John Rolfe,"

Carl grinned, his self-satisfaction evident. The big man leaned over and placed an affectionate hand on his wife's shoulder. Clive stared, non-plussed.

"Nope, I'm afraid you've lost me there, Sir. You're the new John...?"

"John Rolfe," Carl grinned. 'He was the local chap who married a woman you might have heard of: Pocohontas, the Red Indian girl. She's on the village coat of arms. So, just like John Rolfe, it's me and my gorgeous, exotic foreign wife living right here in little old Heacham. So, you see, that makes me the new John Rolfe." Carl Palmer roared as if he'd just cracked the world's funniest joke.

"So, you're a bit of a local historian then, Mr. Palmer?" Clive asked.

"Yes, exactly. I am actually." Carl replied, suddenly growing serious.

"PE teachers aren't all dumb musclemen, you know. I'm very big on history. I've always been into it. In fact, I'm a member of the North Norfolk History Society. It's pretty much my main hobby outside of sport. I'm in the Holkham branch of the Society with Paul Hodson from the school. We meet at a pub in Holkham once a month. There's another, bigger, branch in King's Lynn."

"Paul Hodson? Isn't he the school caretaker? I met him when we discovered Miss Hawkins' body. Mr. Hodson lives here in Heacham too, I believe?"

"Yes, yes he does." said Claudette. "Paul has a cottage on the sea front."

"It's one of the old fishermen's cottages," Carl added. "A much nicer property than ours. He inherited the place from his mother. Paul's an even bigger authority on local history than I am. He knows everything there is to know about this area. He often says to me: 'What I don't know about this county, you can write on a postage stamp.'"

Carl Palmer began laughing again, stopping only to reach for his tea.

"Have you spoken to Paul yet, Inspector?" Carl Palmer asked.

"No, no, I haven't as yet," Clive replied, snapping his notebook shut. "But I shall. Thank you both for your time."

Carl Palmer walked DI Dempsey to the door, still carrying his mug of tea. Clive handed him a business card.

"Don't hesitate to call if anything occurs to you or Mrs. Palmer," Clive said.

"Of course," Carl Palmer smiled, shoving the card in his back pocket. He threw the dregs of his tea on the ground, missing Clive's shoes by millimetres. Then he closed the door with a slam.

23

Sally Hawkins' best friend, Toni Hollins, had agreed to meet Sergeant Tommy Mearns and WPC Abbie Silver at the Saucy Haddock fish and chip restaurant in the centre of Hunstanton.

As a minor, Toni was accompanied by her mother, Jean. It was somewhat unorthodox to interview the girl in a public place rather than in her home or at the police station. However, Abbie had suggested it as she'd wanted Toni to feel totally at ease and neutral surroundings often helped.

Tommy showed his ID to the restaurant manager and secured a quiet corner table. The foursome took their seats. Toni and her mother sat with their backs to the restaurant's panoramic glass window, facing into the restaurant. Abbie and Tommy sat opposite, enjoying a clear view of the windswept seafront flowing across the horizon directly above their interviewees' heads.

Abbie noticed a lone ship in the distance ploughing across the sea, like a snail traversing a mattress. Toni Hollins' dark hair was cut in an angular bob in the same style as Abbie's. To a casual observer, Toni might have appeared to be Abbie's daughter rather than the offspring of the hard-faced peroxide blonde, Jean.

Toni's darting blue eyes gave her a shrew-like quality as she sat low in her seat, nervous and jittery, shrinking in on her thin frame.

What a pair those two girls must have made, thought Abbie – Sally and Toni, both scared of their own shadows. No wonder they'd been best friends. It must have been a totally symbiotic support system – the two withdrawn girls coming together to protect themselves against the big, wide, scary world. At the end of the day, whatever troubles they faced, they had each other.

So, how exactly had one of them ended up strangled and dumped in a field? If anyone knew, Toni Hollins just might. Four laminated menus were grouchily presented by a sullen waitress.

"Just two teas for us," said Abbie, gesturing at herself and Tommy. "Jean and Toni, please have whatever you'd like."

"You can't smoke in here can you?" Mrs. Hollins asked the

waitress. The girl shook her head.

"Look, do I really have to stay here the entire time?" Jean Hollins continued, addressing the remark to Abbie, a pleading look in her eyes. "Couldn't I, you know, just pop outside for a quick gasper while you ask Toni your questions?"

"I'd rather you stay, please, Mrs. Hollins." Abbie said firmly.

"Tea then," said Jean grumpily to the waitress. It was a coin toss as to which of them was the most miserable.

"Three teas," sneered the waitress. "And?"

The question was addressed to Toni.

"Um…"

"Go on, have whatever you want, love," Abbie encouraged.

"Um…can I have plaice and chips, please?"

"No plaice left," the waitress barked.

"Haddock and chips?" Toni asked hopefully.

"Three teas, one 'addock," the waitress grunted. "Any drink?"

"Um…Diet Coke, thanks."

The waitress stalked off. Tommy opened his notebook and placed it on the corner of the table.

"Service with a smile," Tommy shrugged.

"She's always been a moody cow, that one," Jean added with a sneer.

Pot, kettle, black, thought Abbie.

Owner's daughter yet she reckons she's far too la-di-da to be working in a chippie," Jean continued. "Best fish in Norfolk though – fresh off the docks and still fried in dripping. That's what keeps the folks coming back. Certainly ain't the service."

"You're welcome to have some too, Mrs. Hollins," Tommy reminded her. "I can call our friend back."

"Nah. You're alright. I'm on a diet, see. I might pinch a few of Toni's chips, though." The woman cackled.

Toni smiled weakly at her mother's comment. Abbie could see the girl was deeply uncomfortable in her mum's presence. Maybe, if Toni was going to open up and speak freely, it would be best if Jean went outside after all.

"Tell you what, Mrs. H," said Abbie conspiratorially. "You pop out and have that smoke. Tommy will ask them to hold your tea until you return."

"Cheers doll," said Jean, leaping to her feet.

Those still seated at the table barely had time to blink before Toni's mother was out on the street, lighting up, thin grey smoke swirling above her peroxide hair.

"Tommy, tell Princess Charming to hold one of the teas, will you?" said Abbie.

Tommy scraped his chair back and went in search of the waitress. Abbie and Toni were alone.

"Now then, Toni," said Abbie, leaning towards the girl. "Speaking woman to woman, can you tell me anything, anything at all, that might help me catch Sally's killer? Any secrets Sally might have told only to you? Any boyfriends no-one else might have known about? Boys from the school or boys from outside the school? Adult men even?"

Toni looked taken aback by the sudden barrage of questions but she also clearly relished the opportunity to speak to the WPC on her own and, however briefly, to have a confidante back in her life. "Well," Toni said, leaning so far forward her nose was almost touching Abbie's. "Sally did tell me she'd met someone on the internet. She swore me to secrecy about it but I suppose it doesn't matter now. There was some website she used for actors. Paint something. Greasy paint dot com or something like that. Sally said she'd met some man on that acting website who said he could help her. Said he'd given her advice about moving to London, getting an acting job. Said he'd help her get an Equality card or whatever it's called."

Abbie could feel her heart pounding with excitement. She prayed Tommy had the good sense not to return too soon and interrupt the girl's revelations. Abbie cast a glance above Toni's head to ensure Mrs. Hollins was still puffing away contentedly outside.

"Please continue," Abbie encouraged.

"Well," said Toni, sighing. It seemed a huge burden was being lifted from her young shoulders. "About two weeks before Sally died she told me she'd arranged to meet this man from the acting website over in Cromer. I don't know if the meeting ever happened – or even when it was supposed to happen – just that it was planned. Like I said, Sally swore me to secrecy and I haven't told anyone about it until now. Not even my mum knows."

Tommy returned to the table and sat down.

Abbie winced. She gestured to Tommy to stand up again and whispered briefly in his ear. Immediately, Tommy set off.

This time he ended up outside, chatting amiably to Mrs. Hollins to delay the woman's return. Even though Tommy didn't smoke, Abbie watched him expertly cadge a fag from Jean and persuade her to have another one herself.

Good man, thought Abs.

"Tell me more, Toni," Abbie prompted once they were alone again.

"Well, that's about it to be honest," Toni shrugged. "That really is just about the most important thing I can think of to tell you. And that's the only secret Sally had for sure. She'd met some actor bloke on this website and she was going to meet him in Cromer."

"Did she tell you his name? His age? Anything more about him?"

"No. They have user names on the website. He probably had a user name that was different from his real name. He must have known Sally's phone number though because he was also texting her."

"Did you see any of these texts? Did Sally show any of them to you?"

"No. She was very private about it. I asked to see them, of course, but she only told me bits and pieces. She'd clam up if I pushed it, so I didn't push. I just let her tell me as much as she wanted to. To be honest, I half thought she was making it all up and that's why the details were so sketchy. Sally had more of a fantasy life than a real life and that's probably why she wanted to do acting. I didn't really believe her when she said she had a secret boyfriend online. I should have told someone. It's my fault what happened isn't it? For not telling, I mean."

Toni looked as if she might cry. Abbie placed a hand on the girl's shoulder. At that moment the grumpy waitress reappeared. She handed Abbie a mug of tea and shoved a lukewarm tumbler of flat Coke in front of Toni. Even the perfunctory slice of lemon floating limply in Toni's soft drink looked miserable.

"So is it two teas or one?" the waitress barked.

"Look here, missy," Abbie snarled, flashing her police badge at the sullen cow. "Just bring us the food, and do it pronto, or I'll have you arrested for being both stupid and ugly. After that, I'll have this place closed down under health and safety regulations. Now, take that glass of dishwater away and bring my friend a nice cold, fresh Coke with plenty of ice and a decent slice of lemon that you haven't just pulled from the bin."

Shocked, the girl complied, whisking away the offending drink and even attempting an apologetic smile.

"Sometimes it's handy being a copper," Abbie whispered to Toni. "Now, back to this mystery man from the internet – are you sure you can't give me a name? Not even a user name?"

"Um," Toni wrinkled her face in concentration. "No, I'm sorry. I did tell Sally to be careful though. I told her I'd go with her to Cromer, if she wanted – you know, to act as lookout. I said I'd sit in the coffee shop when she met this guy in case he was, you know, a psycho or something. But she never asked me to go with her, which is basically why I think the meeting never happened. She *would* have asked me to go. I know she would. So that's why I didn't report it – not even when I heard she was...heard she was..."

"It's okay, love," Abbie said, handing the girl a tissue. "You mustn't blame yourself. The only person to blame is the bastard who…"

All of a sudden Tommy and Jean were back. A moment later the waitress brought Toni a new Coke and a piping hot plate of golden fish and chips. These were deposited in front of Toni with a grand flourish.

"Hope you enjoy it," said the waitress, through gritted teeth,

"My, that does look rather good," said Jean Hollins covetously, reaching for a chip. "Is it too late to change my mind?"

"Not at all," said Abbie, standing up. "We have to leave now but I'll ask the waitress to bring another plate of haddock and chips over."

"That should cover it," said Tommy, handing Mrs. Hollins a twenty pound note.

"Thank you, Toni," Abbie said to the Hollins girl, who had now recovered her composure. "You've been very helpful. Please bear in mind we'll need you to repeat what you've just told us on record."

Toni nodded solemnly.

"What? She's gotta go through all this *again*?" barked Jean.

"I'll be in touch as the investigation develops," Abbie deadpanned. "Enjoy your meal, ladies."

Tommy and Abbie turned to leave. Abbie caught hold of the waitress and gestured in Jean Hollins' direction.

"One more haddock and chips over there, love, and make it snappy. And, for God's sake, try putting a smile on your ugly mug. Some girls don't even live to be *your* age."

24

At the very moment Tommy was paying for Toni Hollins to enjoy eating some fish, Frank was standing at the docks watching Mary Harris gutting some fish. The girl manoeuvred her knife with practised ease, never once looking down at her handiwork, all the while fixing DCI Homes with a beady gaze.

Mary Harris was thin and bony but nevertheless had a sinewy strength. Her light brown hair was lank and greasy. Several tendrils were plastered to her forehead, protruding beneath the regulation white cap the dock workers were required to wear.

Her eyes were almost the same colour as the blue industrial rubber gloves all the fish-gutting ladies sported.

Mary was one of about twenty five such workers, all standing in a line at their workstations, all grimly busy with their slimy quarry.

"DCI Frank Homes of the…" Frank began, holding up his ID.

"I know who you are," Mary sneered.

"…Norfolk Constabulary." Frank continued regardless.

"I've not done nothing," said Mary.

"I didn't say you had," said Frank, mildly irritated. "I'm just here to talk."

"What about? The price of fish?"

Mary cackled.

"Sally Hawkins." Frank snapped. "A murdered child. A girl who happened to be only one year younger than you when her life was brutally terminated."

"Who?"

"Don't you read the papers, Mary? Watch TV? Listen to the radio? Go online? Are you so busy filleting fish you don't even notice what's happening in your own town?"

"Oh, her."

"Yes, *her*. Several people at your old school have told me you two didn't get along. Some of them say you bullied Sally. And now she's dead. So, I have a few questions I'd like to ask you, Miss Harris."

"What people said what things about me? It's all bollocks!"

"You can talk to me here or at the station," Frank said angrily. "Your call, missy."

"I've got nothing to say."

Frank began jangling his car keys.

"Alright, already. Ask your stupid questions then."

"Can you stop messing with those bloody fish for five minutes? Let's take a walk and have a chat where it doesn't stink."

Mary Harris put the filleting knife down and removed her cap and gloves. She folded the cap into a small handkerchief-sized parcel and tucked it into her pocket as she shook her hair loose. The shaking didn't make much difference, though, and her greasy locks remained stubbornly glued to her scalp.

"Let's walk to the far end of the docks and back again," Mary suggested with a shrug. "It's all gonna stink of fish, I'm afraid, but you'll get some cleaner air further out."

The pair carefully picked their way along the slippery dockside – the girl's industrial boots giving her good traction through the obstacle course of fish guts and plastic crates.

By contrast, Frank skidded comically a few times in his leather slip-ons, grabbing hold of Mary for support more than once. The ships seemed to magically grow bigger as the two walkers approached the open sea.

As the dockside buildings grew correspondingly smaller in the ever-diminishing background, increasing numbers of seagulls swirled around them, screeching their banshee wail.

"They tell me you used to run a gang at school, Mary?"

"Who's 'they'?"

"Never mind. Is it true?"

"More or less."

"More or less?"

"Look, what's your point?"

"They say you ran a girl gang that used to terrorise most of the other girls and some of the boys too?"

"We're not all sugar and spice, Inspector."

"And you especially hated Sally Hawkins? Is that true?"

"I didn't hate her. That's too strong. She was just there and she irritated me. She was so dreary and dreamy and mousey. She had the kind of face that's asking to be kicked. She was a loner and a weirdo. She went round looking all stuck up – as if she was somehow better than everyone else. I just reminded her of the pecking order. That's all."

"So you attacked her?"

"Don't talk shite. I never needed to attack her. I just *threatened* to attack her. That was plenty good enough, believe me. She couldn't give me her pocket money fast enough after that. Lots of 'em gave me their pocket money. I was coining in about five quid a week from every spastic round the school. Easiest cash I ever made. You might think it was all about Sally Hawkins but it weren't. I was a horrible bitch to all of them kids."

"You freely admit that?"

"I admit it, Inspector, because it's my past. I admit it, Inspector, because I've put it behind me and moved on. The leopard has changed its spots. And no, before you ask, I've not found God or seen the light or anything wussy like that. I've grown up so I've grown out of all that juvenile bollocks. I'm on the straight and narrow now, gutting sodding fish for my sins."

"Did you also extort money from Toni Hollins?"

"Who? Oh yeah, you mean that puny little lesbo pal of Sally's? Of course I bloody did. Frankly, *Frank*, you're better off trying to find a girl at school who I *didn't* scam any money off."

Mary cackled loudly, greatly enjoying her own pun.

They walked a little further. Suddenly, Mary stopped. She pulled a crumpled roll-up and a plastic lighter out of her pocket and sparked up. The pungent tobacco smoke, mingling with the salty sea air and the overpowering whiff of fish guts, made Frank feel nauseous.

"You really were a winning personality back then, Mary, weren't you?"

Mary chuckled. This time it was a quiet laugh, wistful and reflective. She exhaled a thin stream of smoke in Frank's direction.

"Like I said, I can't help you with your enquiries, Inspector, but I do hope you catch the scumbag who killed Sally Hawkins and, when you do, you can send him directly to me. I'll be more than happy to gut the bastard for you."

25

After he'd spoken to Mary Harris, Frank drove directly to the seafront in Hunstanton. He needed time to think and he definitely needed some fresh air to clear the stench of fish guts from his lungs.

Ever since his childhood in Essex, when he'd visited his grandmother in Southend for his annual summer holiday, he'd found a brisk walk by the sea to be the best way to clear his mind of any troubles. As Frank walked past the Saucy Haddock restaurant he realised Abbie and Tommy would only recently have finished questioning Toni Hollins. Frank took out his smartphone and tapped the screen.

"Abs," Frank barked as soon as WPC Silver answered. "How'd it go with the Hollins girl? Get anything useful?"

"Absolutely, Sir. She told me Sally had arranged to meet some actor type in Cromer; some guy she'd encountered on that Greasepaint social networking site. This was only two weeks before Sally was murdered."

"Great work, Abs. So, did this meeting between Sally and her mystery man ever take place?"

"Toni didn't know. She'd offered to accompany Sally to the venue – a café – to keep an eye on things but, as we know, Sally was secretive. She could have just gone on her own without telling anyone."

"Okay. That's a major line of enquiry. We'll need Harry's input on the technical side. And, hang on a minute, didn't Sally's class tutor, Jasper Collins, tell Clive that the Drama teacher, Tim Powell, was on that Greasepaint website all the time?"

"Indeed he did," said Abbie. "We talked about it when you were in hospital."

"And I told you to monitor Powell. Any developments?"

"Nothing yet, Sir," said Abbie. "But Tim Powell is definitely our number one suspect."

"Perhaps," said Frank coolly. "We certainly need to speak to Mr. Powell again. However, let's be careful we don't go putting two and two together and making five. What's certain is one of them is lying but we don't yet know which one; it could just as easily be Collins as Powell."

"I hadn't thought of that, Sir," said Abbie meekly.

"That's why I'm the DCI," Frank laughed. It was a friendly jibe, not a slight, but he could still detect a hurt silence.

"But, listen," Frank added quickly. "Tim Powell is undoubtedly our starting point. After all, he could well be the person using that website to arrange a meeting with Sally in Cromer. If so, he's got some explaining to do. Where are you right now, Abs?"

"At the station, Sir. We're all here. Where are you?"

"On the seafront. I'm taking a quick stroll to gather my thoughts. I'll join you soon."

"Any joy from Mary Harris?" Abbie asked.

"No. Waste of time, I reckon. She had to be checked out though."

"Regarding Powell, do you want me to ask Tommy or Clive to bring him in?"

"Not yet, Abs. I want to bring him in myself; put the frighteners on him in person. No, the best thing you can do just now is get hold of another of these characters we need to interview: Paul Hodson, the caretaker. One of you bring Hodson in. After that, we'll put the thumbscrews on Powell.'"

"Yes, Sir. How long before you're back, Sir?"

"I'll be back within the hour. I just need to clear the smell of fish guts from my lungs."

"I'm not sure a walk by the brine is the best remedy, Sir."

Frank laughed.

"You're probably right, Abs. But I do my best thinking by the sea. It must be the salt in the air. It purifies my thoughts and clears the cobwebs like nothing else."

"See you in an hour, Sir."

Frank slipped his phone back in his pocket. As he continued along the seafront he passed a clutch of kiosks offering an assortment of seaside delights: garish plastic buckets and spades, pink candy floss, greasy hamburgers and smooth white ice cream cones. Frank bought himself a '99' cone.

Ice cream in hand, Frank wandered far from the smattering of holiday makers on the seafront path. In between gulps of smooth vanilla, Frank inhaled the sea air deeply.

The experience was calming – just what he needed after all those visions of the ghostly black hound and the trauma of his recent hospitalisation. Now, Frank hoped, all this weird stuff could be put behind him and he could focus solely on the case.

Having eaten his ice cream, Frank realised he'd walked far

beyond the caravan park that hugged a fair stretch of the coastline. He was now completely isolated. Only a small section of empty beach lay below him while an endless grey stretch of churning sea extended away to the far horizon. Frank descended some narrow concrete steps and walked the length of an adjacent boat ramp.

He stopped at the water's edge, just out of reach of the lapping waves. There he stood, hands in pockets, his mind slowly emptying of troubles. Time passed in a deceptive blur. The light gradually began to take on an oddly misty haze. Frank was aware he was growing cold; as cold as the ice cream he'd just eaten. As he grew colder, Frank found himself shaking – slowly at first, then uncontrollably. And then he saw it!

Moving as swiftly and skilfully as a spider on a thread, at first invading only the outer edges of Frank's vision: a gigantic black hound! Only this time it was not running on dry land, it was *gliding* across the surface of the sea!

The dog was a long way out to sea – halfway to the horizon – and yet it was charging at full speed over the waves as if they did not exist.

Frank rubbed his eyes. Surely this could not be happening. Not *again*! And yet, as Frank looked back, there it was.

There was no doubt it was the same huge black spectral creature he'd seen several times before; the same black dog that had put him in hospital; the same ghost dog that had spewed its putrid breath over him beside the Lynn War Memorial. And it was most definitely a dog, despite its enormous size.

Yet could this vision *really* be called a 'dog'? If so, it was a dog that could both walk and run across the surface of deep water. It was a dog that could appear from nowhere, and disappear back into nothingness, seemingly at will.

What in God's name was going on? Why was this dreadful phantom haunting him? What did it all mean?

At last the mist obscuring Frank's vision began to clear. He watched the dog closely, transfixed. It was gliding over the waves in such an ethereal manner it was truly mesmerising. The dog suddenly stopped.

Frank felt a shudder coursing through his bones. The dog turned to look directly at him. Despite the distance between them, Frank felt the animal's glowing red eyes burning through him.

Then the dog rocked back on its powerful haunches and let out a howl – a blood-curdling banshee wail.

Frank was paralysed with fear.

The gigantic dog began to charge – running straight towards Frank, snarling and growling. Its speed was unreal. It had been miles out to sea but now it was gaining ground as if three more strides might bring it to the shore.

This was it, thought Frank – death itself was approaching; his own *specific* death; his death personified in this terrible creature. Frank closed his eyes and waited for the inevitable.

The creature was almost upon him. Frank could hear its breathing. Its snarling penetrated his torso like a knife. And then, silence.

So this is what it feels like to be dead, thought Frank.

He opened his eyes cautiously only to find there was no ghost dog. There was only the sea, grey and heavy and churning. Frank looked every which way; he scoured the coastline and stared back out to sea. There was no phantom hound anywhere.

There was nothing untoward, nothing to fear. There was only himself and the dense, grey brine. Suddenly Frank felt weak.

His vision began to fail, his head felt light.

He sat on the hard concrete of the boat ramp, placed his head in his hands and tried to decide whether he'd rather sob, scream or laugh hysterically. He was losing his mind and he dared not tell another soul.

Frank sat bereft. Then he began rocking back and forth like a trauma victim. Once more, DCI Frank Homes found his entire world was spinning wildly off its axis.

26

DI Dempsey was furious. He didn't like being used as an errand boy. As he saw it, Frank was bang out of order.

Coordinating operations through WPC Abbie Silver was an insult. She was just a lowly uniform. He, Clive Dempsey, was a fully-fledged DI. Yet it was Abbie who'd spoken to Frank on the phone just now. Abbie was also the person in whom Frank regularly confided regarding the Sally Hawkins case.

It was Abbie who'd informed Clive that Frank wanted him to go and fetch this no-mark school janitor, Paul Hodson, and bring him to the station for questioning. It was nothing short of an outrage. Anyone would have thought Abbie was the DI.

Clive was all for teamwork but this was ridiculous. Why was Frank so obsessed with Abbie anyway? He wasn't going to get in the WPC's knickers. Everyone knew she'd been shacked up with the same boyfriend since she was eighteen. She was totally besotted with that dozy cretin who ran a half-arsed business repairing windmills. No-one had any idea what Abbie saw in the loser. However, they were a rock solid couple.

"No chance, Frankie boy," Clive said out loud as he turned the wheel of the Astra and pressed his foot down, gunning the car towards the small coastal settlement of Heacham. That was another thing – when it came to allocating the Force's cars, Frank got an Insignia and Clive only got an Astra. Life was unremittingly unfair.

Paul Hodson was a distinctly unpleasant looking individual. A walking, talking mountain of gelatinous fat. He seemed to have been poured over his own skeleton from a bucket of lard and some of the residue seemed to be dripping over his waistband where he spread out alarmingly at the hips like a melting jelly.

I'm meeting the real-life Tweedle Dum, thought Clive, as he shook Hodson's clammy, pudgy hand. 'Billy Bunter', the kids called him, or 'Billy Munter' or simply 'The Munter.' Whatever you called him, Paul Hodson was a pretty scary prospect to have as your school caretaker, thought Clive. A six foot four, twenty stone troll of a man emerging from his murky cave to tell you off for running across the school's freshly mown lawns. It would have scared the young Clive Dempsey rigid.

"Will this take long?" Hodson asked breathlessly as he pulled the front door of his cottage closed and waddled towards Clive's Astra.

"Not too long, I expect, Mr. Hodson. Hard to say." Clive replied. He still felt irritated at having to collect the fat man on Frank's behalf.

Clive felt the car's suspension groan as Paul Hodson lowered his enormous bulk into the passenger seat. The caretaker's knee brushed against the gear lever, so broad were his hulking thighs. Clive and Hodson eyed each other with mutual discomfort as Clive's hand inadvertently brushed the giant man's leg while checking to see if the Astra was in neutral.

Embarrassed, Hodson shifted his outsize frame to the left, bouncing the car in the process. The fat bastard is going to burst a tyre if this continues, thought Clive. Finally, Paul Hodson settled, albeit in an unnaturally cramped position. Clive fired up the Astra and pulled away.

"Nice place," said Clive as the car picked up speed.

"Eh?" Hodson grunted, turning to look at Clive.

"Your cottage. Those fisherman's cottages in Heacham have

always looked attractive, in my opinion. Right by the sea front yet only a short drive from Lynn and far cheaper than Sunny Hunny."

"What are you – an estate agent or a cop?" Hodson laughed.

It was said in the guise of a joke but there was also a hint of menace that took Clive aback.

"I might be an armchair estate agent, Mr. Hodson but I'm definitely a fully-fledged copper, I can assure you."

"No, no, I just meant..." Hodson stammered, suddenly apologetic.

"I was just making conversation, Sir," Clive continued. "As I was saying, I've often admired those cottages from afar. I could see myself living in a place like that someday. Have you lived there long?"

"All my life. I inherited it from my mother about ten years ago. My dad was a fisherman – from a long line of fishermen. He died at sea in a fishing accident soon after I was born. My mother was allowed to keep the cottage as widow's benefit." Hodson looked pained at the memory.

No way *you* could be a fisherman, thought Clive. You'd sink the boat the moment you stepped into it.

"You didn't fancy going to sea then?" Clive said.

Paul Hodson snorted.

"Look at me. I've always been a fat bastard. No chance of

following in my father's footsteps."

"How long have you been the caretaker at Stenham High?" Clive asked.

"About five years, give or take," Hodson replied.

"And what did you do before that, Sir?"

"Sold vacuum cleaners door-to-door," Hodson said flatly. "The job sucked!"

Clive laughed. His mood of hostility – borne out of resentment at being designated as errand boy by Frank's uppity amanuensis – was finally softening. Now he almost began to feel sorry for his overweight passenger. More to be pitied than despised, perhaps. Clive cast his mind back to the interview he'd recently conducted in Heacham with Hodson's near neighbours, the Palmers.

"You know the Palmers quite well, don't you?"

Paul Hodson hesitated. The pause seemed unnaturally long. When he replied, it was with an unsteady voice.

"I...er...yes. They...er...live in a nearby cottage...by the lavender fields. We all...er...work at Stenham High. I know him much better than her. She's a Frenchie."

"Belgian," Clive corrected him. "She told me so in no uncertain terms."

"Belgian then. Same difference." Hodson snorted. "She's a bit stuck up, if you ask me. I get on better with him. We go for a few beers now and again. We're both in the Holkham branch of the North Norfolk History Society. We attend Society meetings once a month at a pub near Holkham Hall. Gets us both out of the house, I guess."

"So you know a fair bit about this area?" Clive asked as he guided the Astra smoothly into the police station car park.

"Well, put it this way," Paul Hodson said confidently, staring out of the window at the police station. "Nothing much goes on around this place without me knowing about it."

27

Frank sat up and gazed out to sea. His consciousness was only slowly escaping the black void to which it had been banished by the vision of the ghost dog running across the waves.

Gradually it dawned on Frank that he was still on the boat ramp by the water's edge. He then realised he was sitting in the water. His feet were submerged and his trousers were soaked. If anyone saw him, he'd appear to be stark, raving mad. A modern King Canute!

Frank checked his watch. How long had he been here? Well over an hour! He'd been out like a light – sitting on a boat ramp in a rising tide, conscious of absolutely nothing...for over an hour.

How was that even possible? He stood up, water pouring off him and his clothes clinging uncomfortably to his body. He felt clammy, cold and drenched. Everything carried the smell of seaweed and brine. He may as well have been sleeping in the carcass of a beached whale.

As Frank swayed unsteadily back to the pathway he realised how nauseous he felt. Could this episode be something to do with his recent fall? Should he phone the hospital or his GP? Should he – *could* he – talk about this to anyone? Why was this giant ghost dog repeatedly appearing to him in all these bizarre visions? It couldn't be real. It just couldn't. A dog running across the water? A dog with luminous red eyes? A dog the size of a small horse?

This was utter madness and, if he dared admit this insanity in public, he'd lose his case to a rival team from Norwich. The case! Abbie! He should have been back at the police station by now, questioning Paul Hodson.

Frank reached for his mobile. Luckily the phone was safely tucked inside his top pocket, free of the water. Frank called Abbie, fumbling with the phone's screen.

"Abs! It's me."

"Where the hell have you been…er…Sir?"

"I had an accident."

"Oh my God. Are you alright?"

"Never mind. I'm fine. Listen, I've no time to explain. What's going on there? Have you got Hodson?"

"Yes, he's here. Clive brought him in a while back. We gave him a coffee and tried to wait for you but, well, there are limits, Sir. Clive went in with Hodson about five minutes ago."

Clive. At heart he was a good man and he was certainly a decent cop, thought Frank. However, his DI also wanted nothing more than to fill Frank's shoes and take over not just the case but also Frank's position. This delayed, cocked-up interview was just one more bullet in Clive's armoury.

Still, there was nothing Frank could do right now. He was on the sea front while Clive was back in the station sitting opposite Paul Hodson and taking the man's statement. Frank sucked his teeth.

"Alright, fine. Clive is just as capable of interviewing Hodson as I am. I want a copy of the statement on my desk, though, and I want it the moment the interview concludes."

"When will you be in, Sir?"

"I'm going home to change then I'll head directly to the station."

"What sort of accident did you have if you need to change? Are you hurt? Do you need the hospital?"

"Stop fussing, Silver. I didn't piss my pants, if that's what you're thinking. I'll be there as soon as I can. Just make sure the interview transcript is waiting on my desk."

"Yes Sir."

Frank hung up and plunged the phone back in his pocket. His recurrent bouts of lunacy were turning this investigation into a damnable mess. A trail of water spread out behind Frank as he squelched along the pathway, hurrying back to the Insignia. Frank hardly dared look towards the sea now. Instead, he kept his eyes on the ground, focusing mainly on his sodden shoes.

The thought of seeing that hellish dog again was too much to contemplate. A short time later, Frank walked up to the Insignia and blipped the fob to unlock the driver's door.

Once inside, he switched the heater to full blast, keeping the windows shut. Perhaps his trousers might dry out sufficiently for him to go directly to the police station rather than traipsing back home to change. Perhaps he would even catch the tail end of Paul Hodson's interview.

Frank flipped the radio onto a classical music station and put his foot down as the car reached the A149. He was painfully aware this road was the scene of his first sighting of the ghostly black dog. He decided not to look in his rear-view mirror for the entire journey.

What did the dog want with him anyway?

Why did he keep seeing the bloody thing?

What could it all *mean*?

Don't be stupid, Frank, the dog is *not* real!

As the Insignia reached the outskirts of King's Lynn, Frank faced a decision – cop shop or home? Home won. It was a close call but Frank wanted a quick breather before facing his colleagues. He needed to compose himself – to banish his latest sighting of the phantom from his mind – and to get changed into fresh, dry clothes.

When Frank arrived home he was glad to find Mrs. Gostage and Spider were out. Mrs. G. meant well but he was in no mood for her kindly interventions on this occasion.

He sat down heavily on his bed. Maybe he should delay going in to work completely. Maybe he should just go and see Jo. Perhaps he *could* tell her about the visions of the ghost dog after all? Perhaps she'd be the perfect shoulder to cry on. No! It was a stupid idea. Nobody would understand. Nobody *could* understand. Not even Jo.

It would be bad enough having his colleagues thinking he was mad – it would be ten times worse to put Jo in that position. No, this was something Frank would just have to resolve for himself.

But *how*?

Through sheer strength of will, Frank brought his mind back

to the Sally Hawkins case. Now he switched tack – driving the spectral hound from his consciousness by replacing irrational concerns about something that may not exist with very real and rational concerns about something that most definitely did exist... Sally Hawkins' killer.

What was the murderer's motive? Who was in the frame?

What had forensics turned up of further value?

Frank forced himself to think through all the evidence he'd gathered so far. Finally, Frank could feel himself returning to his default setting; the workaholic cop who'd leave no stone unturned to see justice delivered.

Having checked his new outfit in the mirror – grey trousers, pale blue shirt, shiny black Oxfords – Frank grabbed his car keys. It was time to discover exactly what Clive had garnered from the school caretaker, Paul Hodson.

It was time for police business once more.

28

Paul Hodson had gone home by the time Frank arrived at the police station. Still agitated, Frank waved away all enquiries about his well-being and gruffly demanded a cup of coffee and the transcript of Clive's interview with the overweight school caretaker.

With his Colchester United mug planted squarely on the desk and all colleagues banished from his office, Frank began to read. His trained eye picked out only the salient details as he rapidly skimmed the document.

'I visit Stenham High every day in my capacity as caretaker. This includes the holidays. I have been doing this

job for approximately five years…On the day the body was found I arrived at the school shortly after DI Clive Dempsey (who was attending the scene following the discovery of the victim's body)…I had not been alerted to anything untoward and I was visiting the school solely as part of my normal duties…'

Frank's eyes travelled quickly down the page.

'I knew Sally Hawkins by sight and spoke to her on occasion but I did not know her well. I knew her only as one of the many students who attend Stenham High and I did not know her full name until her murder became prominent in the local and national news media. I do not make a point of fraternising with the students although I do socialise with staff. My impression of Sally Hawkins, such as I knew her, was of a quiet and studious girl who kept herself to herself.'

Frank skipped through two paragraphs.

'I live in Heacham and consider myself to be a friend of Carl Palmer, the boys' PE teacher at Stenham High, and his wife, Claudette, a French teacher at the school. Carl and I share an interest in local history and are both members of a local history society (Holkham branch). Carl and I also share an interest in classic cars and stock car racing. We sometimes attend stock car races at the Great Yarmouth track. Carl,

Claudette and I often visit The Victory pub in Heacham for Sunday lunch together. I also sometimes drink with the school Drama teacher, Tim Powell, at The Clifftops pub in Old Hunstanton – usually on Fridays at the end of the school week. I do not socialise with any other school staff.'

Frank threw the transcript back on the desk and took a swig of coffee. He'd fleetingly scanned Hodson's various platitudes at the end of the statement concerning the man's apparent sadness at the Hawkins' family's tragic loss and his willingness to help the enquiry in any way possible.

There was little of obvious value in the entire text but Frank nevertheless felt something wasn't quite right about Paul Hodson. It was one of the reasons he'd wanted to interview the caretaker himself.

Caretakers usually knew anything and everything that was going on at their place of work. Much like hotel doormen, caretakers often functioned as the eyes and ears of any place that employed them.

However, reading between the lines of his statement, it appeared that Paul Hodson was spending most of the interview carefully distancing himself from events at every turn. Frank suspected that Hodson's name would be reappearing later in the enquiry – he just didn't yet know how.

Frank stood up, walked to the kitchen and made himself another coffee. This time he ladled in two teaspoons of sugar, calculating the sugar rush would give him a burst of energy.

He took the coffee back to his office and sat down. The sugar seemed to do the trick and Frank soon felt rejuvenated. Paul Hodson's statement lay on the desk where Frank had thrown it.

He'd catch up with the school caretaker at some point, no doubt about that. Right now, however, Frank was preoccupied by a different concern. He booted up his computer and logged onto the internet. I'll find you, you mutant freak, thought Frank as he typed a phrase into a search engine: 'black dog ghosts, norfolk.'

To Frank's astonishment 103,000 separate results were returned. One name appeared over and over again: 'Black Shuck.' Frank was transfixed. He visited website after website and read report after report. Black Shuck – the Hell Hound of East Anglia – had apparently been present in the region since the Viking era.

The ghost's most famous appearance had been in 1577 in the Suffolk villages of Bungay and Blythburgh. It was reported that Shuck had appeared among the congregations inside both town's churches during a terrible storm and killed at least two worshippers at each site before leaving a giant ghostly claw mark scorched into Blythburgh Church door – a mark that apparently remains visible to this day.

Furthermore, in 1890, a young boy, rescued from the sea, said he'd been forced to swim far from shore by a huge black dog that had chased him into the waves. During the 1930s there were reports from several fishermen near Sheringham describing hearing a blood-curdling howling from the cliff tops during stormy nights – a sound just like the one Frank had heard when he'd seen the dog out at sea.

In 1970 a sighting of Black Shuck made the headlines in the local papers when an abnormally large hound was seen pounding over the beach at Great Yarmouth. In 1980 a woman claimed to have met Shuck while out walking. She described the ghost dog as having 'fur as black as the night, glowing saucer-like eyes, fetid breath and huge teeth' – just like the apparition Frank had seen at close quarters beside the War Memorial.

There was an even more recent sighting; some novelist who claimed to have seen Shuck while driving on the A149 – apparently at the very same spot where Frank had experienced his own first vision.

To see Shuck, it was said, was an extremely bad omen – you could be dead within the year or someone connected to you might die instead. Frank's entire body chilled to the bone.

Could all these sightings be *real*? Could even *some* of them be real – after all, there were so many across so many centuries.

Surely they couldn't *all* be hallucinations? Could this Black Shuck – 'the Devil's Dog' as one site called it – really be walking among us today? Had Frank himself witnessed this unholy creature?

Frank logged off and began pacing. Had anyone observed him they'd have concluded he was lost in thought over the Sally Hawkins case. Only Frank knew the inner turmoil he was facing.

How could he not have known the legend of this Shuck creature? He'd grown up in Essex – not so far away. He'd worked in Suffolk and Norfolk – both counties in which Shuck had been spotted.

And then it dawned on Frank with a new sense of horror – perhaps he *did* know about the Shuck legend after all. Perhaps it had been known to him for years and he had simply somehow forgotten it – until now.

Perhaps he'd suppressed all knowledge of it; banished it from his psyche for some unknown reason. Now, with the trauma of the Sally Hawkins case and with the added pressure of finding the killer, he was projecting his forgotten memories of this uncanny legend into a series of distracting and disturbing visions.

Yes, that was it – it was simply a manifestation of the stress he was under. He was quite literally visiting a waking nightmare upon himself. The theory Frank now constructed for himself as he paced his office presented itself as a strange kind of self-sabotage. However, at least it was a rational theory. At least it was *scientific*. At least it offered a sane and palatable alternative to the utterly crazy notion that a rabid ancient Hell Hound was on the loose and had, for some reason, chosen to haunt him repeatedly and with increasing frequency.

Frank felt dizzy and the room seemed to swim around him. "No, no, you can't black out here – not again!" he told himself. He gripped the edge of the desk for support.

As he did so, his fingers spread across Paul Hodson's statement. The paper bent backwards to reveal a sentence that burned itself into Frank's brain.

Hodson said: **'Carl and I share an interest in local history and are both members of a Norfolk local history society (Holkham branch).'**

An idea formed instantly in Frank's mind. He would find out who ran the Holkham branch of the local history group and visit them. Under the guise of investigating Carl Palmer and Paul Hodson, he would ask – as casually as he could – all about Black Shuck.

Regaining his composure, Frank logged back onto the internet and navigated to the search engine. Now he carefully typed in a new phrase: 'norfolk local history society, holkham branch.'

29

Frank parked the Insignia a few streets from home. He had no choice as parking spaces were at an absolute premium. All he wanted was a decent night's sleep.

Things were closing in on him. He couldn't face chatting to Mrs. Gostage or offering to take Spider for a walk; not tonight. He wasn't even going to cook. Just pour a beer, eat a bag of crisps and hit the hay.

It was a full moon. The blue half-light of Earth's closest cousin mingled with the harsh yellow electric light of the street lamps to create a soupy, misty glow. It might have spooked Frank if he wasn't so darn tired.

Now all he needed was that damned ghost dog to appear, he thought sourly. Frank turned the corner at the top of his road and cursed. Although he'd just driven past, he'd somehow forgotten about the road works the council had begun that morning.

It was the main reason parking spaces were even harder to find than usual. There'd been some problem with the drains and a major excavation had taken place that had required not only the closing of the road but also the re-routing of even pedestrian traffic. A sign apologised in glib weasel words for the 'inconvenience.' It meant Frank had to walk on until he reached the road that ran parallel to his own. After that, he'd have to walk halfway down that street in order to cut through the alleyway that connected the two roads. Then, finally, he'd be home.

Frank's tiredness felt unnatural. All he wanted to do was sleep. In fact, he wanted the comfort of sleep so much, he wondered if he could actually make it home at all. Each step felt as though he were wading through quicksand.

His eyes were drooping, his vision blurring.

At one point he had to stop and hold on to a fence post for support. He thought he was going to faint again. It was like the time the dog appeared on the surface of the sea, charging across the waves before a surge of nausea had pitched Frank into the void.

Yet the dog was nowhere to be seen.

Maybe so, thought Frank, but I can *sense* it. Eventually, feeling steadier, Frank walked on. All was well until Frank turned into the entrance of the alleyway and …there it was!

The beast was standing, surrounded by mist, looming so large it seemed to occupy the entire alleyway – a hulking black mass blocking Frank's path. Frank instinctively backed away.

Had it seen him? It was unmoving – its four powerful legs spread across the width of the alleyway in a stance of suppressed readiness; the slightest forward movement from Frank seemed likely to provoke it into a vicious attack.

What was it called on those websites he'd seen earlier? *Black* something? All Frank could think of was Cerberus – the mythical three-headed dog that guarded the entrance to the Underworld. Well, this dog may only have had one head but it was every bit as fearsome. A jet black head as large as a lion's, incandescent glowing red eyes (entirely without cornea or pupils and yet somehow deeply watchful), teeth as razor sharp and densely packed as any T-Rex and sticky, acidic drool leaking from its blackened lips. There was a fetid stench; the cloying, musty odour of death and decay.

Frank felt nausea rising within.

There was no way past except to walk towards the dog and then to attempt to walk *through* the dog.

This was it, then. The final showdown. If the creature was just a vision, Frank should steel himself, walk towards it, keep on walking, close his eyes and walk straight through it. That would prove there was nothing there. Once and for all, he could banish these insane apparitions.

His mind had played tricks on him for long enough. Now was the time to take control. Face your fears and confront your demons. That was always the advice of the sages, wasn't it? The self-help gurus, professional counsellors, head shrinks of every hue and colour. Perhaps one of them should be here with him right now, seeing exactly what he was seeing; then he could tell *them* to walk jauntily forward without a care in the world.

Frank looked at the gigantic ghost dog. It was still there. This time, however, it *moved*! It suddenly began pawing at the ground, digging and clawing, preparing to attack. Unbelievably, the concrete pathway was being churned up by the dog's actions!

Frank stood transfixed as the animal's monstrous claws eviscerated a solid layer of pavement as though it were the softest clay, revealing the dark, dank, soil below.

The dog took a step forward. When it placed its paw down, the ground shook. Frank felt the world tilting on its axis. There were houses all around him, could *none* of the occupants see – or even hear – this?

Why were there no lights on?

Why no twitching curtains?

The dog's fangs were bared. Shark's teeth had nothing on this. These were dinosaur enamel; prehistoric incisors – deathly white tombstones, sharper than razor wire. This creature was primordial, elemental; older than time itself.

Frank could sense its permanence, its eternal energy. Frank's logical mind could dismiss it all he liked but, to his tortured subconscious, deep in his heart, it was real. It had *always* been real; always and for all time; for longer than Frank could even imagine.

Frank now faced a dilemma – fight or flight? Flight won!

Adrenaline, survival instinct, panic, fear and desperation – all of these unseen forces urged Frank to flee. There was no way to out-run this unholy creature but it certainly wouldn't stop Frank trying. Frank turned and ran. In a millisecond, he felt the dog upon him. Its looming presence cast a hideous shadow.

Horrified, Frank looked over his shoulder; those teeth, that jaw – coming for him. Frank tripped and fell; all was darkness.

30

"You okay, mate? Hey, mate, are you alright?"

Frank heard the man's voice echoing somewhere in the distance as he regained consciousness.

"Mate, you've had a fall. Shall I call an ambulance?"

That was the last thing Frank wanted. Thank the Lord this Good Samaritan hadn't already acted on his initiative and called one anyway.

Frank rubbed the side of his head as he sat up. He was sore but alive. Frank looked around. There was no gigantic devil dog anywhere – just a concerned citizen, crouching over him. Frank stared at his helper. Despite the deep voice, he looked like a student. Probably a local college student aged around eighteen. He was a boy trying hard to be a man. He had a light growth of stubble, long dark hair and the established student 'uniform' of charity shop coat and black jeans.

Frank gripped his young saviour's arm as he pulled himself to his feet. Frank dusted himself down and checked himself for injuries.

"Are you *sure* you're alright, mate?" the student asked again.

"I'm fine. Thank you for your concern. I'd had a few beers after work. I was walking home and I tripped. It's my own stupid fault. I should watch where I'm going. There's no-one else to blame." Frank was aware he was babbling.

"Look, I really think I should call…"

"No!" Frank snapped. Then, in a pacifying tone: "Sorry, honestly, no. I'll be fine."

The last thing Frank wanted was to return to hospital. It had been bad enough last time. He'd definitely be off the case if it happened again.

"Do you live around here?" the student asked.

Frank nodded.

"Right," said the boy. "I'll help you back to your house. But promise me you'll call an ambulance if you feel bad. You can't take chances with a bump on the head. They always tell me at rugby training that if you get..."

"So, you're a rugby man, eh?" said Frank, seizing a chance to change the subject.

"I play a bit," said the boy. "Which way's home then?"

Frank hesitated.

"Down the alley," he replied at last. "Then we turn left."

Frank did not want to walk down that alleyway. He didn't even want to look in that direction. However, thanks to those wretched street repairs, the alley was not only the shortest route home but currently the only route home. However, it was also where Black Shuck had been standing moments earlier.

Aided by the boy, Frank took a wary step in the direction of the alleyway. Then, he stopped in his tracks, gripping the student's arm like a vice. The boy sensed Frank's tension but it took a moment for the student to realise what Frank was looking at with such horror.

Only a short distance in front of them, in the middle of the alleyway, was a large pile of churned-up ground. It looked as if a huge chunk of concrete had been scooped up by a giant hand and casually cast aside.

"You can see it?" Frank asked excitedly. "You can see it too?"

The student nodded.

"Is that what you tripped over? Bloody disgrace. You could sue the council, mate. In fact, you *should* sue the council. If that happened to you in America you could sue for millions. It's probably something to do with the street repairs. One of the workmen must've gouged out a lump of pavement by mistake. Bloody dangerous. No wonder you fell. They should have cordoned that off. Bloody ridiculous."

The student was still shaking his head at the council's irresponsible workmanship as he guided Frank past the torn-up section of pathway. However, all Frank could think about was the fact the boy could also see the hole the giant dog had created. And that could only mean one thing – if someone else (an independent witness, no less) could see the damage Black Shuck had caused, then, undoubtedly the 'phantom' *was* real.

Or was it? Was this really *sufficient* proof?

No sooner had Frank's heart skipped a beat at the prospect he had finally gained independent confirmation that the ghost dog was real than his rational side popped up to counter the notion. That annoyingly logical, sceptical part of Frank's psyche now suggested to him that the ruined pathway might *always* have been like that and Frank's insane subconscious had somehow constructed his most recent ghost hound delusion around that mundane reality.

What to believe?

The student helped Frank as far as his garden gate.

Frank leaned heavily against the gate-post, insisting several times that he'd be fine.

"Is there someone at home who can help you?" the youth asked.

"My wife," Frank lied, hoping Mrs. G. wasn't about to appear at the front door to contradict him. Frank could hear Spider barking inside. The little dog must have heard the latch on the gate.

"Listen, give me your address. I'd like to send you a small 'thank you' for your help this evening," Frank said to the student.

"No, you're alright, mate. You just take care of yourself, yeah?"

The student gave Frank a pat on the shoulder before wandering off. Frank watched his new friend turn the corner before putting his key in the door, sending Spider into a further frenzy. Frank ran up the stairs to his flat.

Later, lying in bed nursing a decidedly sore head, Frank's thoughts returned to his latest encounter with the ghost hound. So, was it real or not? What did it want and why did this keep happening? Was this torment ever going to end?

Clearly, it was set to be yet another sleepless night.

31

The following morning Frank arrived early at the police station. He was becoming an expert at functioning on little or no sleep. Usually, the mornings were fine. It was mid-afternoon one had to be careful about. The trick was to drink plenty of coffee, preferably black. That, and avoid loud noise – not easy in a busy cop shop. Once the others had arrived, Frank told them to assemble in the Incident Room."Okay everyone," Frank said. "Let's get the Sally Hawkins case wrapped up. We've got most of the witness statements completed. Forensics needs a jog, though. Tommy, get on that pronto. Give Kate Ross a ring. So, come on then, who's left to be interviewed?"

Blank faces stared back at the DCI. Chairs scraped on the floor, a few strangled coughs punctuated the awkward silence.

"Come on, for God's sake," Frank hollered. "Wakey wakey, people!"

Clive responded first, flipping hurriedly through his notepad.

"The interviews are pretty much completed, Sir, as you yourself just stated. The only interviews remaining are the two schoolboys…er…" Clive flicked through a few more pages in his notepad. "…Gavin Hurlock and Danny Booker…the two boys whom the History teacher, Jim Clarke, said used to tease and bully Sally."

"Do we really think they'll have anything useful to add?"

"No stone unturned, Sir. Isn't that what you always say?"

Frank frowned. It was true. He believed wholeheartedly in the value of spreading the net as far as possible – interviewing anyone and everyone who might have any information to impart, no matter how seemingly trivial.

Yet, here he was, implying they could let a couple of potential witnesses slide by – and all because he was dog-tired and in an unseemly rush to get the case solved. It was deeply unprofessional and very out of character.

Maybe he *should* tell someone about those insane ghost dog sightings after all? Maybe he should just hand over the reins to DI

Dempsey right now? How tempting it now felt to jack it all in and crawl back to his hospital bed.

"Tommo and I can speak to the two boys, Boss," Clive continued.

Frank shook his head. He had to see this case through – come what may. It was time he took full responsibility once more and gave the Sally Hawkins enquiry his proper care and attention. Devil dogs be damned!

"No, you're alright, Clive. I'll do it. I'll take WPC Silver with me."

Frank couldn't help but notice the sly whistle of displeasure from Clive at this pronouncement. He was well aware his second-in-command was almost at the point of rebellion over Frank's apparent reliance on the lowly uniformed drone otherwise known as WPC Abbie Silver. Frank wouldn't apologise for this favouritism, though.

He genuinely saw Abbie as future DCI material. He wanted to encourage and mentor her through the ranks. He also saw her as his personal security blanket.

It was hard to explain but he felt comfortable when Abs was around. She was his lucky charm; a living, breathing mascot. Most significantly, Frank felt Abbie somehow protected him from the mysterious ghost hound.

He couldn't explain the sensation – after all, it was wholly illogical. It was just that Abbie's presence somehow made Frank feel able to focus on his police work rather than on any crazy supernatural distractions.

"The decision has been made." Frank said firmly. "Come on then you lot, let's get cracking. Abbie, a word."

The others dispersed, Clive giving Frank a churlish glance and a brief shake of the head. Abbie followed Frank into his office. Frank took a seat and gestured for Abbie to do the same.

"Okay, Abs, here's what we'll do. You find out where we can locate these two boys, Booker and Hurl-up or whatever the other one's name is. Make sure you find out by lunchtime. Set up a meeting – somewhere low key where the kids will feel comfortable. Then meet me back here at two o'clock. Wherever we're going, we'll take the Insignia. You'll be driving."

Abbie nodded, hiding her surprise as best she could. It was highly unusual for Frank to allow anyone else to drive the Insignia, let alone actively request them to do so.

Furthermore, Abbie was becoming increasingly embarrassed at her boss's continuing reliance on her. She'd noticed the resentment building inside Clive as the ostensibly lowly Abbie was repeatedly selected for key roles in the investigation.

Still, Frank was the boss. The buck stopped with him.

"Two o'clock. Yes, Sir, see you then."

Abbie stood and turned to leave. She was at the door when Frank called out to her.

"Abs," The WPC turned back to face him. "I'm actually following another line of enquiry today, so I'm going to be out for most of the morning. If I'm late back, don't worry."

"Two o'clock, Sir." Abbie repeated. "See you then."

Once Abbie had left, Frank consulted the scrap of paper on which he'd hastily scribbled the telephone number for the Holkham Branch of the North Norfolk History Society – the organisation to which both Paul Hodson and Carl Palmer belonged.

Frank took out his mobile and punched in some numbers. He was still on the phone, in mid-conversation, when Abbie re-entered the room without knocking. She was carrying a piping hot tea in Frank's Colchester United mug. Frank scowled in displeasure at the sudden intrusion but softened when he recognised the kind gesture behind the unsolicited cuppa. Frank smiled as he beckoned Abbie forward and gestured for her to place the mug on his desk. As an added reassurance, Frank gave Abbie a quick thumbs-up and a broad smile.

"Two sugars," Abbie mouthed quietly as she placed the mug next to her boss. Frank gave her another thumbs-up and an even wider smile.

Just before Abbie left the room, she caught the final sentence of Frank's telephone conversation.

"Yes," said Frank. "It is police business. I'll be there within the hour."

32

As Frank accelerated along the A149 he reflected that his real intention in visiting the North Norfolk History Society was to investigate Black Shuck to see if this apparently legendary 'Hell Hound' could be the explanation for his recurring visions. Having poured over various Shuck-related websites, it now seemed vaguely plausible that Frank's ghost hound and Black Shuck were, in fact, one and the same. At least, in the small hours it seemed plausible.

However, there was no way Frank could even obliquely hint at any of this to the Head of the History Society, Tom Bell, to whom Frank had spoken earlier on the phone. Indeed, Frank couldn't admit anything of the whole ghastly business to *anyone* – and yet the terrible pressure of this burdensome secret was becoming too much to bear. Frank sighed. He needed a convincing cover story for driving all the way to Holkham on the pretext of police business. Luckily, Carl Palmer and Paul Hodson's membership of the History Society gave him the excuse he required. As far as Tom Bell was concerned, Frank was simply investigating the two Stenham High School employees. He'd just have to find a way to somehow work a few questions concerning Black Shuck into the conversation. He wasn't sure how he'd manage it, but that was the plan.

Holkham was a picturesque upmarket village dominated by the stately home, Holkham Hall. Tom Bell lived in the village but rented a room above The Avocet pub for meetings of the North Norfolk History Society.

It was in the pub that Frank met Mr. Bell. Tom Bell was a slight, genial-looking fellow in his late fifties. His thick but prematurely grey hair was styled in a wrap-around semi-circle, leaving a shiny bald crown poking out of the top like a dome.

Viewed from a distance, his heavy side-flaps of hair gave Bell a spaniel-like appearance, as if he had big, floppy ears. Seen up close, Bell looked like a textbook mad professor. His pince-nez spectacles only added to this fusty image.

Tom Bell was the only customer at the bar as Frank entered. It had barely turned 11am and the doors had only recently been thrown open. Despite the summer heat, Tom Bell wore bottle green corduroy trousers, a thick Tattersall shirt and a heavyweight tweed jacket with leather elbow patches. Bell met Frank with an outstretched hand and a welcoming smile.

"Tom Bell, good to meet you. You must be…"

"…DCI Frank Homes of the Norfolk Constabulary, yes."

"Can I get you a drink, Detective?" Bell asked amiably.

"No, thank you. I'm on duty. Well, perhaps just a sparkling mineral water. I am a little parched."

Once the drinks had been purchased – Bell ordering a foaming pint of bitter for himself despite the early hour – the two men occupied a discreet corner table.

"So, how can I help you Inspector?" Tom Bell asked.

Frank took a sip of his mineral water and looked Bell squarely in the eyes.

"My line of enquiry concerns the murder of a local schoolgirl, Sally Hawkins. I am interested in your History Society and, in particular, two of its members; Carl Palmer and Paul Hodson."

"Carl and Paul?" Bell practically spat out his beer. "My God! Do they have something to do with the death of this poor child? I can't believe it."

"I'm not at liberty to disclose the precise nature of my present line of enquiry, Mr. Bell. Furthermore, I would ask for your absolute discretion in keeping our conversation private – not least from Carl Palmer and Paul Hodson. Have you told anyone I was coming to speak to you this morning?"

"No, no, I've not told anyone and, of course, I will keep this conversation strictly *entre nous*. No, wait a moment. I *have* told someone, now I think about it. Julie. She's the only person I've told. I told her I was meeting you here on police business this morning. Sorry, I forgot I'd mentioned it to her."

"Julie?"

"Julie Morton, the History Society's Social Secretary. She keeps a record of all our members, sends out the newsletters, maintains the website and so on. Julie's completely trustworthy. I'll ask her not to mention this to anyone."

"Thank you, Mr. Bell. Now that your memory's returning, is there anyone else you might have spoken to about my visit?"

"No. Just Julie. As I say, fervent apologies. I only mentioned it to her in passing. No, there's no-one else I've told. I'm quite certain of that."

Frank nodded and pulled out his notebook and pen.

"So, what can you tell me about Carl Palmer and Paul Hodson?"

"Well, where to begin? Paul and Carl are both very enthusiastic members of the Society. Paul introduced Carl to the Society when Carl joined the school's staff and was newly settling into the area. I think they share similar interests and they do tend to fraternise quite a lot. In fact, I think the only thing that possibly eclipses their passion for local history is their passion for rebuilding classic cars."

"Classic cars?"

"Yes, Paul Hodson has long been a classic car enthusiast. He owns a disused petrol station just outside Brancaster, on the A149. He bought it with some inheritance money when it was decommissioned. People said he'd be better off using the money to buy a house but he said he was perfectly happy at his mother's place, thank you very much. He said he saw the garage as an investment. He wanted it for its workshop facilities, which he still operates. He had the idea of running a side business in classic car sales and repairs. He said it would make him a fortune but I don't think it ever really got off the ground. Now he just tinkers with old vehicles for his own amusement. He was beside himself with joy when he discovered Carl had the self-same passionate for old bangers. He introduced him to his car workshop and, later, to his other passion – our humble little Society. And the rest, if you'll pardon the pun, is history. These two men are among our most loyal members."

Frank wrote some notes.

"How long have you been running the History Society, Mr. Bell?"

"So long I've rather lost track, to be honest. I took over some time in the late 1980s. 1988, I think. I can check the exact date, if you like?"

"No, that's fine. The point is, as you've been in the area for quite some time, you'll know a great deal about its recent history as well as its past?"

"I like to think so," said Bell, sipping his beer before holding the glass up to the light for a closer inspection. "Wee bit cloudy don't you think?"

Frank shrugged.

"What can you tell me about a local legend?" Frank asked hesitantly. Tom Bell was still examining his beer.

"Hmm?" Bell asked, taking another sip of the dark liquid to satisfy himself it was actually potable. "Legend? As in a celebrity? We don't have too many of those around these parts, Inspector. A couple of rock musicians from yesteryear festering in country piles here and there is about as good as it gets."

"No, no, I mean legend as in folklore. To be precise, I'm hoping you can tell me something about a local ghost dog – Black something…"

"Shuck! Shucky!" Tom Bell laughed and took a large gulp of the supposedly dodgy beer. He seemed to find nothing wrong with it now.

"Black Shuck is definitely a legend. I'm surprised you haven't heard of him. Aren't you a local man? I rather think Shuck's fame has spread far beyond our humble parish. He's a true legend amongst ghost-hunters and believers in the paranormal."

"Nevertheless," Frank harrumphed. "I'm still hoping you can enlighten me further regarding this particular legend."

"Absolutely, I'd be happy to tell you all I can about Black Shuck." Bell smiled, his eyes positively twinkling. "Is this somehow part of the case?"

"This is one line of enquiry, Sir, yes." Frank replied testily. "However, I'm not at liberty to say any more."

Frank knew he was bluffing – and taking a considerable risk in doing so – but he very much doubted Tom Bell could tell he was lying. Besides, he'd already told the man to keep their entire conversation secret and, having secured Bell's assurances in that regard, there surely couldn't be any fall-out from picking the historian's brains over the legend of the ghost hound.

It was a risk worth taking, thought Frank – especially if it provided him with some clear answers about the terrible visions he'd been having ever since the case began.

Frank glanced at Tom Bell's beer glass and saw the man had thoroughly drained it. Thin strands of foam were sliding down the inside of the glass.

"Sign of a good pint, that," Frank said with a smile, indicating the foam. "Same again?" Frank's cordial manner had returned now he knew he was about to find out about the ghost dog.

"Yes please," Bell replied. "Then I'll be more than happy to tell you anything and everything you might care to know about our infamous local ghoul."

33

Frank placed a fresh pint of bitter in front of Tom Bell and sat down, notebook at the ready. Bell nodded his thanks and sipped the beer.

"Fine pint that," said Bell. Satisfied, he leaned forward. "Now then, about our chum, Black Shuck; what *exactly* would you like to know, Inspector?"

"Anything and everything."

"Right, well," Bell began, rubbing his hands at the prospect of delivering a lecture to a captive audience, albeit of one. He took a quick gulp of beer before launching into his address.

"Black Shuck is one of the oldest ghosts in Britain – with

sightings recorded as far back as Roman times. The most famous sighting of Shuck took place in 1577 when Shuck is said to have brought death and mayhem to two Suffolk churches during a thunderstorm. It is reported that, as people cowered within St Mary's Church in Bungay – fervently praying in the midst of a truly unearthly storm – there suddenly appeared within their frightened midst a ghastly black Hell Hound; Black Shuck."

Bell's eyes grew wide as he became more involved in his tale.

"Shuck began racing around the church like a demon, attacking people with huge teeth and claws. The devil dog broke the necks of two parishioners as they knelt in prayer, snapping their heads back so quickly and with such violence they were almost decapitated. Then, just as suddenly as Shuck had appeared, he ran out into the night."

Frank sipped his mineral water and wrote a few desultory notes.

"Go on," Frank prompted.

"Well, the next thing is, Shuck instantly reappeared some twelve miles away in Blythburgh, entering their church and running up the nave – killing a man and a young boy and causing the entire church roof to fall in. It's said the scorch marks from Shuck's claws can be seen burned into Blythburgh's church doors to this day."

Tom Bell leaned back and sighed. He swept up his pint glass and clutched it for comfort, like some bizarre talisman. Frank grunted and sipped more mineral water.

"What about more recent sightings?" Frank asked. "Anything from the present day?"

"The present day?" Bell repeated.

"Indeed." Frank pressed him. "Any 21st century sightings?"

Tom Bell drank some more beer. Over half the pint had gone and this was his second of the morning. Could Frank really trust anything Bell said when the man appeared to have a booze problem? Tom Bell screwed up his eyes, wrinkled his nose and looked to the ceiling in a parody of strained recollection. Eventually he spoke.

"Depends how recent you'd call 'recent'," Bell began tentatively. "There's been nothing this year and nothing for a few years now. But there have been some sightings since the turn of the millennium. Most notably there's some writer who said he saw Shuck while driving on the A149 in around 2000/2001. Corbett or Corbin or something like that. He documented the sighting on his website. I can email you the link, if you like."

Frank nodded and smiled, even though he'd already checked out the writer's report during his own internet searches.

"Then," Bell continued. "There was a report from a mother

and daughter holidaying in Hunstanton in around 2012. They both say they saw Shuck running across the surface of the sea." Bell chuckled. "The bloody dog walks on water now, apparently!"

Frank's spine turned to ice. *Running across the surface of the sea*. It was just like one of his own sightings; the huge dog pounding relentlessly towards him over the waves. Frank turned pale and felt faint. Bell noticed the change in Frank's pallor.

"Are you alright, Inspector?" Tom Bell's voice held a tremulous note of genuine concern.

Frank grabbed his mineral water and took a gulp.

"I'm fine thank you, Mr. Bell. Please continue. Modern sightings...you were saying..."

"Yes, well, if you're sure," Tom Bell said cagily. "The 20th century had a few quite remarkable sightings of Shuck, some of which are well documented. During the 1920s and 1930s fishermen near Sheringham frequently reported seeing a giant ghost hound silhouetted on nearby cliff tops on stormy nights, raising its huge head and howling at the moon. In 1970 a sighting of Shuck pounding along the beach at Great Yarmouth made it into the local newspaper. I think there was even a photograph. In around 1980 a woman out walking with her son also claimed she'd encountered Shuck. Every detail matched the many previous descriptions of our fearsome friend, except she claimed her ghost dog had yellow eyes when everyone knows Black Shuck has red eyes."

"And what does it *mean* to see Shuck?" Frank asked. "What do these sightings actually mean?"

Frank knew his tone sounded a little desperate. He coughed loudly in an attempt to disguise his embarrassment as Tom Bell finished his second pint.

"Fancy another?" Frank asked, eager to find an excuse to walk away and try to regain his composure.

Tom Bell hesitated. Could he really drink three pints in quick succession on an empty stomach while faced with a Police Inspector acting on police business and asking him a bunch of rather weird questions?

"Well," said Tom Bell, drawing the word out to its fullest extent. "Maybe just a half, thank you."

"Right you are," said Frank, standing up.

"And while you're at the bar," Bell added, "I'll just pop to the little boys' room. I'm not really used to drinking quite so much of a morning, to be honest."

"Half it is," Frank said, smiling.

Frank opened his notebook on the bar and attempted to take stock. What had he learned that was actually *factual* about the legendary ghost hound? It was known as Shuck or Black Shuck.

Sightings had been reported for centuries. There had been several sightings on record in the 20th century and at least three other people besides Frank claimed to have seen Shuck during the present century. Many sightings were a matter of clear public record. All of this was *fact*. But what did the sightings actually *mean*? Tom Bell had not yet provided an answer.

Once both men had reconvened, Frank placed a half of bitter in front of Tom Bell and tore open a bag of crisps for them to share, adding a full packet of peanuts into the midst of the crisps.

"Thought you might need some sustenance," Frank explained.

"Very considerate, Inspector," Tom Bell smiled, scooping up a handful of crisps.

"So," said Frank, notebook poised again. "These sightings of Black Shuck – what do they actually mean?"

"I'm not sure there's too much consensus or any real understanding of the term 'meaning' in this regard," Tom Bell began, through a mouthful of crisps.

"Some say Black Shuck is a symbol of malevolence or a portent of evil – a sighting of him is, to them, a sure sign that the observer themselves, or someone within their close family, will die within a year. Yet others say Shuck is completely harmless, even quite benign. Some say he's lucky. Some lone women travellers have reported Black Shuck walking alongside them and acting as their protector on lonely country roads. So, it's all very different. As I said, there's no real consensus. It seems to depend who you're talking to – and in what era you're conversing. Perhaps there is no meaning. Does everything in life always have to have a meaning? Is nothing just a pointless, random anomaly? Consider: why would the concept of an anomaly even exist if nothing at all adhered to it?"

Tom Bell laughed heartily and picked up his drink.

"I rather fear, Inspector, we are now entering the realm of the philosophical. And where, pray, will that get us?"

Bell laughed loudly again.

Frank glanced at his watch. It was clear Tom Bell had little more to tell him of any value. Frank drained his mineral water and pushed his chair back.

"So," Bell piped up. "Do you think this poor girl's killer is somehow inspired by Black Shuck? The killer believes he actually is Shuck or something like that? Is that why you're asking me all these devil dog-related questions?"

Frank stood up.

"I'm asking you these questions, Mr. Bell, because I'm entitled to ask you these questions in the course of a murder investigation." Frank replied, more testily than he'd intended. "Furthermore, I am not at liberty to divulge details of an on-going investigation. And, you'll no doubt recall, you agreed at the outset of our discussion to keep this meeting – and all matters discussed – entirely confidential."

"Aye aye Captain," Tom Bell replied, giving Frank a salute.

This local brew is strong stuff, thought Frank.

"Thank you for your time, Mr. Bell," said Frank, turning on his heel.

"I'll forward you those links," Tom Bell called as Frank walked away.

Frank cursed himself as he pushed through the pub's front doors and stepped into the sunlight. Had he really learned that much more from Tom Bell about the ghost dog than he'd already found on the internet? Frank had barely placed a foot on the pub's gravel driveway when he was suddenly – and very forcefully – grabbed by two hands tugging urgently at his sleeve; desperate hands yanking so hard that Frank almost crashed to the ground.

34

Frank spun rapidly as his sleeve was tugged a second time. Instinct kicked in and Frank was a millisecond away from taking a swing at his assailant when he realised he was being accosted by a woman – a fragile and frightened-looking woman, albeit one possessed of a surprisingly wiry strength. Frank grabbed the woman's arms and pinned them to her sides.

"Easy." Frank soothed. "Take it easy, love."

The woman stared back at him with wide blue-green eyes. It was hard to guess her age. About 45, maybe 50, Frank surmised. Her dark hair was pinned in a tight bun with some premature grey showing at the roots yet her skin was smooth, her lips full and rosy. It was as if she couldn't decide whether to present herself to the world as a siren or a matron. She wore a long, multi-coloured summer dress and a thin pink shawl. The shawl fell to the ground as Frank pinned her arms to her sides.

Frank stooped to retrieve it and handed her the garment.

"Inspector?" she said.

"Who wants to know?" Frank replied gruffly.

"Oh thank goodness," the woman continued, oblivious to Frank's tetchy response. "I hoped it was you. I'd be mortified if I'd grabbed the wrong man."

"Would you now?" Frank growled. "And do you make a habit of grabbing men as they emerge from public houses? Mrs? Miss?"

They moved aside as a group of drinkers headed for the door.

"Ms. It's Ms. Not Mrs or Miss. Both are archaic concepts in this day and age," the woman told Frank, putting on her shawl. "I see no reason why you – or anyone else for that matter – should learn my marital status simply by my title."

"Begging your pardon, Ms." Frank retorted, stretching the 'Ms' into the sort of noise bees make. "But I still don't know why you suddenly launched yourself at me and I still don't know your name."

The woman held out her hand. "Julie Morton," the woman stated. "Pleased to meet you, Inspector Homes."

Julie Morton, thought Frank. Why did that name sound so familiar? Julie Morton seemed to read Frank's mind.

"Secretary of the Historical Society," she said, smiling. "Tom said you were meeting him here today and I urgently needed to see you. Clearly, I only just made it in time. I'm sorry for my lunge but I feared you might simply stride past me, get in your car and be gone before we could speak."

Julie Morton. Yes, Tom Bell had mentioned her in the pub just now. Bell had admitted the Society's Secretary had known about their meeting but he'd also insisted she was discreet and trustworthy. So, why on Earth was she here? Once again, Ms. Morton seemed to read Frank's mind.

"I'm psychic." Julie said, deadpan.

Frank's heart fell and he began to walk away. Julie scurried after him, sorely tempted to grab hold of his sleeve once more.

"Wait!" Julie Morton called, a rising note of desperation in her voice. "I have things to tell you, Inspector. Important things. You need to hear this."

"Yeah, right," Frank sneered. "And then I cross your palm with silver, I suppose?"

Julie ignored the barb and ran ahead of him. She spread herself across the driver's door of the Insignia. Frank blipped the fob to unlock the car.

"Step aside Ms. Morton," Frank ordered. "Or I'll arrest you for obstruction or loitering or *both*."

"Just listen to me!" Julie cried. "I know you've seen the dog."

Frank froze.

How *could* this woman know *that*? Was this a trick of some sort? Something she and Tom Bell had cooked up between them to amuse themselves at his expense? Had she been at the bar, listening in unnoticed as he spoke to Bell?

Frank couldn't remember seeing anyone else in there. Had Bell phoned her when he'd visited the Gents, quickly filled her in on Frank's incessant questions concerning Shuck?

There had to be a rational explanation – Frank always wanted *rational* explanations.

"I thought that would get your attention," Julie Morton continued, moving away from the car door. Frank stood motionless; angry but listening.

"You're in danger, Inspector. That's what I came to tell you. I saw it. I saw it in my visions and in my dreams. It's hard to explain. That's what happens to me. Fragments. That's what I get – at first, anyway. They're like video-shaped pieces of a visual jigsaw that eventually becomes a whole movie. Only I don't get the whole movie in one go – or even in sequence. I just get extracts – like a trailer running out of sync. The thing is, I saw *you*. I saw you encountering the dog and I sensed you were in danger. That's why I came here – to warn you to be careful."

"Get in." Frank said, gesturing towards the Insignia. Julie Morton complied.

Frank turned to face his new friend.

"Buckle up. I'll drive us to a lay-by where we can talk. I presume you don't want Tom Bell to come rolling out of the pub and spot us chatting."

Julie nodded but looked apprehensive.

"How do I know I can trust you?" she asked. "How do I know you're not about to arrest me for wasting police time and we'll just end up driving straight to the police station?"

Frank smiled and fired up the engine.

"I thought you said you were psychic," he chuckled.

They drove in silence for half a mile before Frank pulled into a lay-by. Frank switched off the ignition and turned to face Julie Morton once more. He needed to know exactly what this strange woman knew.

"So, you're a psychic are you?" Frank began. "I suppose you know who the killer is and you've come to help me solve the case?"

"If that's all you have to say, I think I should go," Julie snapped.

"Hold on." Frank held up his hands in a pacifying gesture. "I know some police forces use psychics to help with cases – difficult cases, cold cases, cases in which forensics have struggled. I've seen it documented and I've heard colleagues speak about it. I've just never encountered one of you people before and I don't really have the time to…"

"It's not about the case," Julie said emphatically. "It's about *you*."

"Me?"

"Yes, you Inspector. I've not had any visions concerning the case you're working on, whatever case that might be. I've just seen you and the dog and I've had a terrible sense of foreboding on your behalf."

"And what dog might this be?"

"You're denying you've seen it?"

"I'm confirming and denying nothing. I want to know exactly what dog you mean."

"I see. If you're not prepared to admit it to yourself then you're unlikely to admit it to anyone else."

"What *dog*, Ms. Morton?"

"We're going in circles, aren't we, Inspector?"

"I'm just seeking clarity, Ms. Morton."

"Please, call me Julie."

"I'm just seeking clarity, *Julie*."

"And I'm just trying to help." She reached into her handbag. "Here's my card. Please, call me anytime. Come and see me. I know you're in danger and I'd like to help. If I get any visions concerning the case, I'll call you. But you *must* take care."

She held out a card. Frank hesitated.

"So, you're a *professional* psychic? This is how you earn money?"

The cynical tone again; the implication Frank was being scammed. Julie Morton frowned.

"No, this is my card from the Historical Society. Tom had them printed. Unnecessary really, but he's a stickler for formality as you likely found in the pub. Still, the card has my mobile number and my landline. Call me on either."

Frank took the card and tucked it in his wallet.

"For your information," Julie continued. "I earn a living running a tea room in Holkham with my twin sister. It converts to a fish restaurant in the evenings. You should try it sometime. I refuse all payment for my psychic readings – it wouldn't feel right to profit from that."

"I see," said Frank, remaining steadfastly non-commital.

Suddenly Frank's mobile vibrated.

"DCI Homes."

Julie sat awkwardly as Frank spoke, aware the policeman was trying to say as little as possible in front of her.

"Right," Frank grunted. "Good work, Tommo. I'll head to you now." Frank hung up and sparked the engine.

"I can get the bus," Julie said quietly.

"What? Oh, yes." Frank said as the car sped out of the lay-by. In his haste to return to the police station, he'd completely forgotten the woman sitting beside him.

"Just drop me at the nearest bus stop, if you'll be so kind. I'm sure there'll be a bus along presently."

You'll be lucky, thought Frank.

"Psychic about the bus timetables, are we?" Frank laughed.

"So cynical," said Julie. Still, she laughed too.

Presently, Frank pulled the Insignia onto the hard shoulder opposite a stop for buses in the direction of Holkham. Julie stepped out of the car but then leant in and stared Frank in the eyes.

"You're in denial, Inspector, and that puts you in grave danger. Seeing the dog means something. It always does. Call me when you're ready to talk."

Julie closed the car door before Frank had a chance to reply. Frank sucked his teeth, hit the accelerator and disappeared in a squeal of tyres. This whole damned business was getting weirder by the minute.

35

Frank hated it when events moved on behind his back – just as they had when he'd been lying in that hospital bed. Now it had happened again. On returning to the police station, he'd intended to take Abbie with him to interview the schoolboys, Booker and Hurlock. However, that now had to be put on ice.

While Frank had been fruitlessly interviewing Tom Bell about Black Shuck and humouring some mad 'psychic', the real police work had continued without him. Forensics had come back with clear evidence from Sally's laptop and the ISP that the person she'd arranged to meet in Cromer on the day of her disappearance was none other than the school's Drama teacher – Tim Powell.

Tommo had wasted no time bringing Powell in under caution. The man was sitting in an interview room awaiting Frank – as well as his inevitable brief.

Frank sat behind his desk in his office while Tommo, Clive and Abbie crammed in to bring their DCI up to speed before Frank and Clive formally interviewed the suspect. No time for any psychic ramblings or howling devil dogs now.

"Okay, shoot," said Frank.

It was Tommo who took the lead.

"Right, Sir. In a nutshell, Harry has come up trumps. It turns out on the day she disappeared, Sally had arranged to travel to Cromer to meet someone calling themselves 'Iago' on that smellofgreasepaint website."

"Iago?" Frank asked.

"Shakespeare, Sir," said Abbie. "Iago is one of the Bard's most evil villains, if not the most evil one of all. He's a schemer, a manipulator and a murderer."

"Shakespeare, eh?"

"Well, it fits with the fact Powell is a Drama teacher." Clive added.

"So Powell posed as this 'Iago' character and hid his identity behind that user name to lure Sally Hawkins to Cromer?"

"Exactly," said Tommo. "They'd been communicating on that

website for quite some time. Under the guise of 'Iago', Powell had promised her all sorts – an Equity card, stage roles in the West End, you name it."

"And we have concrete proof?"

"Rock solid, cast iron proof," said Clive. "Harry has the IP addresses of both parties and transcripts of the various threads and emails that passed between Sally and 'Iago.' Basically, Tim Powell is bang to rights."

"It's open and shut," said Abbie.

"Slam dunk," Tommo added.

"*Bastard*," said Clive. "I never trusted him."

"Sounds like we need to have a word with Mr. Powell." Frank said, standing up. "Clive, you come with me. Has Mr. Powell's brief arrived yet?"

Clive shook his head.

"Excellent," Frank continued. "Okay, Clive, you know the drill."

Clive nodded.

"Let's put the thumbscrews on this shithead good and proper."

Frank and Clive headed for the interview room. They'd put Tim Powell in the smaller room to make the bastard sweat even more. As Frank and Clive entered, the uniformed officer who had been guarding Tim Powell squeezed past them and left. Tim

Powell sat behind a small table, back to the wall, facing the door. An old-fashioned tape recorder sat on the table. The recording would be transferred to digital media after the interview had concluded. A plastic cup of tepid tap water sat in front of Powell.

Tim Powell looked extremely sorry for himself. His greasy black 'mop top' looked even more slimy and unkempt than usual. There was an unwashed odour about him and his overweight frame was sweating profusely in the small, airless interview room. His wide-apart eyes seemed to have shrunk even further into his skull and he looked even more pig-like than when Tommo had interviewed him in the school's drama studio.

Tommo had been upset that, having conducted the original interview, he wasn't accompanying Frank in this interview and that Clive had been chosen instead. However, that was a privilege of rank and Clive and Frank had a well-rehearsed routine worked out for suspect interviews that often paid dividends.

Frank kept thinking of the unkind nickname Tommo said the kids had given to Powell – 'Porky Powell.' It was as much as Frank could do not to address the man as such. Porky looked miserably at Frank and then at Clive.

The policemen allowed the suspect a few moments of silence before anyone spoke. This was deliberate. A hiatus sometimes forced a suspect to crack. Often the whole sorry tale then came tumbling out. Not so with Tim Powell, though. Porky sat in determined silence, staring at his feet. After a few interminable minutes, Frank spoke.

"Do you know why you're here, Mr. Powell?"

"No comment," said Porky, gazing at the floor. Frank sighed.

"Do you know why you're here, Mr. Powell?" Frank repeated.

"No comment."

"You'd be well advised to comment," said Clive. "Because, quite frankly, it's not looking too good for you, Mr. Powell. We've got evidence – good, solid evidence that *will* stand up in court – that you've been going online under a pseudonym and grooming a murder victim."

"No comment."

Frank drummed his fingers on the table.

"We have you grooming Sally Hawkins online. We have you enticing Sally to meet you at a café in Cromer on the day of her disappearance," Clive continued. "We have you on record denying you used the internet when you were on that smellofgreasepaint website virtually 24/7."

"Where's my legal adviser? Has he been called?" Tim Powell said unhappily, scowling at Clive.

"*Now* he comments," Frank sneered.

"I'll comment when I have legal representation and not

before." Tim Powell whined, rounding on Frank and delivering a petulant scowl.

"Your lawyer is on his way," said Clive, reassuringly. "Perhaps just answer a few questions for us before he arrives, eh?"

"No comment."

Frank laughed – a hollow, mocking sound.

"If I had a tenner for every utterance of 'no comment' from every shithead who's sat in this room, I'd have retired long ago. Let me tell you, Mr. Powell, it won't go well for you if you choose to 'no comment' everything you're asked. The facts repeatedly show, innocent people don't do that. Innocent people shout their innocence from the rooftops. Innocent people won't shut up about their innocence; *they* can't speak out enough. The *guilty*, on the other hand, always hide behind the coward's catchphrase – no comment, no comment, no comment. Like some demented parrot!"

"No comment." Porky was staring at his feet again.

Frank turned to Clive.

"How predictable was *that*, Clive?" he grunted.

Clive leaned across the table towards Tim Powell. Porky flinched and shrank in his seat. "It would be wise to speak to us, Mr. Powell. If you *are* innocent – if there is some innocent explanation for your behaviour, we can help you. On the other hand, if you tell us nothing..."

Clive shrugged. "No comment."

Suddenly the interview room door opened and a uniformed officer walked up to Frank and whispered in his ear. Frank stood up, tapping Clive on the shoulder to encourage him to also rise.

"Mr. Powell's legal adviser is here."

A thin man in a pale grey suit squeezed past Frank and Clive as he strode into the interview room.

"Some time alone with my client, if you please, gentlemen," the man stated.

"Of course," said Frank, through gritted teeth as he and Clive exited.

"We'll see you soon for Act Two," Clive called to Porky as a parting shot.

36

After allowing Tim Powell half an hour with his brief, Frank and Clive returned to the interview room. Powell was deep in conversation with the lawyer. Frank knew the lawyer – Matthew Lindsay. He was a state employee, provided to those who couldn't afford their own legal representative. Not a bad bloke – a bit prissy during working hours but still someone you could have a pint with when the day was done.

Stick thin with wire wool hair and gold pince-nez specs, Matthew Lindsay had an abrupt but professional manner that immediately instilled both confidence and respect. If Frank had been in trouble, Matthew Lindsay would have been the very chap he'd have wanted sitting in his corner. He was a boon for the cons but a pain in the rear for the cops. Frank sat forward in his chair while Clive trotted out the routine spiel before turning on the tape and formally opening the interview.

"Interview started at 3pm precisely," Clive intoned.

Porky Powell looked at Matthew Lindsay who nodded encouragingly. Frank coughed irritably.

"Mr. Powell, where were you on the afternoon and evening of 21st July…the day Sally Hawkins disappeared?"

"No comment."

Frank sucked his teeth. Clive shifted in his chair. Matthew Lindsay remained poker-faced.

"Mr. Powell, do you deny contacting Sally Hawkins over the internet?"

"No comment."

"Do you deny adopting the persona and user name 'Iago' on the thespian website smellofgreasepaint.com?"

"No comment."

"Even though we have evidence that your IP address was used to contact Sally Hawkins on a number of occasions and to subsequently invite her to an assignation in Cromer on the 21st July?"

"No comment."

"Do you recall telling my colleague, DS Mearns, that you never used the internet?"

"No comment."

Frank brought his clenched fist up to his mouth and coughed. It was the signal Clive had been waiting for. Clive flicked the tape recorder off with a sarcastic "Whoops!" Frank stood up and leaned across the table.

Powell shrank back and cringed although Matthew Lindsay neither moved a muscle nor batted an eyelid – the lawyer had seen this particular pantomime act before.

"Listen here, Powell. You have precisely two choices. You can carry on giving us this 'no comment' bullshit or you can start talking and attempt to save your fat, greasy neck. Because, as it stands, you're heading to the slammer, my friend. Furthermore, you'll be going there with a label round your big, fat, greasy neck identifying you as a groomer, an abductor and a kiddy killer. And I can promise you this; if you keep giving me this 'no comment' crap, I will personally ensure that every single one of the lags on your wing knows they've got a Grade A nonce living in their midst called Tim fucking Powell."

Frank sat down and mopped his brow.

"On the other hand," Frank said, smiling at the startled Powell, "if you *do* decide to talk – and you tell us the truth, mind – I will ensure you're kept well away from any would-be vigilantes. It's your call, Mr. Powell."

Porky looked at Matthew Lindsay in a panic.

"Can he say all that to me?" Porky asked in a trembling voice. "That's threats isn't it? Police brutality."

Clive laughed raucously.

"Tape's not on," Clive said helpfully. "I accidentally switched it off. Silly me, eh?"

"And while Mr. Lindsay's recollection of our conversation might well differ from the two of us," Frank added. "I can only recall advising you that your cooperation is in your best interests. Nothing else. Isn't that right, Clive?"

DI Dempsey nodded.

"Threatening my client is an unwise course of action, DCI Homes." Matthew Lindsay said to Frank.

This was the litmus test; the gamble Frank had taken. Matthew Lindsay no doubt had a dictaphone running under the table and could easily have wrecked Frank's entire strategy. However, if Lindsay himself had concluded that Porky Powell was probably just some child-murdering scumbag concealing evidence then he might let Frank and Clive's 'mishap' with the tape recorder slide by without any serious challenge.

"You should impress upon your client that cooperation in a

murder enquiry is in everybody's interests; not least an enquiry into the murder of a child." Frank remarked sternly, directing his gaze towards Matthew Lindsay.

"We can give you a few minutes, if you like," Clive suggested pleasantly.

Powell looked at Lindsay – an expression of pure despair. Frank thought Lindsay did a pretty good job of hiding his distaste for his client.

"It might be better if you would simply try to answer their questions," Lindsay eventually said to Powell, in soothing tones. "If there's anything you're not sure about then refer it to me and I'll answer for you. It's true that your cooperation will be a matter of record, which will stand in your favour."

Tim Powell meekly nodded his assent. The questions could resume.

"Thank you, Mr. Powell," said Frank, signalling for Clive to switch the tape recorder back on.

With the tape running and Matthew Lindsay by his side, Porky Powell now sat straight-backed in his chair and looked Frank squarely in the eyes.

"How can I help you, Inspector?" Tim Powell asked.

"Mr. Powell, where were you on the afternoon and evening of 21st July…the day Sally Hawkins disappeared?"

"I don't recall. I'd have to check my diary."

"Mr. Powell, do you deny contacting Sally Hawkins over the internet?"

"No, I don't deny it. I contacted her."

"Mr. Powell, do you deny adopting the persona and user name 'Iago' on the thespian website smellofgreasepaint.com?"

"No, I don't deny it. I did that. I was 'Iago'."

Frank's first three questions were now answered without hesitation and without further recourse to Matthew Lindsay. That wasn't so hard now, was it, Frank thought. Frank pressed on.

"Do you recall, Mr. Powell, telling my colleague, DS Mearns, that you never used the internet?"

"Yes I do. That was a lie and a deliberate fabrication."

Matthew Lindsay reached across and placed a paternalistic hand on Porky's arm.

"You don't need to say any more at this stage, Mr. Powell."

Matthew Lindsay turned towards Frank and scowled.

"DCI Homes, are you planning to charge my client? Please either charge my client or release him to my custody."

Frank gritted his teeth. Matthew Lindsay was clearly now finding this case interesting. Powell obviously knew something but he wasn't quite ready to spill the beans. The cat and mouse game between lawyer and cop was about to begin. Frank decided to chance his arm one last time before Matthew Lindsay brought the curtain down completely.

"Mr. Powell, would you care to confess?"

"Confess to what?"

"To the abduction and murder of Sally Hawkins."

"Good God, no."

"I think we're done here," said Matthew Lindsay, rising from his chair. It was Porky Powell who tugged on the lawyer's sleeve and persuaded him to sit back down.

"Look, my career's clearly over," Tim Powell said sadly. "I may as well tell you everything."

"I'd strongly advise you against that," said Matthew Lindsay. "You don't need to say anything more unless you are charged."

Porky practically swatted the lawyer aside.

"It doesn't matter now. I'd rather clear the air. I *want* to come clean. I didn't kill her. I'd never kill anyone, least of all Sally. Let me tell you what I can."

"Please, Mr. Powell, go on," said Frank.

Matthew Lindsay folded his arms and sat with his chin tucked into his chest. Tim Powell took a deep breath before starting his sorry soliloquy.

"I contacted Sally Hawkins, yes. I used the internet – directing her to the website smellofgreasepaint – just as you've said. I was indeed 'Iago' on the site. The name amused me. It's my favourite Shakespeare character. Sally didn't know I was Iago. I wasn't grooming her though. It wasn't like that. There was nothing sexual about any of this. I admired Sally – from afar, I suppose. I just wanted to help her further her career. I knew it was wrong – a teacher contacting a student outside school. But I felt safe doing it as Iago. My mistake was suggesting the meeting. I don't know what came over me, I really don't."

Tim Powell paused. He looked as though he might burst into tears.

"Mr. Powell, we can stop at this point and confer. If they're not going to charge you…" Matthew Lindsay whispered. Powell shook his head.

"I want to get it off my chest," the teacher said sadly.

"That's right, Mr. Powell," Clive said encouragingly. "Please continue. You'll feel better for it."

"So," Frank said. "You arranged to meet Sally Hawkins in Cromer on the day she disappeared?"

Tim Powell nodded.

"Please confirm that out loud, for the tape." Frank stated.

"Yes." Powell croaked. "I arranged to meet Sally Hawkins in Cromer on the day she disappeared. But I didn't abduct her and I certainly didn't kill her."

"So, someone else just happened to do exactly that on exactly the same day?" Clive sneered.

"Yes, well, yes. That's exactly what happened," Tim Powell cried desperately. "You've *got* to believe me."

Clive and Frank looked at each other. Clive raised his eyebrows.

"It's the *truth*," Powell screamed. "You've *got* to believe me. It's the fucking truth you arseholes!"

Tim Powell stood up. The two policemen stood up. Only Matthew Lindsay remained calmly seated.

"Mr. Powell, once more, I'd advise you to say nothing more. DCI Homes, are you charging my client or will you release him into my custody right now?"

Frank ignored the lawyer.

"Mr. Powell, do you drive?" Frank asked.

"What?" Powell snapped.

"It's a straightforward question Mr. Powell. Do you drive a vehicle? Do you hold a driving licence?"

"No," said Powell. "No, no, and no again. No, I don't drive. I've never driven. I've never even taken a driving test."

Frank sucked his lower lip, lost in thought. Clive looked puzzled.

"Alright, Mr. Powell," said Frank. "You can go. I'm not

charging you at this point. But don't disappear. I'll be requiring you to assist us further with our enquiries."

Matthew Lindsay steered a stricken Porky Powell out of the room.

"Good afternoon, gentlemen," said the lawyer.

"Cheerio for now," Clive chuckled, with a wave. "We'll be in touch, Mr. Powell. You can be sure of that."

37

"Why, in God's name, did you let him go?" Clive asked, closing the door to the interview room so he and Frank could talk without interruption.

"Think about it," Frank said, sitting on the edge of the table. "Tim Powell doesn't drive. How did Sally's body get to the dump site?"

"Van or car," said Clive, the realisation dawning on him.

"Exactly – so, unless he's lying about not driving the way he lied about not using the internet…"

"…he had an accomplice."

"Or he's innocent."

"*Innocent*? The girl goes missing on the very same day he arranges to meet her and then she turns up dead? Innocent, my anus!"

"It's all *circumstantial*, Clive. It's damning, for sure. However, it's circumstantial nonetheless."

"So he walks?"

"For now. But put a watch on him. Every time he leaves his house, I want a tail on him. Let him see us watching him too. Shake him up a bit. If he so much as farts, I want one of you there to sniff it."

"We don't have the manpower for a 24/7 tail, Sir."

"Just for a day or so. I'll call him back for more questioning soon enough. Give one of the uniforms a bit of overtime. There'll be a few takers, I'm sure."

"Abbie?"

"No, not Abbie. I've got other plans for her."

Clive grimaced. Frank stood up, clapped his DI on the arm and left the room. He'd barely reached his desk when Tommo came running up, brandishing a sheaf of papers.

"More forensics, boss. It's all falling into place." Tommo said excitedly.

"Well, I'm glad those boys and girls have got their act together at long last. Gather the team, Tommo. We'll meet in the

Incident Room in ten minutes. It'll be good to share the latest with everyone. Meanwhile, I need a dump."

Tommo scurried off to get everyone assembled while Frank headed to the Gents. Frank entered a cubicle, sat on the closed toilet lid, loosened his collar and leant back against the wall. He hadn't needed the loo at all – he just wanted to go somewhere he could think without any risk of being disturbed.

Frank closed his eyes and took stock. Tim Powell had *something* to do with the case, he felt sure of that. But Tim Powell was no killer.

Maybe Powell had lured the girl for someone else. His accomplice had killed her and dumped the body.

But who was the accomplice?

And why would Powell protect the real killer when he was the one so squarely in the frame? Surely it was better to grass up a murderer than do time for someone else's crime?

And yet, some crucial piece of this repulsive jigsaw was still missing. Maybe forensics could pull the rabbit from the hat. They usually did these days. 21st century forensics were practically omnipotent and omniscient.

When Frank's dad had been in the force in the early 1970s they'd be lucky to be able to tell the suspect's blood group. These days they could probably clone the murderer for a laugh.

Frank left the cubicle, walked to the hand basin and splashed cold water on his face. He stood blinking into the mirror, letting water drip from his chin. Frank's eyes were bloodshot. They were red, although not as red as Black Shuck's. Jesus Christ! The damned devil dog again! It seemed Frank couldn't last a single day without thinking about the beast. Even in the interview room with Porky Powell, thoughts of Shuck had kept intruding.

Thankfully, none of the other men had noticed Frank suppressing his unwelcome thoughts. Not even Matthew Lindsay – who was normally as rapacious as a hawk, clocking every tic or nuance of anyone seated opposite him in search of any weakness. Frank knew he couldn't keep fooling everyone indefinitely.

But who on Earth could he tell? And who could he tell while the case remained unsolved? But now, it seemed, the case was finally nearing its conclusion.

Be patient, Frank, he counselled his reflection. Frank dried his face on a paper towel. After the case was solved, he'd take some time off. He'd take Jo on that holiday to Paris – but first he'd see a shrink. No-one needed to know. There'd be one in Norwich or, more discretely, Cambridge. He could go on the hush-hush. He'd unburden himself. All the visions would be explained quite rationally; everything would return to normal. Reassured, Frank headed to the Incident Room to see what Tommo had found out.

They were all there, sitting on chairs they'd wheeled in from their desks. There was one unoccupied seat at the front. Frank took it.

"Okay, Tommo," Frank said gruffly. "Care to share?"

DS Mearns cleared his throat, looked briefly at the clutch of loose papers in his hand then dropped his arm to his side. He ad-libbed a quick summary.

"Forensics has matched the tyre tracks at the dump site," Tommo began. Then he paused. Either consciously or subconsciously he ratcheted up the tension in his listeners.

"…to the school mini-bus," Tommo continued.

Someone whistled. Probably Clive, thought Frank.

"Yes," Tommo said excitedly. "One of the tyres had an unusual tread pattern and, as the earlier database search had already showed, it was some cheap shit South Korean brand – Ying Tong Tyres or some such."

"You sure it wasn't Teriyaki?" Clive guffawed.

"Koo-Rog," said Abbie, scowling.

"Anyway," Tommo continued. "These particular tyres are quite rare and when we checked the school mini-bus, sure enough, the back right tyre was that very Ying Yong brand."

"So, who drives the school mini-bus Tommo?" Frank asked eagerly.

"I'm ahead of you there, Boss," Tommo grinned. "The insurance policy has only three named drivers – Terence Asquith, Paul Hodson and Carl Palmer."

Frank turned to look at Clive. No words passed between them but Clive understood – Tim Powell had no driving license and didn't drive; if he *was* involved then one of these three named drivers was involved alongside him.

"So, we need to know who had the school bus signed out on the day Sally Hawkins disappeared." Abbie said.

"And Uncle Tommy can tell you that too," Tommo chuckled.

"Well, well, you have been a busy bee, haven't you?" Clive said, somewhat peevishly.

"Come on, spit it out, Tommo." Frank ordered.

"Paul Hodson," said Tommo, deadpan.

Tommo let the silence hang in the air as the latest information was digested by the team.

"Paul Hodson drives the school bus almost exclusively," Tommo continued. "Carl Palmer drives it on occasional school trips and Terence Asquith's name is on the policy purely as emergency cover. Paul Hodson is definitely the main driver on a day-to-day basis."

"And you've checked whether the bus was signed out to Paul Hodson on the day Sally Hawkins disappeared?" Frank asked.

"Yes, Boss. The School Secretary confirmed it."

"Great work, Tommo." Frank said.

Frank put a hand on Tommo's shoulder and squeezed.

"We're getting there, folks. The net is finally closing on the killer or killers. Okay, here's what we'll do. First thing tomorrow, Tommo, you impound that mini-bus. I want Forensics crawling all over it, inside and out. Meantime, Clive, you bring Paul Hodson in. I want another chat with that fat bastard. You can warm him up, Clive. Do it *before* his brief arrives. If he's in it with Powell, we'll crack the pair of them. Abbie, you and I will go first thing in search of those two schoolboys – Booker and Hurler, or whatever they're bloody well called. They're the last two names on our interview list."

"Do we really need to, Sir?" Abbie asked. "I mean, since it appears Hodson and Powell are our number one suspects – and Forensics is backing that up – do we really need to speak to those two boys or…?"

"No stone unturned, Abs." Frank said firmly. "Okay, it's looking very promising indeed. However, don't forget, it's still only circumstantial. So far, there's no confessions, no smoking gun, no case to put before the courts. Okay, let's pack it up for today. You all know what you need to be doing tomorrow."

Everyone dispersed in high spirits.

So, it appeared Paul Hodson and Tim Powell were acting in tandem. Frank shuddered. Tweedle Dum and Tweedle Even Dumber – child killers. Weren't fat people supposed to be jolly, thought Frank. Well, those two bastards certainly confounded the stereotype. They'd lose a fair bit of weight on a diet of porridge, though, Frank chuckled to himself.

He swept up the keys to the Insignia with a happy flourish. Tomorrow it would finally be 'case closed.'

38

It was late when Frank arrived home but not too late to take Spider for a walk to The Linnet Tavern to catch last orders. Mrs. G. handed the dog to the policeman with a broad smile.

"I've not had time to walk him today, Frank," the old lady said. "You'll be doing me a favour."

"I might be quite late back, Mrs. G." Frank said cautiously.

"Here's a spare key to my door," said Mrs. G. "Just pop him inside the flat when you get back."

Frank pocketed the key, patted Spider gently and the pair set off into the night. Frank hadn't intended to see Jo at all during the investigation. He didn't want any distractions and she understood it was nothing personal. Still, Frank needed a drink and, truth be told, he needed to see 'his' woman. He needed some human warmth. He wanted the reassurance that he wasn't going mad, that the world wasn't populated entirely by evil child killers, that life could be good and clean and decent. But mostly, he wanted a *drink*.

Spider hopped joyously beside Frank; straining at the leash as if the little scamp somehow knew Frank's destination and wanted to help him arrive there even sooner. The Affenpinscher was fearless – showing no signs of the trauma he'd endured when the pair had encountered Black Shuck by the War Memorial.

Frank was emboldened by his companion's happy demeanour. The DCI had heard it said that animals had a sixth sense where the supernatural was concerned. As long as Spider was content, there was no need to fear that the devil dog might be about to put in an appearance. Spider was Frank's canary in the mine, his own personal early warning system.

The pair continued on their merry way until they approached the War Memorial. Instinctively, Frank hesitated. In his mind's eye, he was reliving the moment the ghost dog's gigantic head had materialised out of the ether. He could almost smell the spectre's fetid breath. Frank looked down at Spider. His scruffy little companion remained wholly untroubled. Clearly, it was safe to proceed.

"Come on, lad," Frank said to Spider, flicking the lead to set the small dog walking once more.

They were almost upon the War Memorial, Frank chuckling to himself at his stupidity, when he noticed a figure half hidden in deep shadows just beyond the statue. Frank stopped. He looked at Spider – still no sign of any upset in the dog's demeanour. Frank walked on, determined, if the need arose, to confront whoever was lurking with the fact he was a policeman.

As Frank and Spider drew level with the Memorial, the would-be mugger jumped out from the shadows. Spider flinched and barked. Frank balled one of his fists.

"No, please don't hit me," a voice cried. It was a woman's voice.

Spider was growling and barking. The woman stepped forward so Frank had a clear view of her. An instant calm seemed to overtake Spider.

"It's me, Julie Morton," the woman said. "From the Historical Society."

Frank could hardly believe his eyes. It was indeed the same woman who'd grabbed him just after he'd interviewed Tom Bell in Holkham. The same woman he'd driven to a lay-by to interrogate after she'd claimed to be psychic. Now, stepping closer, Frank recognised the slight and slender figure, the garish clothing. This woman was no physical threat to anyone. But was she *sane*? And what was she doing here at this very moment, confronting him out of the blue?

"What do you want?" Frank asked curtly.

"I apologise for tracking you down like this, Inspector, but I had to see you urgently," Julie Morton continued breathlessly.

"Are you following me?"

"Not following you, no," Julie laughed. She seemed amused at the possibility. "I was told where to find you."

"Here? Now?" Frank asked incredulously. "By whom?"

"By Torben, my spirit guide."

"Spirit guide?" Now Frank felt he'd heard it all. "Don't tell me, he's also a Red Indian chief. Whoo whoo!" Frank did a pastiche of a rain dance, brandishing an invisible tomahawk and laughing hysterically at his own joke. Julie Morton was unimpressed. "Look, I don't have time for this mumbo jumbo, Ms. Morton." Frank snapped, ceasing his mocking dance.

Frank picked Spider up whereupon the little dog settled happily in his arms.

"If you must know," Julie replied, clearly offended. "Torben is a raven. He mainly comes to me in my dreams and he communicates by telepathy. It's hard to explain. I've seen him ever since I was a little girl."

She clutched anxiously at Frank's sleeve. Spider licked her hand in a sign of his acceptance of her.

"Torben is never wrong. He said I must find you and I must find you *tonight*. You are in danger; *grave* danger. Please, DCI Homes, let me help you."

Frank looked at the woman. Could this situation get any madder?

"I also think I can help to solve your case," Julie Morton continued. "I'm not exactly sure how but I do now believe it's all connected. You, the dead girl, the ghost dog sightings. There's a *connection*. Please, let me help you, Frank."

Frank felt his resolve softening. He must need his head examined but what did he actually have to lose by humouring this strange woman? What if she *did* know something after all?

"What are you suggesting?" Frank asked quietly.

Julie was busy making a fuss of Spider.

"What a charming little dog," Julie said. "He's very special. Is he yours?"

"If you're psychic, you'd know," Frank laughed.

"It doesn't work like that," Julie said tetchily.

"Relax, I'm joking," Frank said, touching Julie's arm in a reassuring gesture. "No, he belongs to my landlady. I walk him sometimes."

"What's his name?" Julie asked.

"Spider."

"Great name. He's a wise old soul. He's lived before. I can sense it."

"If you say so."

Frank put Spider on the ground. The dog sat patiently at his feet as the humans resumed their conversation.

"I want you to come and see me at my home," Julie said.

"Do you now?" Frank laughed.

"Tomorrow night," Julie said. "Tonight would be better, if you can."

"You aren't backwards at coming forwards, are you Ms. Morton?"

"Not like *that*, Inspector," Julie admonished. "I want to hold a séance. I think it will help. It can give you the missing information you need. You need to come to my house. After all, I can't do it here in the street."

"No, you can't. I'd be forced to arrest you for creating a public nuisance."

"Be serious, please Frank. This is a matter of life and death. I can go into a trance and I can communicate with the spirits. I can tell you the things you need to hear. Torben says it's urgent. Please, won't you come tonight?"

Julie Morton grabbed Frank's sleeve.

"I'm not going anywhere tonight," Frank said, breaking free of the woman's grip.

"Please, just think about it," Julie urged. "That's all I ask. I'll be waiting for you at home tomorrow. Come around 9pm. I'll have everything ready."

Frank hesitated.

"At least promise me you'll *think* about it." Julie urged.

"Alright, I'll think about it," Frank growled, unsure if he actually meant it or if he was just pacifying this lunatic in order to escape her clutches.

"Do you still have my business card?" Julie asked.

Frank nodded.

"Good. Until tomorrow, Frank. 9pm. Please come."

Julie Morton turned and walked away. Frank looked forlornly at Spider before pulling gently on the lead, encouraging the little dog to head back in the direction from whence they'd come.

There was no longer any point in going to see Jo. There was no way Frank could concentrate on mundane pleasantries after this latest bizarre encounter with Julie Morton. It was every bit as unsettling as if he'd seen Black Shuck himself.

Back home, Frank deposited Spider in Mrs. G's flat, unclipping the dog's harness and leaving it neatly folded on a side table. He closed the door and trudged upstairs to his own flat with a heavy heart. Was he *really* going to visit Julie Morton tomorrow night? Would that *really* be the action of a sane man?

Best to sleep on it – if he could sleep at all.

39

The next morning, all thoughts of Julie Morton and séances were banished from Frank's mind. The demands of the Sally Hawkins case were paramount and that was where his focus belonged.

On waking, Frank had concentrated only on the practicalities of washing, dressing, feeding himself and collecting Abbie from the cop shop. Now the pair of them sat opposite the two schoolboys, Danny Booker and Gavin Hurlock, who represented the very last names on Frank's interview list. The quartet had met on the seafront at Hunstanton.

As he'd parked the Insignia, the location had reminded Frank of his sighting of Black Shuck running across the waves...but that was quickly purged from his consciousness. Frank and Abbie had walked to a small café with a sea view that was open for breakfast.

The two boys were already waiting for them. Danny Booker was eating three scoops of ice cream while Gavin Hurlock nursed a mug of foaming coffee with two chocolate flakes poking out of the top.

"Nice breakfast," Frank said gruffly, nodding at the boys' unusual choices.

"What of it?" said Hurlock.

"Free country," Booker snarled, swirling his ice cream round the bowl.

"Will you please thank your father for allowing us to interview you here," Abbie said pleasantly to Danny Booker, defusing the tension.

"Better than the cop shop, eh?" Frank added, picking up on Abbie's diplomatic intervention.

"Have your folks owned this place long, Danny?" Frank asked Booker. The boy shrugged.

"Long before I existed," Booker said, finishing his ice cream and pushing the bowl across the table.

"Family business from way back. They probably expect me to take over. Fat chance." Danny Booker looked slyly at Gavin Hurlock and both boys chuckled.

"Not interested in carrying on the family tradition, then?" Abbie asked.

"That's what sisters are for, innit?" Danny Booker smirked. "And I've got two of 'em. Women's work, running a café." Booker added, eyeing Abbie defiantly.

"Is that what your dad says?" Frank interjected. Danny Booker struggled for a reply.

"You didn't tell me we were interviewing Beavis and Butthead," Frank whispered to Abbie. Abbie suppressed an urge to laugh. Frank took out his notebook and laid it on the table.

"Okay boys," said Frank. "Time for you to drop the 'tough guys' act. I want to know precisely what you know about the Sally Hawkins case."

"Is he always like this?" Danny Booker asked Abbie. She ignored the question.

"Right," said Frank, bringing his fist down on the table. "I've had enough of this. Come on then, it's down to the station with the pair of you – we can talk there." Frank stood up.

Gavin Hurlock now interjected hurriedly.

"Look, I'm sorry, Sir. Danny's just nervous, that's all. He didn't mean anything by it, did you Dan?"

Booker shook his head meekly.

"Can we just tell you what we know, please?" Hurlock

continued.

"I wish you bloody well would," Frank sneered, sitting down again.

Frank looked at the boys. They were two pimply, insignificant-looking seventeen-year-olds. They might have seemed the most fearsome pair of toughs back in the classroom – terrorising little schoolgirls like Sally Hawkins – but, out here in the big wide world of adults, they were still finding their feet.

Seventeen was a difficult age, as Frank recalled. It was perfectly natural these two swaggering youths wanted to appear 'cool' in front of each other. Frank decided to cut them some slack.

"Can you fetch us a couple of coffees, there's a good lad," Frank smiled to Danny Booker. The boy stood up and hurried away.

Frank and Abbie were now alone with Gavin Hurlock. Whereas Danny Booker looked like an otter, Gavin Hurlock was more of a shrew, thought Frank. Both boys had a shifty, untrustworthy appearance and could easily have been mistaken for brothers.

They probably got judged by their shifty looks every day of their lives. They weren't proper delinquents, though, despite their childish posturing. Frank had checked the boys' records before setting off – both youths were spotlessly clean; not a rap sheet between them. Still, Gavin Hurlock was clearly the more mature and by far the more approachable. If they could get Hurlock talking before Booker returned, the other boy would be more likely to open up.

"I've heard you used to bully Sally Hawkins," Frank said to Gavin Hurlock, leaning forward and placing his forearms on the table. Hurlock sat back, crossing his arms defensively.

"Says who?" the boy asked.

"Mr. Clarke at your school. Your History teacher. Remember him?"

"That wanker? You shouldn't listen to him."

"Why not?" Abbie asked.

"Because he's full of shit," the boy said flatly.

"So, you *didn't* bully her?" Frank grunted.

"We teased her. It was banter. Harmless stuff. She liked it – gave as good as she got. Old Clarkey couldn't tell the difference."

"Would you say you were a *friend* of Sally's, then?" Abbie interjected.

"Not a friend. I knew her. That's how I know it was her I saw that day, getting into the car. Danny saw her too. We *both* saw her. It was definitely her."

"Woah, hang on a minute, son," Frank exclaimed. "Let me get this straight – you're telling me you and Danny Booker both witnessed Sally Hawkins getting into a car on the day she disappeared?"

Gavin Hurlock nodded, shame-faced.

At that moment, Danny Booker returned carrying the two mugs of coffee Frank had ordered. He placed the drinks clumsily on the table, slopping liquid over the sides.

"Got any sugar?" Frank smiled.

Booker fished in his pockets and skimmed some crumpled packets of brown sugar onto the table, straight into the pool of spilled coffee. The boy sat down next to his friend. Frank grabbed the least drenched sugar sachet.

"Spoon?" Frank enquired.

"Fuck's sake," Danny Booker said, standing up again.

Gavin Hurlock pulled the teaspoon out of his coffee mug and offered it to Frank. Frank motioned for Danny Booker to sit down again.

"Probably best you *don't* go into the family business," Frank chuckled, stirring his coffee. "You won't have any customers left after a week."

Danny Booker scowled unhappily.

"Now then," Frank continued, looking all the while at Danny Booker, "Your pal, Gavin here, has been very helpful in your absence. He tells us you and he witnessed Sally Hawkins climbing into a vehicle on the day of her disappearance."

Danny Booker looked at Gavin Hurlock. Gavin Hurlock looked resolutely at the table top.

"Don't look at him for cues," Frank continued, sipping his coffee. "Tell us what you know, Danny. Is what Gavin said true?"

Danny Booker nodded.

"Danny," Abbie said quietly. "You need to tell us what you know."

Danny Booker took a deep breath and slumped back. It looked as if a weight had been lifted from him.

"Okay," the boy began. "Here's what happened. Gavin and I were in a field just outside town – just beyond Old Hunstanton. The field just after the curve in the road by the farm shop."

"Yes, I know it," Abbie said. "On the 149," she whispered to Frank. "Go on, Danny."

The boy was now addressing Abbie rather than Frank.

"Well, we were drinking cider and smoking. It's where we go to do that. There's a huge tree there with big branches. We climb up in a branch each. And we can see the road from there. We sit there and we drink and smoke. It's what we do most days when the weather's good." Booker sounded defensive.

"I'm not judging you," Abbie said. "I just want to know what you saw."

"Okay, so, on that day, we were up in our tree as usual and we saw this girl standing at the bus stop on the far side of the road. There's a bus stop there, we can see it clearly from the tree. And I said to Gavin, that's Sally Hawkins at the bus stop."

"And I said, yeah, it was." Gavin added.

"And then she sticks her thumb out, hitching a lift, and this car stops."

"Yeah," said Gavin. "I remember we thought it was strange as Sally wasn't really the hitch-hiking type. And then the car came into view."

"And," Danny continued. "It was Paul Hodson's car."

Frank looked at Abbie, Abbie looked at Frank. Then they both looked at the boys.

"Paul Hodson's car?" Frank exclaimed. "You're absolutely sure about this?"

The boys nodded in unison.

"Except it wasn't Hodson who was driving," Booker continued.

Frank and Abbie exchanged glances a second time.

"It was Carl Palmer," Gavin Hurlock said.

"Palmer. The PE teacher?" Abbie asked. "You're absolutely sure of that?"

"Saw the bastard clear as day," Danny Booker replied. "I'd

recognise that dickhead anywhere. Fancies himself big time. It was him at the wheel, I'm sure of it."

"Definitely him," Gavin Hurlock added.

"And you're sure the car belonged to Paul Hodson?" Frank asked urgently.

"Damn right," Danny Booker chuckled. "How many lime green Ford Capris do you think are floating around these parts?"

"Hodson and Palmer restore cars in their spare time – 'classics' they call them. Then they drive them round town thinking they're the dogs' bollocks."

"So I've heard," Frank said.

"Well, this lime green Capri was Paul Hodson's pride and joy." Hurlock stated.

"And you didn't think to volunteer this information to us sooner?" Abbie asked incredulously. "You knew Sally Hawkins had been murdered and you'd both seen her hitching a lift on the day of her disappearance and neither of you said a single word to anyone about it until *now*?"

The boys looked at each other.

"We were going to," Gavin Hurlock said.

"It's just that, well, we were smoking and I mean *smoking*, if you catch my drift. We didn't know if we'd be believed or if we'd just be nicked for...er...having substances. Then, after a few days went by after Sally was discovered, we figured it would look suspicious that we'd apparently withheld what we'd seen. So we decided not to say anything."

"It looks *more* suspicious that you *didn't* come forward," Frank warned. "And let me tell you boys, murder trumps wacky baccy any day of any week."

"You should have come forward sooner," Abbie said.

"We're doing it now, aren't we?" Danny Booker pleaded.

"Okay lads," said Frank, standing up. "You'll need to sign witness statements to make what you've just told us official. We'll be in touch."

Abbie and Frank walked away, both lost in their thoughts until they reached the Insignia.

"Can you believe it?" Frank asked. "Our two star witnesses are a pair of dumb teenagers we very nearly didn't speak to. The very last names on our interview list."

"Two teenagers out of their heads on dope, you mean," Abbie said scornfully. "Can we really rely on a single word they're saying? Will it stand up in court?"

"These are eyewitness sightings," Frank replied gruffly. "It's the best we've got to date. So, it turns out it's Paul Hodson and Carl Palmer in the frame for Sally's abduction – not that clown Tim Powell, after all. Alright Abs, here's what we'll do. I'll drop you back at HQ. You and Clive get the ball rolling by putting the thumbscrews on Paul Hodson – see if the fat bastard cracks. Meanwhile, I'll pick up Carl Palmer. I'll interview that bastard myself. We can hold them side by side in separate interview rooms and jump from one to the other. We'll crack them in minutes."

So, it was Palmer and Hodson rather than Powell and Hodson. Case closed.

40

Frank dropped Abbie at the cop shop and set off for Carl Palmer's cottage in Heacham. As Frank drove, the revelations so recently afforded to him by Danny Booker and Gavin Hurlock kept replaying in his mind: Paul Hodson's car, driven by Carl Palmer stopped for Sally Hawkins on the A149 on the day of the girl's disappearance; Sally got in the car and was never seen again.

This was eye witness testimony from *two* eye witnesses. It was *dynamite*. But how did Tim Powell fit into this scenario? Was he really just some foolish innocent with appalling timing or might he somehow be involved in the guise of an accomplice? Was he the bait, luring the poor, gullible schoolgirl directly into Carl Palmer's clutches? How deep did this depravity lie within the body of the school's staff? Was Frank on the verge of uncovering some sort of paedophile ring within the local High School? It wasn't clear yet.

As Frank parked the Insignia outside the Palmers' cottage he wondered how long it would be before Clive and Abbie had taken Paul Hodson into custody and begun softening him up.

Frank rapped the front door with his knuckles. He stood and waited. Nothing. Frank knocked heavily once again – this time with the heel of his fist. Nothing. The DCI crouched and peered through the letterbox.

Tumbleweed. The bastard was out.

"Fuck," said Frank, turning on his heel.

Hardly had Frank reached the Insignia when a woman emerged from the cottage and ran down the path towards him. Frank was greeted by the sight of Claudette Palmer wearing a pink bath robe with a white towel wrapped, turban-style, around her head.

"You're that policeman, aren't you?" said Mrs. Palmer, in her sing-song foreign accent.

"Detective Chief Inspector Homes, Madam," said Frank gruffly. "Is your husband at home?"

"I'm sorry. I was in the shower when you knocked," Claudette continued, ignoring Frank's question. "I only heard you just before you left. I thought it must be important if you are coming back so I ran out and…"

"Yes, Mrs. Palmer. It is important. I need to speak to your husband, right away."

"Carl is not here. Is he in trouble?"

"Why would you say that?"

"Say what? That he's not here?"

"No. Why would you assume Carl is in trouble?"

"I didn't assume it. I didn't assume anything, Inspector. I simply asked a question. You are a policeman and you want to see Carl so I was worried something might have happened to him."

"Such as?"

"You tell me, Inspector. You are the one coming here to me; not me to you."

"Do you know where your husband is right now, Mrs. Palmer?"

"*Non.* Je n'ai…I mean, no, I have no idea. Sorry."

Frank stood with his hands on his hips, trying to hide his frustration.

"If you would care to come into the cottage," Claudette Palmer continued. "I can try to call him on his mobile. Although it is summer, it is still a little cold for me dressed like this."

Mrs. Palmer gestured at herself with one hand and clutched

the bathrobe tightly to her slender figure with the other hand.

"Of course. Please, lead the way."

Claudette Palmer turned and walked into the cottage. Frank followed like a faithful terrier. Claudette walked into the kitchen, picked up her mobile and punched in a number. Cradling the phone to her ear, she gestured at Frank to take a seat.

It was the same garden furniture as the time Clive had visited. Frank chose the chair that looked the least flimsy. Claudette glanced up from the phone, lodged between ear and shoulder.

"Would you like something to drink, Inspector?" Mrs. Palmer asked.

"No, thank you." Frank said, looking at his watch.

Silence followed. Claudette Palmer screwed up her face, switched off her mobile and threw it onto the table. "He is not answering," she said flatly.

"I see," said Frank. "Do you know where he went and how long ago he left?"

Claudette Palmer sat opposite Frank. She had the creaky chair this time, which groaned in protest even at her slight weight. "As I said already, I have no idea. I am not my husband's boss. He has a life of his own – as do I." Suddenly, her makeshift turban unravelled and slipped to her shoulders. Claudette Palmer shrieked in surprise and desperately grabbed at the towel.

Frank could see she'd dyed her hair a bright peroxide blonde.

"Suits you," said Frank.

"Thank you," said Claudette, flustered. She threw the towel on the table. "Carl said I should try going blonde."

"Do you always do what he tells you?" Frank asked.

Claudette laughed. The falling towel seemed to have broken the ice.

"No, not always," Mrs. Palmer smiled. "As I said, Carl has his life and I have mine. We may be married but we don't own each other."

"Indeed," said Frank. "And it does suit you, you know."

He wanted to say the new colour made her look less like Popeye's girlfriend but he managed to restrain himself. Claudette Palmer stood up and fluffed her newly blonde hair.

"Are you sure you don't want something to drink, Inspector? Tea? Coffee? Something a bit stronger?"

"Yes, I'm sure, thank you, Mrs. Palmer," said Frank. "I'd just like to speak to your husband, rather urgently in fact."

Claudette Palmer sat down again. The chair squeaked its protest once more.

"Let me see," she said, closing her eyes in a gesture that suggested she was searching for some distant memory. "Yes, that's it. Carl said he was meeting Paul Hodson to work on a car today –

at the place Mr. Hodson owns. No wonder he is not answering his mobile. When they get together on a car they are immersed for hours in whatever they are doing at that garage."

"I see," said Frank. "And where is this garage exactly?"

Claudette Palmer stood up.

"I will write the address for you – but you cannot miss it. It is on the A149, on the left side, after Thornham and before you reach Brancaster."

Claudette plucked an empty envelope from a pile of bills, pulled a biro from a mug of pens and began writing.

"Thank you," said Frank.

Back in the Insignia, Frank checked the address: "Royal North Norfolk Garage, Brancaster, PE31." Frank sparked the Insignia into life. The Royal North Norfolk Garage was about to get an unscheduled visit.

41

The Royal North Norfolk Garage was indeed situated on the left side of the A149 on the approach to Brancaster, exactly as Mrs. Palmer had said.

Outwardly disused and largely dilapidated, it was easy to miss if you weren't paying attention. Locals knew the nearest working petrol station was actually located at Deepdale and would routinely hurtle past the derelict garage but Frank supposed a few outsiders might occasionally mistakenly slow down, pull into the forecourt and perhaps even try to make use of the deregulated petrol pumps before realising their error. Frank slowed the Insignia and pulled onto the run-in road for the defunct petrol station forecourt.

He brought the car to a halt directly beside the empty pumps. Someone had covered them with old green tarpaulins – no doubt to deter all but the most stupid of motorists. Frank cut the engine, stepped out of his car and stretched.

The DCI walked over to the boarded-up petrol station cabin and attempted to peer through the wooden slats. It was too dark inside to make anything out. The place had a musty smell – the stench of decay made all the more stomach-churning in the summer heat.

Behind the shop – set a good distance back – were a series of out-buildings that appeared to be equally decayed but were not boarded up. One building was a dismantled car wash and another, like a mini aircraft hangar, all corrugated iron and rusty tin roof, seemed to have been the original workshops for motor vehicle repair jobs. That must be where Carl Palmer was lurking, thought Frank.

The DCI walked over to the workshop. The building sported a large set of metal doors on rollers. Frank hammered repeatedly on the doors until his knuckles felt raw. If Carl Palmer was inside then not only would he have heard the knocking but he would also have been well and truly deafened. Frank waited for the metal doors to slide open. Nothing.

Frank hammered against the doors again. No response.

Then Frank noticed the workshop was padlocked from the outside. There *couldn't* be anyone in there – not unless they'd been deliberately imprisoned. So, where was Carl Palmer hiding?

Clearly he'd told his wife a porker and buggered off someplace else. Frank pulled out his mobile phone and dialled. He walked back to the Insignia as he listened to the phone ringing in his ear. As Frank reached the car, Clive answered.

"What's up Boss?"

"Palmer's gone AWOL."

"You don't say. Seems Paul Hodson's done a runner too."

"A *runner*? How the fuck did that happen? I told you to bring him in and start questioning him."

"Yes, I know, Sir. I'm sorry, Sir. It's like, well, to be honest, it's like he's just vanished into thin air."

Frank chewed his lip. Eventually, Clive spoke again.

"Sir, are you there, Sir?"

"Yes, I'm here, Clive. I'm just thinking. Holy shit, this is a right fuck up. Two suspects – strong suspects – and somehow they both manage to piss off into nowhere on the very day we're set to haul them in?"

"Yes Sir. I've put the word out among the uniforms. They'll bring them in soon enough."

"Let's hope so. Okay, update me when you can, Clive. As

soon as there's some news, I want to know. As it happens, I'm at Hodson's petrol station on the A149 right now. Carl Palmer's wife told me he'd be here but the bastard's nowhere to be seen. I think she was on the level. It appears he's spun her some yarn and fucked off someplace else. Well, I can't hang around here all day in case he reappears. Tell you what – I'll drive out to Cromer and call in at the café where Tim Powell was going to meet Sally Hawkins for his seedy little assignation. This seems as good an opportunity as any to check the place out and speak to the café owner. We need to see if there's anything missing in the jigsaw. We still can't entirely rule Tim Powell out of any involvement. He might have been *knowingly* putting the bait out that led Sally Hawkins to her doom. Meantime, Clive, do whatever it takes to bring those two cretins in pronto."

"Will do, Boss."

The line went dead and Frank pocketed his mobile phone angrily. He climbed into the Insignia, slammed the door, started the engine and thumped the steering wheel. He could only hope the two missing scumbags hadn't gone to ground overseas. The whole case had been within touching distance of being solved.

The last thing Frank needed was a pair of suspects on the run. Still, for all Frank knew, they might just be getting pissed in some snooker hall in Norwich rather than trying to flee the country.

Stay calm, Frank told himself.

Besides, the sudden disappearance of Paul Hodson and Carl Palmer had afforded Frank a new opportunity to further pursue his own agenda concerning Black Shuck. It wasn't that he especially wanted to visit the café in Cromer – or speak to its proprietor – or that he seriously suspected Tim Powell might be actively involved in Sally Hawkins' abduction. It was more that, on his return journey from Cromer, Frank would inevitably drive through Cley next the Sea – allowing him to call in on Julie Morton for the séance she'd promised to hold for him at her cottage.

Good grief, thought Frank. He must be completely insane to be giving that unhinged woman the time of day let alone contemplating anything as irredeemably loopy as attending a séance. Still, Black Shuck had haunted him incessantly and if this so-called psychic really could explain why that was happening, it was worth a try. After all, thought Frank, what's the worst that could happen?

42

Frank hadn't been to Cromer for years. In fact, the place was a bit of a sore point for him. When he'd been married to Sue, they used to visit Cromer for weekend getaways – lovers' weekends involving nights to remember in grand but crumbling Victorian hotels; overloaded with lust and adrenaline; fuelled by too much booze and excessive quantities of Cromer crab. Happy days – before Sue turned sour and love grew stale.

And then the town became a haven for junkies – exiled there by idealistic social services do-gooders (some of the ne'er-do-wells coming from as far away as London only to be unceremoniously dumped in a Cromer B&B).

Soon there was shooting up on the beach, muggings, mindless violence in the pubs – stuff that, as a serving copper, Frank couldn't ignore. Suddenly, those idyllic weekends with Sue became something of a busman's holiday – Frank heading down to the Cromer cop shop, dragging in some miscreant, filling in forms. It was all a bit of a passion killer. Shortly thereafter, Frank's marriage hit the rocks and those lusty trips to Cromer became nothing but a memory; a vague echo of another lifetime.

Frank parked the Insignia by the seafront and took some deep breaths of sea air. It looked as if the place was on the up again. The junkies seemed to have moved on, several of the older buildings had been tarted up and you could even spot a few trendy Southwold types roaming the streets on the lookout for a flat white.

The sea air made Frank feel hungry. He couldn't bring himself to order Cromer crab – too many memories of Sue from that brief period when times had been good. Fish and chips, though, was just what the doctor ordered. There was still plenty of time for Frank to grab a hot meal before sauntering over to the Blue Lagoon Café to speak to its owner.

After all, Frank acknowledged to himself, this whole escapade in Cromer was largely a wild goose chase and a time-killing exercise before he headed to Cley to see Julie Morton for her séance. No need to hurry himself in Cromer just now – unless

Clive suddenly phoned to say Paul Hodson and Carl Palmer had been located.

Frank walked past the pier and along the coast road, stopping at a newsagent for a copy of The Times. He'd have to double back on himself to find the Blue Lagoon but, as he reminded himself, he had plenty of time to kill.

Eventually, Frank found exactly the type of establishment he was seeking – Janet's Fish Bar; a good old-fashioned Norfolk chippy that reeked of hot dripping and malt vinegar. Frank took a corner table, spread out his newspaper and waited for someone to take his order.

It wasn't long before Frank found himself presented with a large plate of crispy cod and fat buttery chips. Later, happily replete, Frank strolled back the way he'd come, depositing the newspaper in a recycling bin and pausing once more to breathe deeply in the sea air. It was now almost 5 p.m – the Blue Lagoon Café would be closing shortly.

Nobody had phoned Frank so Paul Hodson and Carl Palmer must still be AWOL. It was only a matter of time though, thought Frank. Those bastards would be in custody soon enough.

Frank turned a corner and there it was – the Blue Lagoon Café. The exterior was, appropriately enough, painted a garish Marine blue, interspersed by some whitewashed pebble-dash. A large glass frontage displayed an assembly of cheap wooden tables and chairs. The tables were covered in white paper cloths decorated with a blue anchor motif. The café was empty. A sturdy, matronly woman, wearing a bright white apron with the same blue anchor motif, was reaching for the 'Closed' sign on the door.

Frank sprinted the final few yards and tapped on the glass. The woman, who'd clearly seen him approaching, flipped the sign to 'Closed' and hurriedly locked the door. She pointed at the sign and shrugged her shoulders in mock apology. Frank took out his police ID and pressed it against the glass.

The woman's expression changed to one of astonishment. In a second, the door had been opened and Frank was standing inside. Frank shook the woman's hand.

"DCI Frank Homes of King's Lynn Police. Can I speak to the owner of this establishment, please?"

"Is me."

"I'm sorry?"

"Is me, I boss."

The woman's accent was East European.

"I beg your pardon, Madam. You're the owner here?"

"Yes. My name is Ludmilla Hogan. I am boss here."

"You're from Eastern Europe, I take it?"

"Yes, from Poland. But my husband is British person."

"Hence, the name Hogan?"

"Yes, Inspector. Before I was Pliskova. I marry British man. So, now I am Hogan."

"And you run this place on your own or with Mr. Hogan?"

"This is my business. Me and my daughter. She is not here now. Gone home. My husband, he is a builder – how you say, he put up frames on buildings?"

"A scaffolder?"

"Yes, scaffolder. He do that and other building work – roofing and such. Please, what is this about?"

"May we?" Frank gestured to an empty table.

Mrs. Hogan nodded and locked the front door while Frank took a seat.

"Mrs. Hogan," Frank began, once she was also seated. "I am here to investigate a murder."

Ludmilla gasped and put a hand up to her mouth.

"Is terrible, how can I help?"

"I have reason to believe your café may be involved…"

Another gasp.

"My God." She crossed herself.

"It's possible the killer arranged to meet the victim here at your café. It's possible the killer came to eat here beforehand on recce – I mean, it's likely the killer might have checked out your café to see if it was a suitable venue for a quiet meeting. Mrs. Hogan, do you have CCTV here?"

"I'm sorry, we don't have." She shook her head regretfully.

"Another reason the killer may have chosen this place," Frank said, mostly to himself. Frank pulled out his notebook.

"Mrs. Hogan, do you recall anyone strange or suspicious visiting your café in the past few weeks? Anyone at all? Please, try to think."

Ludmilla stood up.

"Can I get you drink, while I am thinking? We have best coffee in all of Cromer – is official, it win prizes."

Frank couldn't face eating or drinking another thing after his fish supper. Still, he had more time to kill before heading to Cley and Julie Morton. He gritted his teeth.

"Thank you, Mrs. Hogan. That would be very nice."

Ludmilla walked into the open-plan kitchen. Frank pulled out his mobile and checked for messages. Nothing. Those bastards Hodson and Palmer were still on the run. Presently, Ludmilla returned with a strong black coffee and a small jug of hot, frothy milk. She hadn't lied – it was good coffee.

Frank sat patiently, scribbling in his notebook – vague descriptions of various tramps and random itinerants; a motley parade of losers and chancers – none of whom sounded even remotely like the Drama teacher, Tim Powell.

Two coffees later and it was approaching 7pm. Frank reckoned it was time he made a move and headed in the direction of Julie Morton. Frank stood up, thanked Ludmilla Hogan and put away his notebook.

"Thank you for your time this evening, Mrs. Hogan. That was indeed most excellent coffee. I'll be sure to spread the word."

Ludmilla opened the door for the DCI and he stepped out into the evening air. Suddenly Ludmilla called out after him.

"This killer – I hope you catch him."

Frank spun round, a smile playing across his lips.

"Oh, we will, Mrs. Hogan. We will. You can be sure of that."

43

Frank was over an hour early when he parked outside Julie Morton's cottage in Cley. He sat in the car feeling unsure whether to knock on the door or to give up on the whole escapade and drive home. He wondered what Julie would need to do to set up a séance anyway – could her preparations take long?

Frank supposed he could drive up and down the A149 and return to the cottage nearer his allotted time of 9pm. On the other hand, he worried he might see Black Shuck. This was now the longest he'd gone without a ghost dog sighting and Frank very much wanted to keep it that way. He pulled out his mobile and dialled. Presently, Abbie answered.

"Sir?" said WPC Silvers.

"Abs, any news from today? Did you get anywhere tracking down Hodson and Palmer?"

"No, Sir, nothing. I thought Clive had called to say we'd drawn a blank?"

"No, he didn't. So, the bastards have gone to ground good and proper?"

"There could be another explanation, Sir. However, it's not looking too good."

"Indeed. Are you in tomorrow, Abs?"

"Yes, Sir."

"Fine. Remind Clive our absolute priority is bringing in those two clowns. Contact the ports and airports to stay on the lookout."

"Already done, Sir. Will you be in the station yourself tomorrow, Sir?"

"I'm following another lead just now, Abs, so I may be in a little later than usual – but, yes, I'll be in."

"Was there anything else, Sir?"

Frank could hear an awkward timbre in Abbie's voice.

His call had likely interrupted something – perhaps some hanky panky with Windy Miller; that was not a pleasant thought. He had no reason to prolong the conversation anyway – beyond the purely selfish expedient of killing more time before attending the

Julie Morton psychic spectacular.

"No, Abs, there's nothing else. You have a good evening."

Frank hung up and threw his mobile in the car's glove box. Listlessly, he turned on the radio and pushed the auto-tuning dial. The radio came to rest on a broadcast of what sounded like experimental jazz – tuneless, aimless, self-indulgent waffle, thought Frank.

The DCI wondered once again if this visit to Julie Morton was really such a good idea. Even the music was weird round here, he mused. It would have been so easy to start the car and drive away; forget the whole stupid notion of a séance.

If any of his colleagues so much as gained an inkling that DCI Frank Homes was doing something so outlandish…well, it didn't bear thinking about.

Frank switched the radio off and retrieved his mobile. He was beyond antsy and didn't know what to do with himself. It was probably all that coffee he'd had at the café in Cromer.

He closed his eyes. Perhaps Jo was available. He figured he may as well give The Linnet Tavern a bell. That would kill some more time. Frank had barely dialled Jo's number when he saw, through the car's windscreen, Julie Morton's cottage door had opened and a familiar thin woman was standing on the doorstep, bathed in a strip of light emanating from the hallway behind her.

The effect of the back-lighting was to cast her entirely in silhouette and it was undeniable; she looked positively *witchy*. A shudder ran through Frank.

He switched his mobile off as the witchy woman began to walk purposefully towards his car. Jo would have to wait. Frank leapt out of the Insignia.

Julie Morton had let her hair down. It fell, full and flowing, streaks of grey visible among the dark locks. Down it tumbled, below her shoulders to the small of her back.

Frank would never have guessed Julie's earlier 'bun' had disguised this much luxuriant hair. She was dressed entirely in black, sporting a thin tie-dyed cotton dress that travelled to her ankles.

It was as if she'd wrapped herself in a black bed sheet, thought Frank.

"Forgot your broomstick?" Frank sneered, ungallantly.

"I thought you might stay sitting in that car all night," Julie replied, ignoring the jibe.

"So did I." Frank admitted. "I can't believe I'm here myself."

Julie took his hands in hers.

"I'm glad you came, Frank. It's okay to be nervous. It's a brave thing to do, especially the first time."

"I'm not nervous. Clinically insane, maybe."

"So, how do you explain the broomstick comment? Just your usual charm? People make fun of the things they fear."

"Sorry about that. Apologies for being so early. I can go away and come back later, if you'd prefer?"

"Not at all. I'm just glad you're here, Frank. Please, come inside."

Julie Morton marched towards the cottage. In that long dress, she seemed to glide as much as walk. Frank followed, glancing around in case any neighbours might have seen him. He need not have worried – the cottage was completely isolated; an isolation made more intense by several large trees that flanked it almost to the point of encirclement. This was truly the outskirts of Cley.

Frank could make out a few lights in some distant buildings in the main village as he stepped onto Julie's front porch. He hesitated momentarily and glanced over his shoulder – he hadn't known why; it was a kind of sixth sense.

Almost on cue, the sky grew overcast – dark, threatening, black clouds seemed to be gathering directly over him.

"Looks like rain," Frank said to Julie, a tremulous smile playing across his lips.

"Well, it's been a pretty hot summer and I guess we could do with some rain," Julie said soothingly. "The garden will be glad of it. It's not rained for several days now."

Julie Morton smiled reassuringly at Frank and beckoned the policeman over the threshold. Once Frank was inside, she closed the door behind him so forcefully that Frank jumped. Julie chuckled.

"Sorry, this rotten old door sticks unless you give it a good shove. I've been meaning to get a man round to fix it for some time now."

"Perhaps just a bit of WD40," Frank suggested, trying to regain his composure. "Now then, where do you want me?"

Julie Morton led Frank into the front room. The room was dominated by a large oak dining table, cleared for tonight's purposes. Four high-backed wooden chairs surrounded the table. They were upholstered with purple velvet. Ornate carvings at the top of the chairs gave the impression of snakes winding their way around the chair's legs, the snake's heads eventually emerging above the chair tops and curling back to face each other like a pair of bookends.

Julie walked to the far side of the room and drew the curtains. Then she pulled out two of the chairs. Julie sat down and patted the spare chair beside her, enticing Frank to join her as though he were a lap dog. Outside, the storm broke urgently with a huge flash of lightning and an almighty crash of thunder. The cottage windows shook with the sudden violence.

Instinctively, Frank ducked. It sounded as though the building was being bombed. Julie laughed.

"Well now, here comes the rain," Julie remarked calmly. "Won't you sit down, Frank?"

The thunderstorm was now raging; heavy rain was battering the windows as if it was being jet-sprayed directly at them. Frank gripped the edge of the dining table as he sat down. Had the table been made of clay, Frank's fingers would have sunk right in. Julie Morton placed her hands on top of Frank's.

"You don't have to do this if you don't want to," she said. "If it's making you this uncomfortable then perhaps we should…"

"No!" Frank said, with a forcefulness that surprised even him. "I've come this far, let's just get on with it."

Julie nodded and released Frank's hands. The storm intensified. The lightning strikes and thunder bursts were now following so close to one another it was hard to tell them apart.

Julie stood up – a witchy silhouette illuminated by the back-lighting of the storm faced Frank once more, this time at disturbingly close quarters. Julie Morton stood momentarily still, bathed in the eerie light of the storm that flashed on and off like some demonic strobe system.

"Would you like a drink before we begin?" Julie asked. "I've got some brandy tucked away."

"No, no thank you," said Frank. "Let's just get this over with."

Julie sat down and smoothed her dress.

"It's all gone a bit Hammer Horror," Frank laughed, gesturing at another thunder flash.

"We can wait until the storm abates, if you prefer," Julie said, her eyes searching Frank's with what appeared to be a note of deep concern.

"No," Frank replied stiffly. "Let's do this."

44

Julie Morton leaned back in her chair and closed her eyes. She placed both palms flat on the table and extended her arms until her elbows locked. Then she tilted her head upwards as if staring at the ceiling, although her eyes remained firmly shut.

Outside, the thunderstorm rose to a new crescendo. Frank wondered, not for the first time, exactly why he'd placed himself in this creepy cottage with this strange woman undergoing this freaky ritual.

"Don't be alarmed," Julie Morton said calmly. "I'm calling for Torben, my spirit guide. I need to connect with him first so I can contact the other spirits."

Frank wondered if he should reply but decided he'd better not disturb Julie's concentration. He desperately wanted to put a light on; all the electric lights were off and only a few flickering candles provided any illumination. The result was a deeply unsettling half-light. The lightning flashes of the storm gave sudden transitory glimpses of the room in stark relief but these were fleeting instances.

Julie Morton began to moan or was it a type of singing? Chanting, perhaps? An incantation?

Frank didn't like it – it was worse than that experimental jazz on the car radio. Eventually, Frank could make out a few words, emerging through the slow, torturous whining to gradually become a hypnotic mantra: "Torben come, Torben come."

In her trance-like state, Julie Morton repeated these rhythmic resonances over and over. The utterances were slower than normal speech yet weirdly beguiling and, after a time, oddly soporific.

Before Frank knew it, he felt the room spinning, his mind swimming and the sense that he may fall from his chair at any moment. The shocked DCI gripped the table harder, trying to steady himself. Julie Morton was tilting further back on her chair.

"Torben come, Torben come."

Julie's chanting changed pace, speeding up to become a manic refrain. It also grew louder.

As if in consort with Julie's chants, the storm outside reached its zenith. Rain battered the windows of the cottage as thunder shook the frames. The entire building appeared to be under siege from the elements. Julie Morton let out a piercing scream that threatened to burst Frank's eardrums.

The policeman sat rooted to his chair.

Julie Morton stopped looking at the ceiling, her head gradually returned to a normal posture. Now she appeared to be looking straight ahead, looking straight at Frank. Her eyes, though, remained tightly shut. Suddenly, Julie Morton opened her eyes and Frank was horrified. Only the whites of Julie's eyes were visible; the coloured parts had somehow vanished so she looked completely, but unnaturally, blind. How was such a thing even possible?

"He is here." Julie said. Her voice was calm.

"Torben is with us," she intoned solemnly.

Julie relaxed her arms and sat completely still.

"Should I...?" Frank began.

Julie shushed him angrily.

"Wait!" she hissed.

Frank didn't know if he was imagining it, but he thought he could hear the wings of a flapping bird. At first the sound was distant but it gradually grew louder and seemed to be getting closer. Now the sound was coming from inside the room and it could even be heard above the violence of the storm.

Black shadows darted about Frank's head. Some of them passed so close, Frank instinctively ducked. Yet nothing was there.

Could this really be happening? It seemed as if a large black bird – a raven – was in the room with them, flitting this way and that at preternatural speed; far quicker than any normal bird could fly. It moved like some sinister animation – a menacing stop-motion image that only became momentarily visible in the intermittent lightning flashes of the storm that assaulted the room.

Frank felt he'd had more than enough of this terrifying display and tried to stand up to leave but, to his horror, he found himself totally paralysed as if he'd been bound to his chair by invisible rope. The DCI could only watch as the random black shapes coalesced into a perfect facsimile of a huge raven.

The giant bird landed on the table, its wings still flapping. Gradually, it settled. It walked directly towards Julie Morton and then, as suddenly as it had arrived, it vanished into thin air. Julie Morton shuddered and let out a high-pitched moan, as if in horrendous pain.

She closed her eyes once more. As she did so, silence reigned. Even the storm seemed to pause. Frank struggled to catch his breath.

Even throughout his sightings of Black Shuck, he had never been quite this afraid. Julie Morton opened her eyes. They seemed to be back to normal now; no longer opaque and ghoulish.

"Torben is with us," she said serenely, smiling benignly at Frank. "Please, ask him whatever you need."

"I...I..." Frank began.

He hardly knew what to ask, barely knew what to say. He was torn. Part of him wanted to ask directly about Sally Hawkins' killer. Was he on the right track? Had he really already found the killer or killers? Would justice be served?

Another part of Frank wanted to ask about Black Shuck – about his sightings of the demonic hound. Why was it happening to him? What did it *mean*? Frank shifted in his seat. At least he could move again. If he wanted to stand up and flee, this was his moment.

"Well?" Julie Morton asked. A sinister and threatening tone seemed to have crept into her voice. "What is it you wish to know?" Julie continued. "Ask and ask *now*!"

Her last statement had been an angry command, her voice rising in pitch to an unnaturally shrill screech that cut through Frank like a knife.

"I...er...I wish to know why...why I have been seeing..." Frank began.

It was a sentence Frank would never complete. Suddenly Julie Morton began to growl – exactly like a dog! It was low and menacing at first, giving way to sharp yaps and wild yelps. Frank stood up and backed away from the table, sending his chair crashing. He couldn't drag his eyes from Julie Morton.

Next, she leapt onto the table, walking on all fours like an animal, her limbs twisted in a hideous approximation of some malformed four-legged creature – a giant spider missing half its grotesque limbs.

The creature that had previously been Julie Morton was frothing at the mouth. Again, she began to bark. Now her teeth were bared. These were razor sharp fangs that stretched her mouth obscenely. Next, her eyes turned bright red. It was a glowing red; the incandescent red of the eyes of…Black Shuck.

Frank knew those eyes all too well. Once more he felt himself trapped by their hypnotic gaze. Julie Morton's neck now began to twist and elongate as though she were being hanged from an invisible gibbet.

Her head gradually turned to one side, ending up sideways to her body. She was becoming less and less human by the second. The vision now confronting Frank was worse than any painting by Bosch, more appalling than any description of Dante. DCI Homes was now faced by a sickening distortion from the bowels of Hades.

Recovering his senses, Frank knew only one thing – he must escape. As Frank backed away from the horrific spectacle, he tumbled over the fallen chair and found himself lying helpless on the floor. The gruesome fiend that Julie Morton had become scrambled hurriedly across the table top. Frank heard it scrabbling somewhere above him. And then, ominously, silence descended.

Frank lay helpless on the floor, gazing up at the table's edge. Any second now he expected the monster's face to appear above him, its hideous teeth gnashing, its breath fetid and – no doubt – his life about to end. And yet, an awful vacuum of silence reigned.

Did Frank dare to peer over the top of the table? Well, he couldn't stay on the ground indefinitely, he reasoned. However, he had no wish to once again encounter the beast that had previously been Julie Morton.

Tenderly, gingerly, Frank pulled himself into a crouching position. Then, with a reckless lunge, he rose to his feet. Frank found himself looking at an empty table top. There were tell-tale claw marks – deep scratches and vicious scuffs – gouged into the table's dark surface but, crucially, there was no sign of any ogre. It took a split second to register. Alas, the beast was still with him!

It might not have been sprawled on the table top any longer but it was still in the room. It was now clinging to the wall directly opposite Frank.

It hung there, surveying the DCI hatefully with its blazing red eyes. It measured Frank menacingly, frothing at the mouth and growling repugnantly. And then it moved, exactly like a giant spider, traversing up the wall and, defying the laws of gravity, directly onto the ceiling. It scuttled across the ceiling until it was poised right above Frank's head.

Frank was mesmerised. He stood helplessly below this monstrosity; a puny fly beneath a powerful tarantula.

As Frank stared, the creature's eyes momentarily ceased to be red, its poisonous shark-like mouth reverted to that of a human, the neck retreated to its normal length; Julie Morton's tortured features appeared to him once more.

The poor woman seemed in total agony, fighting against whatever malevolent influence held her in its spell as she attempted to reassert her true self. The body of this appalling vision, however, remained entirely that of the gigantic spider-dog hybrid so that it appeared Julie Morton's head had somehow been grafted onto an abomination.

With an enormous effort, Julie Morton struggled to speak. At first she gasped like a landed fish. Then, through sheer strength of will, she shouted at Frank with all her might.

"Murder, murder, killer, murder!" she chanted.

Over and over, she repeated this dreadful refrain.

Unlike the slow, hypnotic chant she'd used to summon Torben, this incantation proceeded at double-speed, growing faster and faster until it sounded to Frank like an old cassette tape being chewed. It was guttural, unnatural.

Somehow Frank found the strength to back away. Hardly had he moved before the woman-spider-dog hybrid fell from the ceiling and crashed to the floor. There it lay beside the table. Frank could hardly bear to look.

As he did so, it resumed a fully human shape but remained horribly twisted; the limbs of the woman it had once been appearing to have been broken like twigs. Julie Morton was surely dead. Frank felt compelled to check on Julie as she lay there, crippled and unmoving.

He was mortally afraid but he also knew he had to see if she'd somehow survived her hellish ordeal. He crept slowly towards the corpse. Julie lay face down. Frank reached a hand towards Julie's shoulder to turn her over to examine the extent of her injuries. However, before he could touch her, she whipped round and thrust her face towards his. Once again, her eyes were bright white and opaque. Julie yelled urgently at Frank.

"Leave!" Julie screamed. "Leave now! This was a mistake. That spirit was unclean. You are in great danger. Go now! LEAVE!"

Frank needed no second invitation. In an instant, he was out of the front door, leaving it wide open in his haste.

He sprinted down the driveway to the Insignia, the newly resurgent storm battering him as he sought refuge in the car. Frank fired the engine, switched on the car's headlights and sped away into the night.

45

Frank drove faster and faster through the rain. His only thought was to get away, to put as much distance between himself and Julie Morton's cottage as quickly as possible. He simply couldn't process all he'd just seen. That such things should exist – in this world, in this century.

Was it really possible or was he losing his mind? Rain battered the windscreen while strong winds rocked the body of the Insignia this way and that. More than once, Frank caught the car at the last moment, barely averting a slide. He couldn't have cared less.

Escape was the only thing on his mind.

The Insignia rounded a bend and Frank immediately

recognised where he was – about to pass Paul Hodson's dilapidated petrol station at any moment. The silhouette of the site loomed into Frank's peripheral vision. Frank turned his attention back to the road.

No, it couldn't be! Surely, *this* wasn't real?

How many more torments must he stand?

There, in the middle of the road, glowing in the darkness and pointing directly towards the abandoned petrol station, stood the figure of Sally Hawkins! The murdered girl was somehow there, her arm outstretched, her finger pointing.

Frank recognised the multi-coloured fingernails, the cold alabaster complexion he'd seen on her corpse. But her eyes – her eyes were *alive*.

Her eyes were burning – ablaze with the fire of hatred and accusation. Frank's car barrelled towards the horrific vision. There was nothing he could do. He felt he would hit the girl at any second.

Girl? *Ghost*, more like!

Frank's vehicle was almost upon her. Instinct took over – just as if it had been an actual person in the road before him, Frank wrenched the steering wheel to the right and sent the Insignia on a collision course with the decommissioned petrol pumps on the gas station forecourt.

At the final moment, Frank pulled the steering wheel in the opposite direction. The attempted correction failed and the car slid into an uncontrollable spin, side-swiping the petrol pumps with an almighty crash and setting off the Insignia's airbags. There was a blinding flash before everything went black.

Frank returned to consciousness only to find himself with a face-full of airbag. The car's engine was ticking over harmlessly in the background– somehow Frank must have flicked it into neutral during the milliseconds before impact; some unconscious act of self-preservation.

Frank switched off the engine and eased the driver's seat back. He took stock of himself – no broken bones, no whiplash. There was, however, a dull ache in his lower back. It seemed he'd been lucky though – incredibly lucky.

Then it all came flooding back – Julie Morton, the séance, the awful creature she'd become, the ghost of Sally Hawkins. A shiver went down Frank's spine. He was in danger; he'd been warned and now he believed it.

He had to get out of the car. The sudden imperative became blind panic. Frank yanked desperately at the door handle. At first it wouldn't open. He pulled and thrashed at the door in a state of increasing alarm. With a final desperate lunge, Frank put all his weight against the door and shoved. In a rush, he fell out of the car and landed on hard tarmac. It was still raining heavily – bucketing like a biblical flood. It was also unnaturally cold. Perhaps this sensation of cold was simply shock, Frank reasoned.

Shivering and aching, the policeman clambered awkwardly to his feet. Torrential rain continued to cascade down, bouncing off the bonnet of the stricken car, soaking Frank to the skin.

Frank staggered to the nearest building – the same set of workshops he'd examined only a few hours earlier. As he approached, he thought he could detect a shaft of light inside. The main doors – previously padlocked – were now slightly ajar.

Someone was inside! Frank slowed his approach. Nothing could be heard except the rainfall, cascading all around him. But, yes, someone was in there.

Surely they'd heard the crash? So, why hadn't they come out, offered some assistance? What the hell was going on in there?

Frank placed a hand on one of the sliding metal doors, steadying himself. Then, it felt exactly as though his head had exploded. He lurched forward, falling through the gap and sprawling onto the concrete floor of the workshop.

Someone had hit him from behind with a heavy object and they'd hit him hard. The world swam on its axis and Frank lost consciousness just as a hefty boot nudged him in the ribs.

In the blackness, Frank felt he was floating.

He was airless, lifeless and yet somehow buoyant. It wasn't unpleasant, it wasn't especially frightening – it just *was*. Reality now had a new dimension, consciousness had a new domain; experience had a completely new set of possibilities.

The darkness coalesced all around him, gathering like storm clouds before enveloping him completely. He hadn't known darkness could be so dark. And then he heard it – the steady, rhythmic barking of a dog. This was low, guttural, powerful barking – the sound of a mighty beast. And it was growing louder; louder and closer.

Now he could see two red eyes emerging out of the darkness. They were distant at first – pinpricks of light across millennia of empty space. But they were closing on him – travelling rapidly – racing towards him; traversing time, space and reality – pursuing him like quarry.

The eyes became a face; the face was that of Black Shuck – sporting mighty jaws and razor sharp teeth. The dog was almost upon him, he could see its sinews straining across its powerful torso. Frank winced as Shuck launched himself at him with an immense, ear-shattering yowl.

At the very last second, Shuck sailed right over Frank, the devil dog passing over him like a freight train over a shivering dormouse caught between the tracks. At that precise moment, DCI

Frank Homes regained consciousness. Frank looked around, trying to take in his surroundings as his awareness gradually returned.

His head throbbed at the back of his skull, where he'd been hit. Frank tried to move his right hand up to feel for the extent of the damage – only to discover his wrists had been bound behind his back. He was seated on a concrete floor, leaning up against a brick wall.

Across from him was the expanse of the motor vehicle workshop – a sizeable space that contained a vehicle pit, two mechanised car jacks and room for at least four cars.

The doors Frank had fallen through after being assaulted stood at the far end of the workshop and they were now closed. Someone had dragged him to his current resting place and bound him. However, he was not gagged.

Someone had done all of this – but *who*?

Rain continued to beat down on the corrugated roof of the workshop. It was still heavy but slowing. Frank flexed his wrists behind him, twisting them this way and that. He wasn't sure what material had been used to secure him. It felt like thin twine – something of that sort.

The binding cut into him as he attempted to manipulate it but the pain was nothing compared to the excruciating pulsing of his injured head.

Frank worked at his bonds – a frantic amateur Houdini desperately trying to save his life. He could feel the ties stretching and loosening slightly. Thank God he hadn't been cable tied – he'd be done for if that was the case. As it was, Frank felt he might just work himself free, given enough time.

DCI Homes repeatedly clenched and unclenched his fists, twisting his wrists as much as he could. Whoever had done this had stepped outside but would no doubt reappear at any moment.

What were they doing? Moving the Insignia? Hiding any evidence of his presence? He couldn't tell if he still had the car keys on him or if they'd been taken.

He couldn't even remember if he'd had them on him when he'd tumbled out of the car after the crash. One thing at a time, Frank, he told himself.

The priority now was simply to break free of his bondage. Frank stopped what he was doing and looked up. To his horror, the doors to the workshop were opening – his captor was about to appear...

46

The workshop doors slid open on screeching, unoiled rails. Frank couldn't take his eyes off the growing gap in the doorway.

Who would appear? *What* might appear? Could anything actually get any more bizarre on this dreadful night? A figure stepped through the doors, turned its back to Frank, pulled the workshop doors closed and shook itself free of the rain. Water pooled at the figure's feet.

It was a sizeable man in navy blue overalls – the sort mechanics wear. The mystery man's back remained towards Frank as he secured the workshop doors against the elements.

Finally, the man spun to face Frank.

Harsh electric light illuminated his pudgy head. It was Paul Hodson.

"Well, well, well," Frank called across the empty space. "Look what the cat just dragged in."

"Good evening, Inspector," said Paul Hodson, striding towards Frank, still brushing rain from his drenched overalls.

"I trust you're sitting comfortably," Hodson sneered.

"So it was you who hit me?" Frank asked as the school caretaker pulled up a mechanics' stool and sat his great bulk directly opposite Frank.

"You're not a detective for nothing, are you?" Hodson scoffed, mopping his brow with a grease-covered handkerchief.

"Correct," said Frank, noticing Hodson had been careful to seat himself beyond touching distance – despite Frank's hands being bound. That meant the fat bastard was still scared of him, Frank concluded. *Good*!

"And you'll be brought to justice soon enough," Frank continued.

Hodson laughed. The arrogance and disdain the fat man was now expressing was the true side of his nature, thought Frank. It had been briefly evident to Clive too. Now it was given free reign.

"Look at you," said Hodson. "The great detective. Sat in a

pool of his own piss. Not looking too clever now, are we?"

Frank looked down at himself. He'd thought it was rainwater. Then again, he had just been knocked out and dragged across a concrete floor. If he had pissed himself, it must have happened then.

"This what you're looking for?" Hodson asked, holding up Frank's mobile phone.

It hadn't been – but Frank now feared the worst. Paul Hodson stood up and let the phone drop to the ground. Then, making sure Frank was watching, Hodson raised a foot and brought his steel toe-capped work boot down on the device. Then he did it again – and again and again – before sitting down, panting from the exertion.

"I hope that was insured," Hodson smirked. "Bit more than a cracked screen, I'd say."

"So, why did you do it?" Frank asked.

"Come again?" Hodson chuckled. "So you couldn't ring your mates for help, obviously. Not very bright for a copper, are we?"

"Sally Hawkins," Frank deadpanned. "Why did you kill Sally Hawkins?"

Paul Hodson paused. Frank noticed his discomfort and took the opportunity to begin surreptitiously working at loosening the ties behind his back.

"I didn't kill her," Paul Hodson said quietly. His tone was almost apologetic.

"Yeah, right," Frank snorted. "That's why you've just bashed me on the bonce and hog-tied me. That screams innocence all over."

"I *didn't* kill her!" Hodson shouted, leaping to his feet. The man was almost hysterical. Despite himself, Frank flinched. Paul Hodson sat down again.

"I didn't kill her," Hodson repeated. "I'm not taking the rap for that."

Frank was puzzled but tried not to let it show.

"So, if *you* didn't kill her, Paul, who did?"

That's it, use his first name. Try to establish a connection, thought Frank.

Hodson looked blank, said nothing.

"Paul, listen to me," Frank continued. His voice was soft, soothing. Behind his back he worked furiously at his bonds.

"Paul, if you didn't do this then we need to work together. You haven't killed anyone, not yet anyway. You need to tell me who did. Paul, who killed Sally Hawkins?"

Paul Hodson sat like a statue, staring vacantly ahead. The silence seemed unending. Suddenly, a vicious smile spread across Hodson's face.

The caretaker leapt from his seat – with surprising athleticism for a man of his girth. Without warning, he kicked Frank hard in the side of the head. Some latent instinct had allowed Frank to duck the blow sufficiently that Hodson only connected with the sole of his boot rather than with the full force of the steel toecap.

Even so, Frank feared a tooth had been cracked, perhaps lost entirely. There was blood running down his cheek. Hodson sat down heavily once more.

"Since you're going to die anyway," the big man said. "I might as well tell you what happened."

Frank stared at him. The salty tang of blood filled his mouth. Paul Hodson shifted his bulk on his perch. He opened his mouth as if to speak, closed it, opened it, closed it. After a few more false starts, he finally spoke.

"Carl Palmer killed Sally Hawkins," Hodson said eventually. "Right here in this garage."

I knew it, Frank thought. Then he recalled the ghost of Sally he'd just seen, pointing at this very spot before he'd crashed the Insignia. A shiver ran the length of Frank's spine. Now that Paul Hodson had revealed the truth there was no stopping him. The entire story poured out like a church confessional. Frank, literally a captive audience, sat and took it all in.

"Sally was hitch-hiking – or waiting for a bus – one or the

other, I'm not sure," Hodson said. "Anyway, Carl picked her up. It was a chance thing. He'd been driving past, saw Sally, stopped. He was in my car– my Capri. She was going to Cromer to meet somebody. Carl said he was going that way too, offered her a lift. Instead he brought her here. It was on the way, after all. He said he had to stop off, fetch something. Anyway, on some pretext, he got Sally to join him inside. We used to bring girls back here to party. Escorts, hookers, slappers from local pubs. Some good times were had in this place, Inspector, believe me."

Paul Hodson was momentarily filled with a dreamy reminiscence. Eventually, he returned to his lurid tale.

"Carl had some GHB. He was going to dose Sally, have some fun with her. If he got the dosage right, she wouldn't even recollect it. When she came round he either planned to drop her off in Cromer just as she'd asked or he'd kick her out somewhere on the A149 close to Lynn. He didn't mean to kill her. It was an accident. Sort of."

Frank grunted. It was an involuntary reaction from deep within – a bass note of pure cynicism. Then, concerned he might deter Paul Hodson from finishing his account, Frank added: "Go on, Paul."

"It was an accident," Hodson repeated. "When I got here, the girl was dead. Carl had phoned me, said I should come round, said he'd got a lively one, said we could have some fun. Like I said, when I got here, she was already dead. She was lying in that mechanics' pit over there."

Hodson gestured at an outsized grave-shaped hole in which car mechanics stood to tinker with the undersides of vehicles.

"Just there she was," said Hodson, jerking his thumb over his shoulder.

"What *exactly* happened, Paul? Come on, this is important." Frank coaxed.

"She was in the pit when I got here, stark naked but for her panties. Carl was standing by the side of the pit, washing her down with the high pressure jet-spray. She still had the scarf round her neck with which he'd killed her. I couldn't look at first. Her neck had shrunk. He'd pulled so hard her neck had been squeezed so small it looked like a tied balloon. He told me to pull myself together."

"And you just did what he said?"

"You don't understand." Hodson yelled.

Frank thought he was about to be kicked again.

"What do you know, you prick, you nosey fucking copper?"

"Nothing, Paul. I don't know anything. You're absolutely right." Frank said calmly. "So, come on, tell me. What happened? Help me to understand."

"I can only tell you what Carl told me," Hodson continued. "He said he went to dose Sally but she knocked it out of his hand. That was the only stuff he had on him. He had no choice after that. She knew him; knew who he was. How could he let her go after that? He didn't *want* to kill her. It was quick. He told me it was quick."

"But you went along with it? You didn't think of calling us once you'd got free of the situation?"

"You don't understand." Hodson bellowed.

"No I *don't!*" Frank hollered back. "What you both did was utterly inhuman. No wonder I don't understand."

"He...Carl...he has stuff on me." Hodson said quietly. "I had to help him. I had no choice."

"Stuff?"

"Yes, *stuff*," said Hodson. "We used to party here, right? We drugged the girls when we had to, we videoed what we did, we didn't ask all the girls' ages. Carl had video of me. Me with...well, you work it out, you're the cop."

"So he was blackmailing you?"

"He just reminded me we were in this together. He had a video of me that would do me no favours if it came to light. But it didn't need to – *doesn't* need to – if I do as he says. So, he cleaned the body with the pressure jet and then he got me to dispose of it. He loaded it in the school mini-van, which I was driving, and I was the one who disposed of it in the field behind the school. We were in it together then, he reminded me."

"Paul, listen, I can help you. We can work something out. I can arrange some counselling for you. You *can* avoid a prison sentence, I promise you that. You need to untie me. You need to give evidence. We need to work together on this. We need to put Carl Palmer behind bars. He's a killer, you're not. Listen, I believe you. Paul, I *believe* you."

Paul Hodson thought for a while. His expressions wavered between hope and resolution. For a moment, Frank thought he'd won the battle. Then Hodson spoke again, shaking his head, an evil smile returning to his outsize features.

"Oh no you don't. You're not playing me for a fool. I've said too much already. I'm phoning Carl. He'll come round and, to put it plainly, he'll kill you. He's done it once so I'm sure he can do it again. Say your prayers, Inspector. I reckon you've got about an hour at the most."

47

Paul Hodson pulled out his mobile and walked to the far side of the workshop. It was clear to Frank what was happening; Hodson was summoning Carl Palmer to kill their captive.

Frank worked furiously at his bonds while Hodson's back remained turned. Was he really able to move his wrists more easily or was he imagining it?

Paul Hodson put the phone away and grinned. He made a cut-throat gesture at Frank and laughed. Then he lumbered back to the mechanic's stool and sat down.

"Forty minutes," Hodson said. "That's how long it'll take him to get here. Your last forty minutes on earth, Inspector."

"You won't get away with it," Frank said. The words sounded hollow even to him. "Never mind getting rid of my corpse, losing that car outside won't be easy."

Hodson laughed – a deep, contemptuous guffaw.

"God, you're thick!" Hodson cackled. "To think they put you in charge of a murder investigation. Look around you – this is a fucking garage, dipshit. Breaking up a car is exactly what we do. Piece of piss, mate. Face it, you're *finished*."

Forty minutes. That's what the fat bastard had said, thought Frank. Forty minutes until Carl Palmer arrived. Forty minutes to free himself. Paul Hodson wasn't going to kill him, that much was apparent, but Carl Palmer, well, that was a different matter.

So, here's the plan: keep Paul Hodson distracted, keep working at your bonds, get yourself free, overpower the fat shit, escape into the night. Do exactly that...or die trying.

"Can you really live with this, Paul?" Frank asked. "Can you *really* sleep at night with not just one murder but two on your conscience?"

Hodson laughed heartily once more.

"What conscience? I sleep just fine. Thanks for asking, though."

"Come on, Paul, that's bullshit and you know it. Palmer's a killer, you're not. Trust me, I've been in this job long enough to distinguish the real scum from the camp followers. You said yourself he's blackmailing you. Come on, man. Strike back before it's too late."

Paul Hodson shifted in his seat, said nothing.

"Like I said, I can help you. If you show remorse, true remorse..."

"*Remorse?*" Hodson yelled. "Remorse for what? I didn't fucking do it! What part of that don't you understand?"

"You disposed of the body, Paul. Your forensic traces are all over the victim, all over the crime scene, all over the vehicle used to transport Sally to the dump site. We matched the tyre treads at the crime scene to the school mini-van; the van *you* were driving that night. You want know how this is going to play out, Paul? It will be your word against his. He'll say *you* killed her, *you* dumped her. He tried his level best to stop you but it was too late; you were hell-bent, crazy, a man possessed. Think about it – it will be your word against his with all the forensics pointing directly at you. What do you *think* a jury will conclude?"

"Bollocks. Don't think your mind games are going to work on me. I wasn't born yesterday. This is a classic cop's trick – divide and rule, promise the earth but deliver nothing. Methinks white man speaks with forked tongue. Like Carl said, if we stick to our story, tie up any loose ends, all will be fine. You, Inspector, are a loose end."

Frank worked frantically at his ties, now almost oblivious as to whether Paul Hodson noticed or not. The rain had stopped. An eerie silence had descended.

"You don't honestly think he'll stop there do you, Paul?" Frank said urgently. "Sally. Me. And then he just stops killing people? It doesn't work that way. They get a taste for it, these killers. Do it once and you've broken a taboo. The first one's the most difficult. Six or seven later, it's like shelling peas. It's you who's the loose end, Paul, not me. I'm victim number two but I'm just an inconvenience to Carl Palmer. You, though, you're the *real* loose end. How long is he going to trust you to keep quiet, Paul? Think about it. You know everything and I mean *everything*. You can put Carl Palmer behind bars for the rest of his days. What if you get pissed? What if you get cold feet? What if you talk in your sleep? Maybe not now but, believe me, these thoughts are going to start running through your sick pal's diseased mind sooner or later. Then where will you be? In that mechanic's pit over there. Think about it, Paul. Come on, untie me, make a statement. Let's get this case solved. You can help me and I can help you."

Paul Hodson stood up and Frank feared he was about to be kicked again. The hulking man paced angrily up and down the empty workshop. Frank had finally got to him, it seemed.

329

The fat nonce was finally giving the policeman's words due consideration. At the same time, Frank could feel his bonds beginning to loosen. Suddenly, Hodson stopped pacing and charged directly towards Frank.

This was it, Frank thought, another vicious boot to the head was coming. Frank braced himself. His only thought was whether it would be brutal enough to knock him out. If so, that was game over. Carl Palmer would arrive, strangle Frank while he was unconscious and dump his body.

Ironically, DCI Homes would himself become another crime statistic. Frank tensed and prepared to duck Paul Hodson's boot as far as possible in his state of bondage. Then, almost as Hodson was upon him, the fat bastard's mobile rang.

"Fuck, shit, bollocks," Hodson yelled, stopping in his tracks and pressing the phone to his ear. "What?" he bellowed into the device. Then, more tamely: "Yes, yes, understood."

Frank worked frenziedly at his bonds as Paul Hodson walked to the far side of the workshop, gabbling into the mobile. Shortly after ending his call, Hodson shot a vicious glance at Frank and left the workshop, banging the doors closed behind him. Frank noticed the fat oaf hadn't bothered to lock the doors.

Arrogance or stupidity? Frank neither knew nor cared – instead, he took the opportunity to work freely at his bonds.

Frank's wrists were raw and bleeding, but he had to continue. He had to take advantage of Paul Hodson's absence, however brief it might be. Hodson was making several trips to and fro between the workshop in which Frank lay captive and some outside storage unit. On average, Frank calculated, Hodson was away for two or three minutes at a time. Each return visit saw Hodson wheeling a large vat of industrial bleach on a trolley. He set each one down near the empty mechanic's pit. Then he looked at Frank and grinned.

"Fresh out of sulphuric acid, unfortunately," Paul Hodson chuckled, mopping his brow. "Might have chucked you in alive if we'd had any – watch you dissolving like a slug in salt! Sssssssss!"

Frank said nothing, only regretted he'd earlier tried appealing to Paul Hodson's better nature – clearly the fat shite didn't have one.

"Have to do to you what we did to Sally," Paul Hodson continued. "Only this time we'll do it better, take our time. We'll wash you down with bleach, jet spray every inch of you, burn your clothes, dump you where the sun don't shine."

It sounded as though Paul Hodson was talking to himself as much as to Frank. Either he was psyching himself up or he was simply revelling in the moment.

A sudden spasm from behind Frank's back told him his wrists were free at last. He worried that Paul Hodson might have seen the tell-tale movement but, fortunately, the fat cretin was still staring stupidly into the mechanic's pit.

This was Frank's chance, he told himself. Scramble to his feet, kick Hodson into the pit, run out into the night, call for back-up before the real killer arrived.

Almost all of Frank's muscles ached. He still had some pain in his lower back from the crash. His wrists were so sore it was as if he'd crawled over broken glass. His legs were cramping from the position he'd been forced into on the ground. It wasn't going to be easy to spring to his feet and launch an attack. However, he had to try.

Frank tensed every muscle he could muster and slowly dragged his feet into position. Then, horribly, hideously, as if in a waking nightmare, the metal doors to the workshop slid open. A second later, Carl Palmer walked in; a large, heavy duty garden spade slung casually over one shoulder.

"Evening ladies," Palmer sniggered.

48

Carl Palmer stood in the entrance to the workshop surveying the scene before him as Paul Hodson rushed to lock the sliding metal doors behind his accomplice. Frank's heart sank.

At the very moment he'd finally freed his hands, that scumbag Palmer had turned up. The trick now was to ensure neither Palmer nor Hodson twigged the fact the policeman had loosened his bonds. Frank was outnumbered two to one, he was injured and Palmer was armed with a large spade.

The odds were not great but, if Frank could retain the element of surprise, there remained a slender hope of escape. Carl Palmer was a big man. Powerful, muscular, toned, well over six foot, fit as a butcher's dog – a typical PE teacher. Poor Sally Hawkins would not have stood a chance. He looked like a warrior from a bygone age as he posed, legs apart, spade slung about his shoulders. Palmer stood right in front of the seemingly helpless DCI, enjoying his quarry's discomfort.

"Alright, Inspector?" Palmer cackled.

He was enjoying his moment of power, thought Frank. Plenty of killers get a twisted kick out of the helplessness of their victims. It's a particularly sick kind of high. Frank sized the man up, saying nothing. Carl Palmer wasn't going to kill him immediately, he reasoned. It was a gamble, of course.

If Palmer raised that spade, Frank would have to react instantly as best he could. However, if Frank could play with the man's mind for a while – get him off guard, distract him somehow; if he could manage that then Frank would have more chance of launching a surprise attack on both of his captors. The main focus was the spade – avoid it, seize it, use it on its owner.

"Why did you do it, Carl?" Frank asked.

Palmer smiled.

"Trying to buy a bit more time are we, Inspector? *Pathetic.*"

Palmer spat on the floor.

"I'd just like to know." Frank said. "You're going to kill me anyway, so what harm can it do? Come on, Palmer, indulge me.

Was the killing planned or was it a spur of the moment thing?"

Palmer looked across at Paul Hodson, now standing a few feet to Palmer's left. Frank twitched; he was considering making a lunge for the spade while Carl Palmer's eyes were averted. No, not yet; the gap between them was still too great.

"What did you tell him?" Palmer asked Hodson irritably.

"N-nothing Carl, honest," Hodson stammered.

Palmer turned back to Frank and lowered the spade to the ground. The heavy implement hit the workshop's concrete floor with a metallic echo. Frank realised the edges of the spade had been sharpened. In fact, they looked razor sharp.

Carl Palmer rested one foot on the spade and leant over the handle – as casual as a gravedigger on a fag break. The PE teacher stared deep into Frank's eyes, saying nothing. The policeman held his gaze.

In his peripheral vision, Frank was aware of Paul Hodson dancing nervously from foot to foot. The eyeball to eyeball stand-off continued for an excruciating amount of time. It must have been only a few moments but, to Frank, it felt like a lifetime.

"Do you know what I'm going to do to you, Inspector?" Carl Palmer asked eventually.

Frank stared back defiantly. It was important not to show any fear.

"Give me a clip round the ear and send me on my way with no hard feelings?" Frank answered, deadpan.

Despite himself, Carl Palmer allowed a half-smile to play across his lips.

"You see this spade, DCI Homes? Multi-purpose tool, this. First, I'm going to bash your brains out with the flat part. Then I'm going to turn the spade on its side and chop your head clean off with the sharp edge. I might just chop the rest of you into tiny little pieces while I'm at it. Then, I'm going to use this same spade to dig a great big hole in the woods and shovel what's left of you right in. Then, I'll fill the hole and pat the earth down all nice and neat. And do you know what I'll be left with? This very same spade. Like I said, a fine example of a multi-purpose tool."

Palmer lifted the spade and kissed it. Frank tensed himself for action once more, careful to keep his hands firmly behind his back to preserve the image that he remained tightly tied. Carl Palmer was clearly insane. That made him unpredictable, which made him doubly dangerous.

"Why did you do it, Palmer?" Frank repeated.

Carl Palmer raised himself to his full height and sighed, swinging the spade casually back and forth. Frank tried to keep one eye on the spade and the other on Palmer.

"Not this bullshit again," Palmer said wearily.

Then, stabbing the spade into the floor once more, he seemed to relent.

"Alright, fuck it. Since you're so desperate to know, I'll tell you."

For a moment, silence reigned. Carl Palmer seemed to be frozen in time; standing motionless in some sort of trance. Frank watched as Paul Hodson carefully backed away from the pair of them, surreptitiously edging himself towards the locked workshop doors. That was a bad sign, thought Frank.

What did Hodson know that the policeman didn't? Did Paul Hodson now expect an attack to be launched on Frank? Was he giving Palmer ample spade-swinging room and keeping himself out of harm's way at the same time?

"They're all bitches at the end of the day, aren't they, Inspector?" Carl Palmer said at last.

"They're bitches and slags. Whores and tarts. Asking for it, most of 'em. Going round with it all on show like a bunch of prick-teasers. Taunting and trying it on for size. Pushing the boundaries, seeing what might happen. It all changes once they get the reaction they're seeking, though, doesn't it? They soon start squealing like stuck pigs then, don't they?"

"Is that what you think Sally Hawkins did? Led you on? Provoked you somehow?"

Frank didn't believe it for one second but, to Palmer, in that man's twisted mind, perhaps that's how he'd seen it. Frank needed to keep the man talking, get him distracted.

"We had us some good times in here," Carl Palmer continued.

He was lost in his sick nostalgia. Perhaps this was Frank's moment? Frank edged one foot slowly backwards, placing it carefully to help lever himself upright. Suddenly, Carl Palmer stepped forward and kicked the sole of Frank's foot, forcing his leg flat once again.

"Stop fidgeting, fuckhead!" Palmer snapped. "You said you wanted to hear this."

Palmer called across to Paul Hodson but kept his eyes firmly glued on Frank.

"Hey, Paul. We used to have us some good times in here, didn't we?"

Hodson said nothing. Instead, he backed even further away; getting ever closer to the workshop doors.

"Please yourself then, you fat cunt," Carl Palmer muttered.

"So, yes, Inspector," Palmer continued. "We'd bring birds back here and party like there's no tomorrow. We'd drug 'em, film it, anything goes. It was fun with a capital 'F'. Except it got boring. I grew jaded, fancied something more, something *different*. I'd seen that Sally kid hanging round at school. Mousey little thing but, I can tell you Inspector, under that school uniform, well, it's a whole other story. So, anyway, one day I'm driving along minding my own business and then – stone the crows – there's the little slapper thumbing a lift. Bold as brass she was, flagging me down. That's what I call a gift horse, Inspector. Anyway, remind me why the fuck I'm telling you this?"

Carl Palmer placed both hands on the spade and tightened his grip. Paul Hodson backed away some more. The fat caretaker was now standing right next to the workshop doors. And that's when Frank saw it. It was gradual at first – just a hint of mist creeping beneath the closed metal doors, seeping into the room, swirling and coalescing until it became thicker and thicker.

Finally, it gathered to form a dense cloud in the centre of the workshop. Paul Hodson now reversed his direction of flight, backing rapidly away from the metal doors and the impenetrable smog. Despite the obvious danger of Carl Palmer and his raised spade, Frank's eyes remained trained on the mysterious vapour. At that moment, nothing else mattered.

"Oh, no you don't," Palmer snarled. "That's the oldest trick in the book, Inspector. Don't think I'm falling for that one. Look out behind you – whoooooo!"

Frank's would-be killer laughed contemptuously as he raised the spade above his head.

"Carl," Paul Hodson wailed. "Carl, I think you need to see this."

"Not now," said Palmer, preparing to strike a lethal blow.

Frank continued to stare at the vapour, oblivious to Carl Palmer and anything he might do. Now, sensing something really was occurring somewhere behind him, Carl Palmer turned and found himself confronted by an unbelievable sight. The supernatural smog had gathered fully now. It hovered in the middle of the workshop; a thick, toxic presence.

A low rumble began to issue from the depths of the mist. It was indistinct at first but gradually it became recognisable as the aggressive growl of an extremely large dog. The noise escalated in intensity and volume, growing deafening as it echoed around the hollow chamber of the workshop.

By now, Frank had realised precisely where he'd seen this mist before – at the King's Lynn War Memorial when Black Shuck's gigantic head had appeared to him out of the same murky ether. Sure enough, as the mist rolled upwards, the distinct outline of a familiar black Hellhound began to emerge.

At first only four huge paws could be seen beneath the rising curtain of smog. Then, as the haze dissipated, travelling ever upwards, four powerful tree-trunk legs, rippling with sinews, came into view.

Finally, with the supernatural vapours completely vanished, Black Shuck stood among the three men.

Shuck's massive head twisted slowly this way and that, picking out each of the men in turn. The Hellhound's flaming red eyes, burning with fire, swept from person to person, sizing up his quarry. Drool fell from his shark-like incisors as the fearsome beast began to snarl. The dog moved position slowly, each footstep shaking the concrete floor. It widened its stance and lowered its frame, preparing to attack.

Paul Hodson shat his pants. Carl Palmer dropped the spade.

Only DCI Frank Homes remained in a state of semi-calm. After all, he'd seen Black Shuck several times before. A small part of him felt gratified that others could now see the beast as well. He wasn't imagining it after all. It was an odd kind of relief.

"What the fuck is that?" Carl Palmer asked Paul Hodson.

"Christ knows," Paul Hodson blurted.

If either man had cared to look behind them, they'd have seen DCI Frank Homes grinning happily from ear to ear.

49

Standing before them, Black Shuck seemed as much a living, breathing animal as an ethereal apparition. At such close quarters, the Hellhound appeared as solid as a flesh and blood T-Rex somehow brought back to life across distant millennia.

Shuck pawed violently at the ground, gouging through the concrete like a knife through butter, just as Frank had witnessed back in King's Lynn. The dog's flaming red eyes sent a laser beam of fear through all three observers.

What happened next happened in an instant. It was hard to tell who – or *what* – had moved first. To Frank, events seemed to unfold as follows: Carl Palmer ran directly behind Paul Hodson, making a desperate dash for the workshop doors. At that precise moment, Black Shuck sprang forwards and seized Paul Hodson in his mighty jaws, narrowly missing capturing both men in one clean swoop. The Hellhound raised the struggling caretaker high into the air, almost dashing him against the workshop roof. The fat man squirmed in the demon dog's jaws like a plump field mouse trying to free itself from the clutches of a ravenous owl.

Frank was on his feet the moment Carl Palmer had started running. Now he stood mesmerised by the spectacle of Black Shuck mercilessly toying with his prey. The devil dog shook Paul Hodson like a rag doll, growling and snarling all the while. Then Shuck began biting through Hodson's torso, sinking those razor sharp fangs through the blubbery flesh.

Paul Hodson screamed; a high-pitched screech that rent the night. Blood began to spill from Shuck's jaws, gushing like paint from a punctured can. Shuck was now shaking the fat man's body so vigorously it was in danger of being torn in two. Blood and guts spilled onto the concrete floor.

From the corner of his eye, Frank saw Carl Palmer had opened the workshop doors and dashed into the blackness of the night.

Black Shuck hurled the remains of Paul Hodson into the air and, as the mutilated body fell, the dog moved his gigantic shark-like head in a rabid frenzy.

Faster than the eye could see, Shuck's mighty jaws lacerated Paul Hodson's corpse into tiny pieces; splattering the walls and floor with blood, guts, brain and bones. Something wet and sticky splashed across Frank's face, perhaps an eyeball or part of a spleen. Frank barely noticed, he was just glad to be alive.

Frank remained motionless and rooted, still as a statue, dripping from head to toe with Paul Hodson's gore, waiting to see what new horror would come next. Shuck stood triumphant amidst the bloody morass that had once been a human being.

The gigantic dog gazed directly at Frank. Frank stared back, perplexed by the strange look Shuck was giving him. It could hardly be called benign but it certainly wasn't the same stare of death the Hellhound had visited upon Paul Hodson. It was, perhaps, a look of recognition. Beyond that, Frank couldn't say.

Shuck turned his huge head away from Frank to glower out into the darkness of the night. The Hellhound's penetrating gaze was now directed at the open workshop doors through which a terrified Carl Palmer had so recently fled.

Beyond the doors came the sound of a vehicle's engine starting up; Palmer was escaping. In two mighty bounds, Black Shuck tore across the workshop and out into the blackness from whence he came.

Frank took a second to process all that had just happened.

Gingerly, he stepped through the gruesome mire that had once been Paul Hodson. Miraculously, within the bloody mess, Frank spotted the keys to the Insignia lying in a puddle of gore. They must have fallen from Hodson's pocket prior to his demise, Frank thought. Resisting the urge to retch, Frank retrieved the keys and dashed out of the workshop.

Once outside, Frank spotted the tail-lights of Carl Palmer's pick-up disappearing onto the A149. Of Shuck, however, there was no sign. Over by the damaged petrol pumps stood the Insignia – lying exactly where Frank had crashed it.

Frank ran to the car and, fumbling with the sticky, blood-spattered keys, clambered inside. He could only pray the car would start and the steering had not been damaged.

Frank turned the key. Nothing.

Frank tried again and was rewarded with a momentary splutter. Frank tried a third time and the car sprang into life. Crunching the gears and burning the tyres, Frank hurtled along the A149 in pursuit of Carl Palmer.

Frank stamped the accelerator to the floor and the Insignia picked up speed. The car's headlights had sustained some damage in the crash and, as a result, the light Frank had to navigate by was uneven. Furthermore, he had to juggle with a steering wheel obscured by an airbag that had inflated in the crash but had, thankfully, now deflated sufficiently to drive. It was more of a switchback ride than a car journey but Frank drove like a man possessed; Carl Palmer was his quarry and the killer of Sally Hawkins was not going to escape.

Several narrowly averted collisions later, Frank spotted two red pin-pricks of light ahead of him. He couldn't help but think of Black Shuck's flaming red eyes but these were undoubtedly the tail-lights from Carl Palmer's pick-up. Tantalisingly, they disappeared into blackness every time Palmer turned a corner.

Frank pressed even harder on the accelerator. The Insignia responded, its bonnet rising and dipping as Frank powered along the A149. The chase continued until the two vehicles approached the outskirts of Old Hunstanton. A straight length of tarmac would soon open out, Frank thought. Then he'd catch Palmer for sure.

Frank recognised precisely where he was – he'd soon be passing the bungalow of the English teacher, Jasper Collins, on the right hand side of the carriageway. There was an open patch of land on the same side as the bungalow and, from there, a pathway leading to the cliffs. A sharp left-hand bend lay just a little further ahead.

However, Carl Palmer probably knew this too.

Even so, Palmer's pick-up showed no sign of slowing. Something – some buried instinct – made Frank glance in his rear-view mirror at that very moment. The sight was so extraordinary that Frank had to look again to be sure what he'd seen was real.

There, bounding along the roadway just behind Frank's car was a massive black beast with two laser-like red eyes, easily closing the distance with every stride.

Black Shuck was gaining ominously on both vehicles – the mighty Hellhound was barrelling along full-tilt, just as Frank had seen him racing across the surface of the waves. However, on this occasion a further air of menace was palpable in the spectral beast.

Frank returned his gaze to the road just in time to steady the car and avoid a pot hole. He'd closed the gap sufficiently on Carl Palmer to read the number plate on the back of the killer's pick-up. Surely he had him now?

Then Frank saw something that chilled him to the core. Standing in the road, directly ahead of Carl Palmer's pick-up, stood the ghost of Sally Hawkins. Her eyes were closed, her skin alabaster pale, her face a perfect death mask. She was unmoving and corpse-like – until, that is, Carl Palmer's vehicle was almost upon her. At that instant, Sally Hawkins' ghost opened her eyes wide to reveal they were a deep, luminous blood red; just like Shuck's. The murdered girl's ghost screamed a piercing banshee wail as she pointed an implacable finger of accusation at her killer that sent Carl Palmer's pick-up careening off the road, bumping over the uneven grassland and heading straight for the clifftop. God alone knew what Carl Palmer made of the events that had befallen him. However, the man somehow wrestled his out-of-control vehicle to a halt.

Having stopped, the killer threw himself headlong onto the grass. Frank pulled the Insignia off the road and bounced over the grass in hot pursuit, his mind focusing only on preventing Carl Palmer from getting away.

Frank's car skidded across the grassy surface as he stamped on the brakes which, at such high speeds and on such slippery terrain, were not as effective as he'd wished. Frank's car headed directly for Carl Palmer's pick-up – and Carl Palmer, only just picking himself off the ground, was in line to be crushed between the two vehicles.

Time now seemed to slow. Frank braced himself for his second car crash of the night. He saw Carl Palmer struggling to his feet and registered – with a small, secret satisfaction – the look of abject terror that haunted Sally Hawkins' killer as he stared in the direction of Frank's rapidly approaching vehicle. Except, Frank suddenly realised, Carl Palmer was actually looking *beyond* Frank and the man's fear had a different source entirely.

An instant before Frank's Insignia hit Carl Palmer, Frank became aware of a powerful on-rushing whirlwind sweeping past him. Its brute force pushed the Insignia to one side as though it were a toy, simultaneously allowing Frank to avoid a collision. The tornado had the appearance of a large black shadow and, instinctively, Frank knew: Black Shuck. Shuck rushed directly at Carl Palmer.

Palmer swayed unsteadily as he momentarily drew himself to his full height. In one mighty leap, the devil dog seized the child killer in his gigantic jaws and launched himself – still gripping his wildly thrashing quarry – over the edge of the cliff; plunging the pair of them towards the jagged rocks below.

Frank's Insignia spun. Only when the car's boot clipped the edge of Carl Palmer's pick-up did it slow sufficiently to allow it to come to rest barely a few metres from the cliff's edge.

All the pain and horror of this dreadful night now seemed to hit Frank in a rush. His back felt as though he was being carved in two. His wrists burned like fire. His brain swam.

DCI Frank Homes slumped forward, placed his head on the Insignia's steering wheel and blacked out.

50

Frank had no idea how long he'd been unconscious. Still, as he came round, there were no sirens, no anxious crowds gathering, no illumination beyond the silvery moonlight. Instead there was only an unnatural calm and a heavy shroud of darkness stretching to the horizon. A thin trail of steam was escaping from the Insignia's bonnet. Frank lifted his head from the steering wheel.

He remembered everything very clearly this time – every horrific moment; the relentless storm, the terrifying séance, his ordeal in captivity, Black Shuck eviscerating Paul Hodson, the car chase at insane speeds, Sally Hawkins' implacable avenging ghost, Shuck launching himself and Carl Palmer over the cliff's edge –

dragging the child-killer to the bowels of Hell.

Frank opened the Insignia's driver's door and stepped gingerly onto the grass. Adrenaline surged through his veins, obliterating any sense of injury.

Frank now had only one objective. He walked slowly forwards, tottering unsteadily at first but soon advancing with increasing confidence. The burgeoning moonlight seemed to strengthen his resolve. Now it illuminated a safe passage for him. Frank walked unerringly towards the cliff's edge, making for the very spot at which Carl Palmer had disappeared.

As he reached the edge of the cliff, Frank knelt down and continued with extreme caution on his hands and knees. Rocks and dirt crumbled away as he hovered at the precipice. Frank extended his torso and craned his neck as far as he dared over the cliff edge.

Then, summoning all his resolve, he looked downwards. There, lying in broken pieces across the blood-stained rocks far below, was the torn-asunder corpse of the evil child killer, Carl Palmer. Of Black Shuck, however, there was no sign.

DCI Frank Homes sat back on his haunches and closed his eyes, offering a silent prayer of thanks for his own deliverance.

Justice had been done.

Sally Hawkins could finally rest in peace.

Only one thought now echoed through the policeman's mind

and that thought was this:

This is HIS land.

This is *HIS* domain.

THE END

Author's Note

Black Dog is my fourth novel to be published. However, in many ways, it is also my first. I mean this in the sense that it represents a return to my first love in terms of genre – horror. My first ever novel (never published because I lost the only copy of the manuscript) was laboriously written at the age of nineteen using two fingers on a typewriter in those now unimaginable pre-internet days. It was a horror novel – *'Vrykolakas!'* – concerning a plague of vampires on a remote Greek island. Though I rather immodestly say so myself, that early novel (actually more of a novella) showed some small level of promise. It was six years later that I decided I wanted to be a full-time author and that writing fiction was a true vocational calling. I then began to follow the literary muse wherever she might lead although it was not in the direction of the horror genre…until now.

As a schoolboy I was an avid fan of Hammer Horror (I still am!) – both the film studio and its iconic movies. Growing up in the late 1970s, one of my favourite treats was to be allowed to stay up late at night watching Hammer horror films on TV so I could later regale my school friends with accounts of the camp Gothic melodrama, blood and bare-breasted glamour that were the Hammer hallmark. Once I became a writer I promised myself I would one day write a Hammer style horror novel. It would appear that day has finally arrived.

Black Dog has its genesis in my time spent living in King's Lynn in North Norfolk where I was staying while undertaking a PGCE (teacher training degree) at Cambridge University. Whilst in Norfolk I actually saw the infamous 'Black Shuck' (the notorious Hellhound of legend) while driving on the A149 road on a bright summer's day. (An account of this sighting may be read on my blog). I duly gave this sighting to Black Dog's protagonist, DCI Frank Homes, as his first encounter with the spectre. In reality, I experienced this sighting exactly as I've written it through Frank's eyes. This entire novel sprang from that one instance.

Having actually seen Shuck myself, I thoroughly researched the legend of Black Shuck (and ghostly black dog sightings in general) and made some fascinating discoveries. Ghostly black dog sightings are the most prevalent ghostly phenomenon reported worldwide and the greatest number of these sightings occur in the UK. The legend of Black Shuck was the same fable Sir Arthur Conan Doyle used as inspiration for *The Hound Of The Baskervilles*. My protagonist, Frank Homes is named 'Homes' as a somewhat mischievous tribute to both Conan Doyle and the great Sherlock.

Fascinated by my discoveries, I posted detailed summaries of my Black Shuck/ghostly black dog research on my blog. These posts proved to be highly popular. Soon after uploading my findings, people began leaving their own accounts of sightings of Black Shuck (and other ghostly black dog sightings worldwide) on my website. I have incorporated several of these reports into the narrative of Black Dog, repackaging them as encounters experienced by my troubled DCI. (In particular, thank you to Brogan and Nicole for the splendidly satisfying scene in which Shuck confronts Frank while running over the waves off the Hunstanton coastline).

I have greatly enjoyed writing this book and fervently hope the same levels of joy and excitement may be gained from reading it. It was especially satisfying to be writing about East Anglia as I have strong connections to the region. My father's family hail from Lowestoft and my roots there go back several generations. I spent many happy times visiting my grandmother in Lowestoft throughout my early childhood. (I must also thank Lowestoft band, The Darkness, for their song 'Black Shuck' – one of several tracks that was played at top volume many times during the writing of this novel!). In later life, I lived in King's Lynn and worked in both King's Lynn and Hunstanton for a year (which is, of course, when I saw Shuck).

Part of the fun I had when writing Black Dog was to playfully insert subtle (and less than subtle) tributes to my heroes, influences and inspirations in terms of several characters' names. I have already mentioned DCI Homes being named in tribute to Conan Doyle. I will identify only one other such instance of self-indulgent whimsy – the name of the pet dog in my story; Spider (the Affenpinscher). Spider is so called in tribute to the great horror author, Susan Hill (incidentally a fellow alumnus of King's College London), whose modern horror classic *The Woman In Black* memorably features a dog called Spider.

Although writing fiction is essentially a solitary occupation, as with all novels, there are a great many people to thank for helping one's book come to fruition. I would like to express my profound gratitude to several individuals. From the outset, I must recognise the extremely generous assistance of a professional forensics technician, Kate Norton-Hewins, in an advisory capacity. Whilst Black Dog is undoubtedly a work of fiction and, falling within the horror genre means it plays fast and loose with the strictures of everyday reality, I nevertheless wanted the police procedural element of the narrative to have some degree of realism. Kate kindly provided me with a detailed forensics report on the 'murder' of Sally Hawkins as though it was a real case. (It was a fascinating read). This invaluable assistance allowed me to shape the narrative in a far more plausible fashion than in my initial draft. (I must, however, add that I ultimately still played somewhat fast and loose with Kate's own report in the final draft of this book. After all, Kate assures me that, even with a jet-wash of industrial bleach, the killers would still have left several forensic traces that she could detect! So, the notion within the narrative that no useful forensic traces could be found is pure artistic license on my part rather than any reflection on Kate's forensic prowess).

Among friends and family, I must firstly thank Leah for proof-reading every single chapter of this book across each and every draft (and there were many drafts!). Thank you for your unfailing enthusiasm and constant encouragement. Also, for services to proofing and beta reading, I must thank my good friend, Julia – including for the metaphorical slaps on the wrist for my habitual over-use of italics and exclamation marks. (I'm now fully cured, Jules...*perhaps*!!!!). My good friend Poppet is also to be both thanked and celebrated for her wonderful cover design and expert formatting – both tasks that are completely beyond yours truly and are hugely appreciated.

Similarly, I am grateful to all those who have encouraged me at every step of the way in completing and publishing this book. In this respect, I must mention Ruth Marie (*hola amiga*!), Jason, Bob, Darren and Val – all of whom have regularly and unfailingly expressed interest in the progress of this novel throughout the several years it has taken to bring it to completion. This unerring support has been a direct factor in my persevering to a conclusion.

Lastly, I should also thank Teddy – a loyal companion and cat of distinction who has stoically endured my writing about dogs!

As with all of my novels, I like to give a percentage of author's profits to a deserving charitable cause. It seems appropriate that this book should directly benefit our canine chums. However, as an avowed 'dog and cat man' in equal measure, I have determined this title should support a charity that cares for both dogs and cats in equal measure – the Celia Hammond Animal Trust (CHAT), which is also the beneficiary from a percentage of sales from my previous novel, Little Bastard. Thank you for purchasing this book and helping me to help this admirable cause.

And finally…if you, dear reader, can kindly find the time and inclination, please do provide me with an Amazon review for this book. Your feedback is always greatly appreciated. If there is sufficient appetite, Black Dog will become the first in a series of supernatural thrillers.

Simon Corbin
November 2017

About the Author

Simon Corbin is an author from southwest London. Simon was educated at Rugby School, London University and Cambridge University. Simon spent over 20 years as a freelance writer/journalist (writing feature articles for newspapers and magazines and completing copywriting assignments for advertising agencies, government departments and blue chip clients) before moving into teaching. (Simon has taught both journalism and creative writing at Richmond Adult & Community College in Surrey as well as GCSE and A-Level English at several west London FE colleges).

Writing novels has long been a vocational calling for Simon, beginning with a vampire-based horror yarn, *Vrykolakas*, written as a teenager (the manuscript sadly lost). Simon's first published novel, *Rude Boy*, (a re-imagining of Catcher In The Rye within the 1980s UK punk scene) was followed by the concept thriller, *Love, Gudrun Ensslin* (positing the question as to how a still active Baader Meinhof Gang might have responded to the banking crisis and its subsequent era of austerity). His third novel, *Little Bastard*, an essay in 1970s nostalgia and a darkly humorous study of a dysfunctional family represented a further leap of genre. With the release of *Black Dog*, Simon has returned to his literary first love – Horror.

In recent years, Simon has branched out into screenwriting – co-authoring a horror movie script for Hollywood investors.

Outside writing, Simon's interests include cartooning and caricaturing (something he has done ever since he first held a pen), playing music (writing songs and performing with good friend Julia in a band/songwriting collective entitled 'Cats Don't Bark') and playing tennis (up to three times a week, if weather permits).

For further information about Simon and his writing, please see the following websites:

Simon's blog:

https://simoncorbin.wordpress.com/simons-blog/

Website for Simon's novel Rude Boy:

http://rudeboybook.com/

Website for Simon's novel Love, Gudrun Ensslin:

http://lovegudbook.weebly.com/

Website for Simon's novel Little Bastard:

http://litbasbook.weebly.com

Simon's Amazon Author page:

http://www.amazon.co.uk/Simon-Corbin/e/B0049AX2FC

Books by Simon Corbin

Rude Boy
Little Bastard
Love, Gudrun Ensslin

Printed in Great Britain
by Amazon